The Wave Theory of Angels

By the same author

The Changeling

The Wave Theory of Angels

ALISON MACLEOD

HAMISH HAMILTON
an imprint of
PENGUIN BOOKS

HAMISH HAMILTON

Published by the Penguin Group
Penguin Books Ltd, 80 Strand, London WC2R ORL, England
Penguin Group (USA) Inc., 375 Hudson Street, New York, New York 10014, USA
Penguin Group (Canada), 10 Alcorn Avenue, Toronto, Ontario, Canada M4V 3B2
(a division of Pearson Penguin Canada Inc.)
Penguin Ireland, 25 St Stephen's Green, Dublin 2, Ireland (a division of Penguin Books Ltd)
Penguin Group (Australia), 250 Camberwell Road,
Camberwell, Victoria 3124, Australia (a division of Pearson Australia Group Pty Ltd)
Penguin Books India Pvt Ltd, 11 Community Centre,
Panchsheel Park, New Delhi – 110 017, India
Penguin Group (NZ), cnr Airborne and Rosedale Roads, Albany, Auckland 1310, New Zealand
(a division of Pearson New Zealand Ltd)
Penguin Books (South Africa) (Pty) Ltd, 24 Sturdee Avenue,
Rosebank 2196, South Africa

Penguin Books Ltd, Registered Offices: 80 Strand, London WC2R ORL, England

www.penguin.com

First published 2005

I

Copyright © Alison MacLeod, 2005

The moral right of the author has been asserted

The publisher is grateful for the permission to reproduce lines from 'Second Elegy of the Duino Elegies'
by Rainer Maria Rilke, published in *The Selected Poetry of Rainer Maria Rilke*,
edited and translated by Stephen Mitchell, Picador, 1987

Set in 12/14.75 pt Monotype Dante
Typeset by Rowland Phototypesetting Ltd, Bury St Edmunds, Suffolk
Printed in Great Britain by Clays Ltd, St Ives plc

A CIP catalogue record for this book is available from the British Library

ISBN 0-241-14261-X

for my father, Hugh MacLeod (1925–2003),
and Hugo Donnelly (1951–2003), with love

But if the archangel now, perilous, from behind the stars
took even one step down toward us: our own heart, beating
higher and higher, would beat us to death . . .

Rainer Maria Rilke
(translated by Stephen Mitchell)

Acknowledgements

I am grateful to the Canada Council for the Arts, the Arts Council of England and the Society of Authors (London) for their generosity and recognition at times of definitive need. This book would not have been possible without their assistance. I am also greatly indebted to colleagues and friends at University College Chichester for their encouragement and support. Thanks are due especially to Hugh Dunkerley (for his unfailing belief in the book), Karen Stevens, Stephanie Norgate, Professor Vicki Feaver, David Swann, Dr Isla Duncan, Dr Bill Gray and Dr Jago Morrison. I also wish to thank Dr Stephen Jefferies and Dr David Peat for their respective expertise, generously given.

Time of the Bells

I

The world yearns. This is its sure gravity: the attraction of bodies. Earth for molten star. Moon for earth. A hand for the orb of a breast. This is its movement too: the motion of desire, of a longing toward.

She slept deeply. There was a commotion outside, some panic at the site, but she didn't wake.

The night before, she hadn't wanted to sleep. She'd told her sister she was hungry, that she could eat a dog, a baby, the moon; that she was hot, too hot to lie there together in bed, the two of them rolling into the dip, their arms and legs smacking in the muggy heat; that the sky was crazy with summer lightning and they should go outside and see; that her bees would be restless under such a sky – they'd swarm come morning if she wasn't careful; that each of her bees was a memory in her head, a syllable of sweetness and light ready to sting her conscience; that she'd seen a bear dancing on the cathedral steps that afternoon and the hurdy-gurdy player had told her that bears will try to make love to women because they mate on two legs, not four; that she'd heard a Dominican tell a crowd by the bathhouse that there are 301,655,722 angels and so many demons in the air, a needle dropped from heaven to earth must strike one; that, *par le diable*, she was hot.

'Marguerite,' she'd said, turning to her sister, 'are you asleep? Marguerite?'

There was an explosion of stone. The man known as l'Ymagier – the Imaginator – ran into the street in the direction of the

lodge. But he only got as far as the scaffolding at what was to be the west tower.

He'd seen it once before.

It took five men three hundred steps on the great wheel to lift even a hundredweight of stone ten feet. The bishop was insisting the vaults of St Pierre would reach an unimaginable one hundred and sixty feet. And the work was to be done faster, so the hoists were growing by the day, and suddenly every drooling halfwit knew the measure of faith: at Beauvais, the cathedral would rise above Notre Dame, above Chartres, above even Amiens. Its towers would scatter the stars.

One of the five that morning had missed the count, lost his footing. The load came crashing to the ground, spinning the treadmill backwards like a frenzied wheel of fortune at a Michaelmas fair, breaking each man's legs over and over again.

Quarrymen, lime carriers, plasterers, pointers, artificers, scaffolders and stone cutters knelt where they stood. L'Ymagier too went down on his knees, if self-consciously. He was not easy with common observances. Somebody was shouting for the master mason. Chalk dust had turned the air to a milky film. Traders from the market were arriving, breathless – they'd heard it too. Loud as God's fist. A monk from St Germer led the crowd in a prayer for the five. Three of them fainted as they were lowered from the wheel on to a stumbling wall of shoulders. The other two were raving with pain. L'Ymagier mumbled the responses, staring at the wrecked bodies from the corner of his eye. He knew his prayers wouldn't save even one of those men from a life spent on his belly hauling himself from year to year, or if lucky on two twisted sticks.

Beside him, a fat shoemaker shifted on arthritic knees. 'Was a glover,' he said confidentially, 'but make no mistake, pilgrims aren't walking to Beauvais on their hands.'

L'Ymagier wiped his face with his shirtsleeve. Then he got

to his feet, knocked the shoemaker to the ground with a blow from his boot, and walked away to the sound of the man's plaintive groans.

'She isn't. That's what I'm trying to tell you.'

'Then for God's sake wake her, Marguerite.'

She stared. Her father had returned distracted, impatient. The knees of his breeches were yellow with chalk dust. His face was rimmed with sweat. He could hardly look her in the eye. Nothing seemed real. Her sister was holding her breath.

'She won't get up.' She could feel her eyes fill. 'You tell her.'

'Tell her what?' He could hear again the woman who had howled, who'd said she'd dreamed it: blocks of cut stone dropping like the Books of the Prophets from the sky. She'd woken terrified. The oneiromancer, who set his stall in the arcade of the charnel house, had told her to expect a fall in fortunes. A temporary loss. And now this! Her only son, shattered.

'Tell her that she has to get up.'

The room was muggy with heat and old breath. L'Ymagier wiped his face in his shirt, then beheld his daughter. 'Christina?' Her face was slack, her chin fallen, her eyes sticky with sleep. 'Christina, get up. You're too old for these charades.'

He laid his hand on her forehead and sank to the edge of the pallet.

'What is it?' Marguerite: her voice as if from the bottom of a well.

He pulled Christina to him. He touched her cheek, neck, breast, wrist. 'She's cold. You can see that, can't you? And on a day like this of all days.' As if his elder daughter was only perverse.

He slapped her cheeks. He rubbed her arms and legs as if he'd pulled her from the river in January, not from a sheet of linen. He shook her by the shoulders until her head lolled.

'Father, don't. Don't.'

When the physic came at last – Marguerite afraid; slipping from the house; the physic at work across the town; the fierce stink of mustard as he drives a woman's womb from over her heart and back into her belly; the woman crying that she can inhale no more, that her chest is on fire – when the physic came at last, l'Ymagier did not look up. 'Marguerite is laying a fire,' he reported, as if to say, You are not needed here. Let us be among ourselves. But the physic, young as he was, prised Christina's wrist from his hold and searched for her pulse. He felt her neck. He lifted her eyelid and touched the membrane of her eye. He laid her flat on the pallet, requested a shallow bowl of water and placed it on the flat of her stomach, pondering it. He held a strand of wool before her mouth. Then he took the candle from the bedside, asked Marguerite to light it, and held it before her sister's slackened mouth.

L'Ymagier blew it out. 'I've told you. She's cold.' He turned to where his other daughter stood terrified in the corner. 'Will you kill her with your gloom, Marguerite?'

He heard the physic tell Marguerite he would send for the priest. 'Why? So he too can tell me my daughter is dead? So we can pray for the repose of her soul?' He knew the words well enough. *Memento, Domine, famularum tuarum qui nos praecesserunt cum signo fidei, et dormiunt in somno pacis.* Be mindful, O Lord, of thine handmaidens who have gone before us with the sign of faith and who sleep the sleep of peace.

Man of science that the physic was – acolyte of Aristotle, Hippocrates and Galen – how could he understand that those words would be the death of Christina? At Paris, at the university, l'Ymagier, like the young physic, had studied the embalmed marvels of human musculature. As a student, at the age of seventeen, he had been encouraged to observe in the newly dead the principle of Anti-Creation, as delineated by Aristotle in *De Generatione et Corruptione*. He had observed more.

Death, l'Ymagier would tell you, possesses us slowly and by degrees. There is the loss of the vital heat; of the replenishing breath, yes. There is the ostensible moment when the soul flies from the mouth, a small naked thing weighing, they were told, three pounds. But death is more than a moment. L'Ymagier knew it. You had only to ask those five who were broken that day on the mason's wheel.

On the wall by the door was the wreath of his dead wife's hair, pale red in the light. Faded now. He'd known, but he'd let the priests take her. He'd known that death is less of an event than a slow transubstantiation: of the body into ruin; of the beloved into a warp and woof of worms; of each one of us into no more than a story that others will tell.

There is a prelude. The hands are folded, the fingers intertwined. Perhaps the rings are removed. The brow is anointed, the obsequies spoken, and the lips kissed. Then we wind words, like we do the sheet.

Yet, beneath that sheet, the body is animated still. The limbs cool and stiffen – in some, a process that will have begun in the final days of life. A greenish colour spreads from the abdomen. The surface veins turn brownish, sketching on the skin a faint aborescent pattern. Bloodstained fluid might escape the mouth, and the eyeballs will begin to liquefy. There is motion. There is energy. Even if it is gone amok.

In time, there is a shedding of the hair and nails, a blistering of the skin. The vulva or scrotum swells. The stomach distends. Within four to five days, a body can swell to two or three times its natural size – the face will hardly be recognizable – and still it will be as much as a year before the flesh slips clean from the bone.

Only upon exhumation will the beloved at last come to rest – to stillness – in that ramshackle display of tibia and skulls at the charnel house. Only then does the beloved depart us.

This, thought l'Ymagier, is what neither Church Father nor physic will have us know: life yields only haltingly to death.

Why do we gaze at statuary? We gaze because it troubles us with that which we've long forgotten. As primitives, as children, we once understood that the animate and the inanimate are not irreconcilable; that one energy is the basis of all matter; that all matter is always, ultimately, possibility. Otherwise, argues l'Ymagier, how is it we eat the body of Christ; that we drink His blood? How is it possible that a strip of willow knows water? That my hand hums when I lay it over my daughter's still heart?

While Christina was with them, while she was yet herself, he would not leave her. He would warm her. He would keep her from harm. He would whisper to her that she was more than a physic's findings or a priest's prayers. More than a story in a eulogizing mouth. He would not let that story begin.

He pressed his mouth to her ear. 'Possedes ton coeur, ma fille.' Possess thy heart.

2

From Helmholtz we know that energy is a quantity just as mass is a quantity. We know it can be transformed but it cannot be destroyed. Where energy disappears from one part of a system, it has to appear elsewhere in the system. Pope John XXII seemed to have an innate suspicion of this, the First Law of Thermodynamics, in only 1331, less than fifty years after l'Ymagier wished his daughter back to life. For in that year His Holiness issued a decree that prohibited the raising of people from the dead.

Someone had to.

The Church needed a crackdown on marvels.

Yet what was the truth of Christina? Think of her as a plant. Or a flower. Every woman, we are told, is a flower, and Christina is fireweed, wild, rangy and high coloured. Fireweed spreads at the edges of Beauvais, springing up where the native woodland is cut back for the grape-growers' terraces; where the ground is suddenly vast after the ravages of flame. As the weed pushes through, its leaves like lances, as it blooms and falls away in an endless exchange of matter and energy, at which point is there a sharp distinction between what is alive and what is not? Clearly, a molecule that crosses a cell boundary into one of its spiky leaves does not suddenly 'die' when it is released again into the atmosphere.

So, even when life is not manifest, might it not be implicit? Is it possible that the life of Christina is there, latent, even in her death? Is this the impossible secret of Lazarus? Of the statue that moves its arm in benediction? For isn't Nature, finally, eternal flux? Heraclitus's everything-flows. Isn't form merely reality's changing cloak?

Or is this simply the madness of l'Ymagier? Is his brain like that of a dead man, feverish with activity even after the heart has stopped? Did the heart of l'Ymagier stop when his elder daughter did not awake?

L'Ymagier was Giles of Beauvais, the most celebrated sculptor on the Île-de-France. Yet this was not his first incarnation.

Years ago, he'd abandoned his studies at Paris. The theologians at the university had wanted blood. The philosophers attempted to save themselves by sacrificing their own so-called radicals. He, among others, was accused of Arabism – a charge that had already ruined reputations. And more. After the tribunal he had been lucky to leave Paris with his life.

He returned to Beauvais to apprentice, belatedly, under a freestone mason, for his native town was burgeoning under the rising cathedral of St Pierre. His own father had been a wood carver who'd specialized in the hands and feet of the saints. Expressive things. Truths unfolding in gesture. As a boy, he'd worked with his father until the day he left for Paris where, he'd heard it said, they taught the pagan philosophers in defiance of the papal ban.

Yet, by the age of twenty-one, he was weary of philosophy. And wearier still of scripture. He wanted to hold a chisel again. He wanted the warmth of wood. He wanted to lift life from the pupae of stone.

From his father, he'd inherited strong hands and a natural understanding of space, ratio and dimension. He'd developed, too, an instinct for the tension of earthly forces at work behind form – of the struggle, as we might know it, between gravity and centrifuge, between attraction and flight.

By the time Christina was born, just five years later in 1264, l'Ymagier was without rival or precedent. You can see his stone-work throughout the Île-de-France: on ornate tombs, on the fountainheads in pleasure gardens, in the arcades of charnel houses. It was said that if you struck one of his leaf-topped columns, sap would ooze out; that dogs couldn't cock their legs against stone effigies without taking fright. He could put wind in granite foliage, fire in a demon's hair, slither in a serpent's tail.

You think I exaggerate.

The imagination was not, in those days, the flimsy abstraction it is now. It was a stranger beast. The word itself was still new, still potent, having only entered the French language the century before. And makers of images – this new breed of imaginators – were demiurges of a territory, an intermediate world the Church needed to colonize.

It would be a full fifteen years from the time of his return to Beauvais before l'Ymagier would accept employment by the diocesan chapter. No time, it is true, in the span of a cathedral's making, but an unusually lengthy wait for the prelates of Beauvais. Finally, there was nothing else for it. The bishop was informed that he himself must request the man's services.

Naturally, l'Ymagier did agree, and the irony he'd long looked forward to was indeed sweet. 'His Grace, it seems, needs me, my girls, and I've said, of course, I will serve where I may.' He scooped the two of them into his arms and squeezed them tight. 'And what better cover for a naughty heretic than the tallest cathedral in Christendom?'

Christina was ten and Marguerite just eight. Both of them had laughed with him, clapping at a joke they couldn't understand. So it happened: under his chisel, 'le forêt' of the rising cathedral came slowly to life, a grove of leafy pillars under starry vaults.

However, it was on the question of wings that Giles of Beauvais's career would begin, unexpectedly, to founder.

When Christina was only twelve she discovered her father, in the watery light of a winter morning, struggling with a dead swan. His arms were outstretched against its wingspan and his head buried in its breast: my mother, she thought sleepily, dead and white and come back to hold him again. Then he lifted a blade, cut back the flesh from the breastbone, and counted with the span of his hand.

Finally he gathered the swan up and carried it away, its tied beak banging at his knees. He hardly knew she was with him, just behind, still in her shift. In the streets, through the market, people joked with him, but he hardly spoke. The old anger had returned: that truth must submit to authorized form; that the common people must be duped by beauty.

In his atelier, his daughters found large pieces, broken things, under hemp sheets, as if he could no longer bear to look.

For he would lie no more. He would no longer cast the impassive angels of the Church's fixed and immovable cosmos. He would no longer pretend that this was all he knew. He would no longer pretend that the Tenth Angel had never been.

'What does it say?' she called from behind. 'The writing, what does it say?'

He turned to find his small daughter pointing to the scrap of hide he had stitched to the tip of one lank wing. He looked at her. Saw the seriousness in her face. He would not lie to her. 'It says, "Fear of the Angel".'

A threat. She knew, not by the words, but by the hard line of his mouth.

He didn't know how much she had understood.

Most birds need a square foot of lifting feathers for every half pound of weight. A swan weighs twenty-five to thirty pounds. That low, undulant flight requires a wingspan of eight feet. Do you see? At even one hundred and fifty pounds, an angel would require a wingspan of forty to fifty feet. To support the force of such wings, its sternum would need to be a colossal trunk of bone; its shoulders two terrifying crossbeams; its spine a disfiguring outcrop. An angel, he told Christina that morning, could only be monstrous.

He dumped the swan, huge and bloody, at the bishop's door. Later, Christina led him by the hand to the water trough behind the market and washed his hands and arms of the blood, as if she were the parent and he the child who needed only calming.

On the day of her long sleep, he found a half-eaten apple in a recess in the wall by the door. He saw her eating it only the day before. He left it there. A trace.

There were others.

The fireweed in the jug, still fresh.

The garnet ring in the water trough. She'd searched everywhere.

The impress of her toes on the soles of her clogs.

Bees stray in the house.

She could not have left them. He would not allow it. He would not allow it for he could not bear it. Christina was the life of the house. And she knew his nature and forgave him it.

3

When the priest left, l'Ymagier said, 'There's no time.'

Marguerite thought of Christina dead in the next room, laid out on their bed with a linen sheet over her. She kept expecting her to appear, sucking honey from a spoon and treading down the backs of her slippers. She needed her. How could she cope with their father on her own?

Marguerite? Are you asleep? Marguerite?

She'd heard her sister in the night but she hadn't opened her eyes. If only she had. If only she'd turned to her and said, 'You're hot. I'll fetch water.'

She didn't tell her father she'd seen Father Joseph blowing into Christina's mouth and touching her ears with his spittle. Or that she'd seen him check her throat and wrists.

When she was alone with Christina again, she crawled into bed beside her sister's cold body and cried into her hair.

Sssh, Marguerite. Go to sleep now.

For a moment, he hesitated. The two of them lying there together. As if the day hadn't started. As if he himself had only dreamed Christina's long dream.

When he woke Marguerite, she'd slept so deeply for a moment she didn't know him.

He told her what she must do. 'There's a good girl.'

At the back of the monastery she found them: the skeps and her sister's wicker veil. As she lowered it over her head, a monk in the rabbit pen across the yard raised his hand, thinking she was Christina.

She turned away, her stomach in spasms. She worked quickly, finding the heaviest of the skeps and plunging them, one by one, into the fish pond until a city of bees floated dead to the surface. She took the net, skimmed the surface clean, raised the skeps and harvested the honey, leaving it outside the larder door as Christina had always done. Then she ran – a relief to run at last, to be gone from the place – she ran, the buckets of creamy comb knocking at her legs.

At home, l'Ymagier broke off hexagons of wax and melted them over a low fire. He oiled Christina's face. He spoke quietly but with ease. He had bought a vigil-cloth of purple and gold for her laying out, and would Marguerite pluck her sister's hairline and eyebrows? To show the smoothness of her brow for the mass.

She stared. She could feel arcs of sweat spreading under her arms.

'Do you think Father Joseph will be denied the opportunity of a death, Marguerite?' He dipped a brush into the warm wax and applied it to Christina's face. He was making a mask, to preserve the image of her, she who was the image of their mother.

Marguerite could only say, 'Why is there a straw between her lips?'

'So she can breathe.' He looked up, studying his second daughter's face. And, as if to clarify: 'So there is no danger of suffocation.'

That afternoon, Marguerite moved to her father's instructions like a startled automaton on a pulley at a Twelfth Night feast. She stripped her sister of her shift and soaked her body in an alum bath to whiten the tan of her skin.

Later he laid her on the flags, and Marguerite painted her from head to toe from a kettle of wax. To stall the marks of time, he said. Layer upon layer. And she remembered clearly: she saw no bruises, no signs of struggle. How could there have been? Hadn't she lain beside Christina as she slept?

The Egyptians were known to preserve their loved ones in caskets of honey, and the Church too, their 'special dead': saints, holy men, those whose bodies yielded not to rot but to the sweet odour of sanctity. Too difficult, l'Ymagier had concluded, though it had not escaped his consideration. The wax would suffice.

Marguerite wanted to snap her fingers before his face. She wanted to seize his arm as he peeled the mask from her sister's face. She wanted to say, Let's stop this now. I *will* weep for my sister. *You*, you too, must weep for her, or she will die all over again at the dearth of your tears.

When the final application had cooled into a translucent shell, she drew the vigil-cloth over her sister's nakedness, and l'Ymagier lifted her from the cool stone floor and laid her upon the bed. The effect was unsettling, for wax holds the light, and in the late-afternoon sun Christina seemed to take on a glow, a static brightness, that unsettled her sister.

Immutability is a terrible magic.

Brother Bernard had not been difficult to persuade. A girl, l'Ymagier had reminded him, would be quieter, less curious in the scriptorium. Brother Bernard had nodded – he did not need add that Marguerite's ignorance would be her chief asset. And l'Ymagier, for his part, felt it unnecessary to tell Brother Bernard that he himself had taught Marguerite to read both Latin and French.

So a page turner was employed to serve the ageing theologians and encyclopedists in the monastery's scriptorium.

Privilege. Palsy. It was all one in the end. L'Ymagier told his daughter only: 'If you remain standing as you work, it gives the appearance of servitude. And your eyes are sharp.'

From her unique vantage point, by the elbow of Brother Vincent of Beauvais, Marguerite studied maps of the world. *Imago mundi.* Over meals with her father and sister, she'd sketch sticky copies on the table with honey, marking east at the top, then the locations of Paris, London, Oxford, Purgatory and Paradise. Or she'd tell Christina and l'Ymagier about the monstrous races that lived at the edges of the world: the Acephili who wore their faces on their chests, the Panotii with ears so large they used them as blankets by night, and the ones that always made Christina laugh, the Sciopods, a one-legged people with a giant foot which doubled as a canopy when they lay down in the sun.

Sometimes too Marguerite delivered adjurations from Books of Secrets for their entertainment. 'I adjure you, O speck in the eye, by the living God and holy God, to disappear from the piteous eye of this servant of God, whether you are black, red or white. May Christ make you go away!' Then l'Ymagier would leap up, blinking and crying all at once, and the three of them would clap and praise Christ.

But there are secrets, and there are secrets. Every Thursday between lauds and prime, Brother Vincent requests a series of volumes that are kept, not in the stacks, but in a set of wooden cages at the back of the scriptorium. Each volume is fastened by a thick metal clasp, for which Brother Vincent produces a key from a ring in the calfskin pouch at his waist.

Watch her now: Marguerite lifts out the heaviest volume from behind the wooden bars. *Picatrix.* Inside, its letters are strange, unreadable. Letters like the claw prints of birds in the snow. Then too there is *Oneirocritica. On Dreams.* A Latin translation. Beneath it, Macrobius's *Commentary on the Dream of Scipio* and its classification of all dream types. She gathers the three into her arms.

At the desk Marguerite knows she is to turn the heavy vellum page when Brother Vincent taps it with the finger that is missing its nail. But she knows more. She knows the monks amass accounts of dreams behind the monastery walls. She knows that theories of dreams trouble their book-strewn, vellum-yellow sleep. She knows that the scriptorium of St Germer is a rampart in the Church's defence against the overreaching hands of the university radicals at Paris. She knows that the Church purchases rare Islamic volumes and translations at huge expense from itinerants in the north of Spain. Not so they will be read, but so they might never be read again.

Reading over the outcrop of Brother Vincent's shoulder, Marguerite fattens with the contraband words she collects, like sugar almonds in her mouth. *Paradrome.* 'Agent of restless sleep.' *Leliourian.* 'A Shining One.' 'A being that inhabits the sphere beyond the moon; that, by the use of imaginative action' – *phantastikos, phantastikos*, she repeats – 'acts upon mortals to provoke images in their minds.' *Incubus.* But here Brother Vincent's elbows obscure and confound. 'Authors of urgent vision, at times by sudden and violent terror.' 'A single nightly encounter can leave . . . *afflicti et debilitati.*'

The old monk slowly rubs the pink crown of his head, weary for the world.

But the world is not weary. In Boulogne a man passed a calf from his bowels. In Lyons a plain girl fell down a well and was lifted out a beauty. In Pierrefonds a priest was cursed with a second skin after battling an intractable demon. He sweats uncontrollably now, so that even his holy vestments are a burden.

'Paradrome,' Marguerite would repeat to Christina in the night. 'Leliourian,' they whispered behind their hands at mass.

4

Christina's long sleep began in the early hours of Friday morning. As Marguerite wakes, tired, anxious, on Sunday, she remembers what her father told her the night before. 'Christina's nails are growing.'

She can't think. She can hardly hope. There's knocking at the door. Father Joseph and the nun they call Sister Paul step inside. Marguerite leans outside and shouts for her father in his atelier but Father Joseph will not wait. He walks through to where Christina lies, covered by the vigil-cloth. Sister Paul follows. Marguerite hovers nervously at the threshold. Will her father never come?

'Asleep in Christ, as you can see,' says l'Ymagier as he enters at last, smacking sawdust from his knees. He will play their game if need be. He will feign piety.

Yet he is brought up short. Grief suddenly wells in his throat. He feels the ache of it in his jaw. He beholds his daughter as the old priest does. He sees her dead.

Father Joseph fingers Christina's waxen forehead but does not refer to it. He merely nods to Sister Paul.

She is calm, resolute. 'Your sister, Marguerite, kept the hives at the monastery.'

The sound of her own name startles her. 'Yes,' she says, 'she was good with bees.'

'Good with them?' She motions Marguerite into the room.

'She understood them.'

'Tell me. What is there to understand?'

(Christina's finger pressed over her lips. A secret. She had a secret. *What is it, Christina? Please,* she begged. *Tell. I know there's something. I've seen you* . . . Then, Christina opening her mouth just wide enough to let the queen bee fly straight out.)

'Marguerite, what is there to understand?' The nun smells of goose fat and old cloth.

'It was something she used to say.'

Father Joseph is impatient. 'You shared this bed with your sister?'

'Yes.'

'Did you notice anything out of the ordinary on Thursday night? No, look at me, Marguerite.'

'There was lightning. Summer lightning.'

'What else?'

'Nothing else.'

'Your sister died beside you but you noticed nothing?'

'She was very hot. She couldn't get comfortable.'

'Did she remove her shift?'

'No.'

'Did she talk in her sleep?'

'She has since we were small.'

'That night. Did she talk in her sleep on Thursday night, Marguerite?'

She wants her sister to wake up and answer for herself.

'Marguerite, when I visited you last, on Friday morning, you told me you woke in the night.'

'Did I?'

'Your sister woke you, did she not?'

(*Marguerite? Are you asleep? Marguerite?*)

'The tanner's dog was barking.'

'As the tanner had tied him in the yard for the night. Yes. But you woke again. Before dawn, you said.'

'As the bell rang for matins. I often wake with it.'

'And when you woke, your sister was restless beside you.'

20

'She often half wakes at the bell.'

'It disturbs her.'

'She has always tossed and turned.'

'Why do you think that is, Marguerite?'

'It is her nature.'

'When she is restless, she speaks aloud?'

'At times.'

'What did she say? That night. What did she say?'

'I can't recall.'

'We'll come back to it.'

'It was nonsense.'

'You remember then. That's good.'

'Night jabber. That's what our mother used to call it.'

'Nevertheless.'

'"You're hurting me." I thought she said, "You're hurting me."'

'Yet you were not concerned?'

'She was fast asleep again in moments.'

'Was she, Marguerite?' He folds his hands across his middle, regarding her. 'Was she truly?'

Later, alone with Christina, Sister Paul will fold back the vigil-cloth, spread Christina's legs, and discover with three fingers the openness of her body, for already the machinery of the Church's authority is in motion.

'You must understand, Monsieur l'Ymagier,' intones the priest. 'In cases of sudden or violent death, the deceased will make every attempt to discover a means, through the divine agency of the mass, to make his or her cause of death known to the assembled mourners. I can assure you that the Church is dedicated to upholding this, your daughter's "bier right". The newly departed soul is unusually vulnerable, especially in cases such as hers. She will therefore have our every attention. It will be a requiem mass. The bishop is quite clear. This is an extraordinary loss, and you will not be alone in your grief. His Grace asks that you are mindful of that.'

L'Ymagier meets his eyes. 'It is a comfort, of course.'

5

Late August. Yet l'Ymagier leaves the door open much of the day.

At first, he was afraid of the fresh air, of direct sunlight, of the late-summer heat. He surrounded her with wormwood, myrrh and pieces of white quartz.

Until he realized there was no need. She was as ever.

That morning, after the priest's departure, did he not observe her eyelids pulsing below the wax? He called out to Marguerite, but by the time she came in from the garden the movement had stopped.

Did he shout at her for being so slow? He cannot recall.

When his daughters were small and tearful, l'Ymagier would cajole them with magic tricks. Out of sight, he'd hide a frog in a scooped-out loaf of bread and make the loaf jump across the table, a thing possessed, as they tried, without success, to break bread. He could make a dead fish dance to life on the plate. He could turn a white rose red. He could make an egg float in mid-air. Their favourite. He'd take an egg from the chicken run, hold it before them – 'A perfectly ordinary egg, you can see that, can't you?' – then flip his hand over as if he'd decided, on a whim, to let the egg fall to the floor and smash. But the egg did not smash. It floated below his palm like a moon in the vault of the night.

Much later, Christina worked it out. He'd blown the egg clean and attached to it a white-blonde strand of Marguerite's hair.

In those days when Christina lay lifeless on their bed, strange in her waxen shell, Marguerite used to think about that suspended egg, and she'd find herself looking twice when her father took his hand away from her sister's brow.

He was fond of Plotinus. 'Every action has magic at its source, and the entire life of the practical man is a bewitchment.'

Did Christina merely dream below her father's willing hand?

'Asleep in Christ,' her father had lied to the priest. The good death as sleep. The eternally comforting metaphor. One finds it labouring still in clumsy epitaphs: 'Here lies Mary Small, who fell asleep on May the 6th, 1981, in the company of family and friends. May she rest evermore.'

Then, too, there is sleep, the eight-hour death. The well-loved face made other, taken away from us, in sleep. Our own face strange to us in the snapshots which catch us napping. Where were we in that sleep? Can we say?

We spend an average of twenty to twenty-five years of our lives asleep and five to six years of that sleeping life in dream, or 'paradoxical sleep' – so called because the brain is as active, if not more so, as it is in waking. Yet we lie as if paralysed. The only muscles which retain tone are the eyes, the dia-phragm and, oddly, the genitals – for there is, unaccountably, an increase in blood flow to both the penis and the vagina. Dream, you see, is not only the stuff of counted sheep and river-bank languor.

Open the cover of a bestiary, that medieval encyclopedia of the natural world. Here you'll find the yale, an animal with the jowls of a boar and the tail of an elephant; and the griffin, which boasts the body of a lion and the wings of an eagle. Behold the beaver, which, pursued by man, will bite off its testicles and throw them into the path of hunters to evade capture; and the hyena, a hermaphroditic beast that lives in the graves of dead men and feeds on their bodies. Turn the page. The cubs of the lioness are born dead and remain so for three days until the father blows in their faces to waken them to life.

All are creatures escaped from the illuminated margins of our dreams, where the human is also part beast. In his *Speculum Naturale* Vincent of Beauvais was penning warnings, even as Marguerite read over his shoulder, of coitus between species.

We expect such fears of medievals. We are better acquainted with the world.

So let us move Christina, for our purposes, from the bed she shares with her sister in the year 1284 to a bed in a sleep lab in a large urban centre in, say, the year 2001. We want, after all, the reassuring hum of state-of-the-art living. We want New World rather than Old, for youth is famously impatient of ambiguity.

Chicago.

We're in Chicago.

Forget for now the church bell's sway over the day and its hours. Forget the clear reckoning of the hourglass. Leave behind the timekeeping candle and its steady-flamed resolve. Blow it out. We need not watch the hours disappear in thin bands of coloured wax. Let us move instead into 'imaginary time', that speculative dimension of late-twentieth-century physics which is represented mathematically by the square root of -1.

It is a time when events are able to move in any direction. It is a time which has some of the qualities of space.

This is a flying visit.

A sleep technologist replaces the priest at Christina's bedside. A qualified respirologist, he also stands in for the young physic and the strand of wool before her nose. Perhaps he once travelled to France. A high-school exchange. The Chicago skyline for French Gothic. Glassy façades and sinews of steel for monumental stone and flying buttresses. Sky-scraping prodigies for vaulted heavens.

In his souvenir album on the final page: the cathedral of St Pierre at Beauvais on an overcast day. Yellowing extravagance in an everyday town. On the back of the snap a long-ago note to himself, a detail from the tour, forgotten now: 'Even the Pontiac Building, reassembled in this cathedral, would not touch its vaults.'

Here, in the sleep lab, the ceilings are seven feet. There are few windows, none that can open, and little natural light. The effect, for anyone entering the lab for the first time, is not so much timeless as atemporal.

He finds Christina, of course, already asleep. Nor does she wake as he tapes four electrodes to her scalp for the EEG, two to the corners of her eyes, three to her chin, two to her ears, and small wires to her upper lip for the airflowthermister. The wires tangle in her hair. He throws back a corner of the sheet and attaches two more cords to her legs, for the measurement of muscle tone, and two to her chest, near the clavicles, for the EKG. Her breasts are small, high. His fingers are cold but she doesn't wake; even reflex twitches are absent in dream, if dream it is. He slips a bright metal probe over her finger, like some strange token of betrothal.

Her history: parasomnia. A confusion of states of consciousness in deep stage three or four of sleep, occurring usually in the first third of the night. Events are commonly referred to as 'attacks'. The result? Sleepwalking or talking. Bed-wetting. Or, in Christina's case, night terrors – the sensation of a body upon her. Which may trigger, in rare cases, an arrhythmia, a disturbance to the heart's electrical system.

Arrhythmia, typically, is brought on by exercise, emotional excitement or distress, even in sleep. Blood flow to the major organs, particularly to the brain, diminishes or stops. The pulse is lost. The victim is catapulted into unconsciousness – into anything from a faint to a coma. Otherwise death itself is the first sign. A young person, sound of heart, dies of cardiac arrest. Coroners find nothing.

(*Possess thy heart.* That's what l'Ymagier whispered to his daughter the morning she did not awake.)

The long, forested sleeps of fairy tales are of no account in the sleep lab, nor the dark raptures of the mystic saints and their sudden transports. Long forgotten too is the medieval taxonomy of paradromes, demonic agents of dream who interrupted the sleep of mortals; who brought on the evil of 'nocturnal pollutions' (wet dreams, swollen genitals); spirits who dissolved the boundaries between love and fear, between this world and another.

Even the occasional real-life scare story of modern days – the retired English woman who woke to find a string knotted around her finger; who couldn't remember what it was a reminder of; who sat up in bed to turn on the light and knocked her head against the steel roof of a mortuary drawer – even these news sensations are far, far away from the concerns of the sleep technologist, lulled through the night by the scratch of the polysomnograph's twelve pens; by the intimate, amplified sounds of others in sleep; by the surety that he, alone, is awake.

But Christina.

The microphone above her bed awaits the sound of her breath. The infrared eye of a video camera is intent on her face. The electrodes on her scalp will pick up electrical activity in the temporal lobes, the most electrically unstable portions of the human brain. Deep within, the hippocampus and the amygdala mediate the neuronal whirl of emotion and perception. Food, sex and smell excite these areas of the brain, which are essentially primitive, though not rudimentary. The hippocampus, for example, seems to be involved in instances where the mind 'splits off' from the brain; where the mind emerges with an apparent autonomy – *spirit* or even *soul*, in the parlance of 1284.

Such instances would seem to suggest we possess an innate capacity for transcendence. Or at least for the delusion of transcendence. Artificial excitation of temporo-parietal lobe circuitry can, for example, generate a profound sense of mystical experience. You may seem to slip gravity's tether, floating near the ceiling and gazing down upon your body below. You may breathe deeply of a rose or hear, from nowhere, the voice of a loved one.

Notably, we do not doubt the reality of roses or the fact of a beloved voice simply because one or the other has been artificially produced, a phantom of desire on the stage of the brain. So could this, this means of somehow rising above ourselves, be the brain's oldest memory?

And where is Christina now? Will she wake suddenly, coming up for air – wires clinging like river weed to her hair – to find she overslept? Might l'Ymagier wish her awake after all?

Wait. The sleep technologist has yet to locate her on his video monitor. He hits a button and moves, channel to channel, room to room.

There she is.

The fixed and limited angle of the camera presents her as if she is a young woman in a box, under glass, and in a sense she is. The on-screen timer reads 23:42:36, and already in Beauvais l'Ymagier has taken the measure of her body for the bier upon which she'll rest; for the litter that will bear her to the grave. Already, behind the closed door of his atelier, her effigy – no mere *memento mori* – has taken form.

It is faithful to the circumference of her head, to the distance between her eyes, to the position of her ears. It knows too the breadth of her shoulders, the reach of her arms, the ratio of her torso to her legs.

Rewind a little.

L'Ymagier planes the rough-out and sees her again in his mind's eye, running like a boy to her bees; kicking off her clogs at the stile. Long legs. Yet the legs and feet can only be crudely hewn. There is no time, he argues to himself. It is the head, face, breast and hands that must serve. Her wooden hands will clasp a wooden lily to her wooden breast. No one, he reminds himself, will see the feet.

He raises the vigil-cloth once more, observing it as it falls lightly into place, unruffled as the standard-issue white bedspread and sheet that cover her now in the lab.

One day, thinks our technologist, observing her on the screen, brain imaging – MRI, PET scans – will look crude. One day, implants will track, record and translate the activity of individual neurons as a patient sleeps. One day we will have footage of her dreams.

6

Can you hear her?

It had started to rain. A shower, but sudden and heavy. I marked the tree with the hive and stood waiting beneath its dripping branches. I saw something, a muddy shoulder, a flash of white arm behind a dead trunk, then nothing.

You knew how to hide. You were so easy in the undergrowth. You could disappear with a handspring in long grass.

Now you climb even into my dreams.

What was the knowledge of Sister Paul's three fingers?

On a windy afternoon in May, Marguerite had followed Christina past the town walls and the crumbling chalk quarry, up the vine-covered hills and into the wood beyond. She called out, but her sister moved too quickly. When she came suddenly upon a camp of tree-bark pullers, she stopped short and ran for home.

That night in their bed, Christina didn't smell like herself. She smelled of damp earth, Friday fish and woodsmoke. There were pieces of twig caught in her hair. And honey. Honey in her hair, on her neck.

From that night on – or did Marguerite imagine it? – her sister's sleep was broken. She'd open her eyes and speak incoherently to the dark. Sometimes she'd wake rigid, unable to get her breath.

For the first time in her life, Marguerite was no longer certain who her sister was, and this uncertainty spread like a drizzle over the brightness of spring. Nothing was clear any more. Christina was secretive, impatient. When she combed out Marguerite's hair at night, she'd sigh, exasperated by the knots. When one of her clogs went missing, she flung the other at the tanner's dog. When l'Ymagier said he wanted her home more often, that he wanted her to help him in the atelier as she once had, there were tears of frustration in her eyes.

Your mother was a travelling acrobat who left you in the hollow of a tree when the troupe moved on to Clermont. It's all your father told you.

An ashman, you said, with a wasted leg. The wood, his home before it was yours.

You can skin a fox or a rabbit as easily as I remove a glove. Sometimes I watch you hoard acorns and truffles, for you know what it is to live half-dead for weeks at a time, like an animal in a hole.

There is a winter in you.

You are more solitary than a bark puller. You've never even been as far as the town. The new cathedral is an impossibility at which you squint from the edges of the grape-growers' terraces. When you told me you didn't believe in it, I laughed.

Your eyes are black, luminous. Hard to turn from.

Only in 1972 did Pope Paul VI abolish the formal order of the exorcist. A belated concession to modernity. Five hundred years before, exorcists were unapologetic. Giles of Beauvais – still a student at Paris in 1258 and not yet the imaginator he was to be – was ordained to lower orders as a matter of course, and fortified with a book of exorcisms.

Today, one in five of us will experience what is still known, clinically, as the incubus, though, statistically, few will ever speak of it. From the mote-filled distance of the thirteenth century, William of Auvergne, in *De Universo*, recounts numerous stories, recognizable today, of this dark stranger: *in* from the Latin for 'upon', *cubare* meaning 'to press'. So, a burden or a weight. He is more commonly known, however, as the crusher. The choker. The shaggy defiler of women. The restless woodland demon. The wild man. The damaged angel, outlawed from heavenly climes.

'There is nothing wonderful,' writes William, 'that demons should make love to women.' Officialdom was unwilling to raise an eyebrow. Folk wisdom, too, is matter of fact: it describes a sexual organ that is freezing cold, made of iron, or even double-pronged.

Victims recall the sound of footsteps, of breathing. They remember the sense of suffocation, of being wide awake, of helpless paralysis, imminent entombment or near heart attack. Even today, more than 80 per cent of those who have experienced the incubus remain convinced of a highly personal encounter with something other.

Only rarely does the incubus come gently, a love partner, a spirit whose habit it is to invade hearts torn by grief; a spirit, we are told, women once beseeched, seeking him out, sleeping alone in his forested temples and metamorphosing under the weight of him. Is it for these reasons that the incubus was notoriously difficult to exorcize?

In the language of this century: a chronic sleep disorder. Cause unknown.

We know it is not a case of sluggish humours stopping the passage of the animal spirits so that the body cannot move. It is not a case, as Paracelsus argued, of menstrual flux engendering phantoms in the air. It is not due to incongruous matter from the blood mixing with the nervous fluid in the cerebellum, nor poisonous gases, *miasmata*, congesting the brain. It is not a matter of undigested food pressing on the diaphragm – for the early Greeks, incidentally, the seat of the soul. Nor does the incubus loom at certain phases of the moon.

He is not, it would seem, abolished by shaving one's head, scarifying the throat, bleeding the ankle or ingesting any of the following: wild carrot, the black seeds of the male peony or ten milligrams of diazepam.

In this century, the incubus comes to us in what is known as 'delta' sleep – a dreamless sleep, the sleep of the cathedral crypt. While most of us shoot out of deep sleep to the surface when disturbed, like a lift speeding upward, some of us unaccountably get stuck between floors. We experience a double consciousness, and the incubus, it seems, gains entry through this portal.

Of course, the experience of a presence in the room may be nothing more than the result of pressure on a limb as one sleeps; of chronic electrical discharges within the temporal lobe structures; of repressed mental conflict regarding sexual desire, usually incestuous. For Freud, the demon and its crushing weight represent the authoritative father and the guilty aspects of an incest symbolism.

Or, take a variation on that theme. Remember the pressure on the victim's breast, the terrible inevitability of self-surrender, the genital emissions. The incubus represents a repression of the natural masochistic component of the female sexual instinct. (Picture, we are instructed, the fear of being entered, of being impaled. Consider the conflict associated with yielding.) Or is this diagnosis merely the mid-century Freudian's denial of his own repressed feelings of dominance, resurrected by the fantasy of a narcoleptic femininity, by the eros of a young woman at rest?

In any case, angst, we are reminded, has a voluptuous quality.

In predisposed subjects, attacks of parasomnia, including the incubus, may be elicited by forced arousals.

Our sleep technologist will experiment with arousals as Christina moves into delta-phase sleep. At his desk, the eight intercoms breathe sonorously. On channel 1 of the monitor, we find Mrs H, aged forty-eight. She has been gaining weight unintentionally. In the morning she discovers plates, cups and saucers around her bed, and crumbs in her sheets. She is concerned about her lack of control. Recently she defecated in her bed one night and, understandably, this has disturbed her.

On channel 2, Mr R, a newlywed. Mrs R has woken repeatedly at night to discover her husband masturbating in his sleep. When she awakens him, he is always unaware of his behaviour and very embarrassed. The couple claim to have good sexual relations. Now, however, in the night of the sleep lab, nothing. No sign. Mr R scratches his groin haphazardly under the blanket. That is all.

On channel 3, a suspected case of sleep apnoea. The same on 6. Beds 5, 7 and 8 are empty tonight. No last-minute referrals. No midnight visionaries from the night shelters.

On channel 4, there, Christina. Dead to the world.

The technologist slips out of the office and buys himself a weak cup of coffee from the machine in the corridor. The animated metal hand selects and holds the cup, ready for the greater workings within. Coffee. Milk. One sugar. The only other sign of life in the lab at one in the morning.

He will confirm Christina's entry into delta sleep before forcing arousal. He would expect to see slow waves, with a frequency of only one half to two cycles per second. He would expect to see the pens of the polysomnograph sketching the shape of stalagmites on the page, close narrow peaks in the cave of sleep.

Is the image not reminiscent of something he once longed for as a child? He dimly remembers pouring packets of coloured crystals into a fishbowl and awaiting a bright, underwater world of stalagmites to spring up, cathedral towers for his goldfish. Did it ever turn into the picture on the box? He cannot recall.

He sips his coffee slowly. He is not usually susceptible to idle moments of fantasy. Christina, it seems, has caught his imagination.

Is that why he is unable to read the data properly? Suddenly, bells are ringing. He moves from computer screen to amplifier; from video monitor to oxygen-saturation monitor. Coffee spills over a keyboard. He rips a recording from the rolling paper output of the polysomnograph. The last three minutes of her sleep. Why can't he interpret?

The automatic writing of the twelve pens is wild. The EEG says delta. No, delta moving into theta. Non-REM into REM. Deep sleep into dream. She is only dreaming. The oculogram confirms it. Yet airflow indicates arousals. Chest and abdomen effort is maximum. Nothing will correlate.

He makes a dash for her room and throws open the door. Her blanket is on the floor. So are the leads that were connected to her legs and chest. He doesn't understand. He goes to her bed. Beneath her lids, her eyes pulse in dream. Where is she?

(Flat on her back as debris rains in upon her from high above. She's turning her face, trying to breathe, spitting grit and earth from her mouth, when someone wanders past. A thin man in an open bathrobe. 'Tastes awful, doesn't it?' he says, grimacing.)

The technologist covers her once more. He listens at the door for a moment as she cries out in her sleep.

He checks his other patients. Normal. He fills out an incident report, minimizing the evident discrepancies. He thinks of the girlfriend he once had who threw out every wristwatch she wore; who seemed to turn off street lights as she passed.

He writes 'ghost in the machine' and overcompensates with a spree of exclamation marks. It will amuse his colleague who replaces him in four hours.

7

It was like a wild root. When I took it in my mouth, I sucked as I had once sucked at my mother's nipple, drawing you to life. Afterwards, you pressed me to you, so hard I thought you'd crush me.

I didn't know you would. I didn't know you'd leave me for dead.

That's how it was. A wild root, and my mouth, my maidenhead, the bloom of you. A fragile pairing.

Without me now, you know only the dark and cold of leaf mould and stale earth again. You know only to hide. Poor tuber. Poor burrowing thing.

Hear me. I wish for the days when I didn't know that a life can break.

'O King of virgins, who lovest the chaste of heart and undefiled, do thou with the dew of thy heavenly grace quench in my body all flames of unlawful feeling that I may evermore abide before thee in innocency of body and of soul. Mortify in my members the sting of the flesh and repress in me every dangerous passion.'

Who's there?

Christina was taken from the home of l'Ymagier on Sunday night, the eve of her funeral, before the curfew. She was carried to the new cathedral's Chapel of the Holy Sepulchre and laid upon the bier her father himself had once hewn. Three priests attended her. They assured l'Ymagier that a vigil would be kept; that she would not be deprived of the Office of the Dead and its petitions. For yea, was not a single day in Purgatory an entire year of mortal time?

Before she was taken, father and sister were permitted to kiss her. Marguerite was surprised by the sensation of wax against her lips – moist to the touch, like a cold sweat on her sister's brow. She wanted to run from the house. But run where? Her grandparents were long dead. And while her father was admired in the town, he kept himself – he kept the three of them – aloof from it. People smelled pride.

Only she and Christina knew. Their father was not easy enough within himself to be easy among others. It was their mother who had completed him. It was their mother's death that had left him broken, fragmentary, like some cast-off piece under sheets in his own atelier.

Now there was talk. And only that morning something on the threshold. A large amulet stuffed with faeces, black fur and blood. She threw it into the river and said nothing to her father.

Would he have heard in any case? He'd hardly left his atelier since the day before. Once – to see Athalie. The Egyptian, he sometimes called her, as if it were a title, while in the town she and her overgrown son were spat at as gypsies.

Then, that evening, he'd come into the house from the atelier, still in his leather apron, and found her keeping vigil at her sister's side. She looked up, surprised, unused to him suddenly. He said he needed something. She expected him to say supper. Or a jar of beer. Or candles, better light. Maybe a hole to be mended in the sleeve of his tunic, for the mass. Not a volume. Not a stolen volume.

He wasn't making sense. She must find it, he said. In the scriptorium at St Germer. Before her sister's mass tomorrow. Avicenna's *Philosophia Orientalis* – or any of its parts. She must go before first light. Before the monks rose for matins.

Marguerite noticed his hands, bruised and nicked; the leather thimble still on his thumb. And when was it – late Friday afternoon? – that the door of his atelier was ajar? Inside, the huge rough-out of ash clamped on the carving horse. Was there a commission?

'I saw it once,' he continued. 'I read from it. By the university walls, where the prostitutes leaned. Priceless, the stranger said. One of those unexpected moments. My hands trembled, as they did when I held Christina and then you for the first time. It was made from vellum, uterine vellum, which is the most dear. Calfskin plucked early from the womb. It was a bound copy, itself of fragments, for the original was plundered in Avicenna's own time. The copy was the only one that escaped the purge at the university. It's said to be in fragments again. A surer means of its preservation, I suppose. Even so, the monks will have got their hands on something of it. His commentary on *De Anima*, I am certain. Perhaps the "Epistle on the Angels". Probably. Do you see? Here, Marguerite. Not at Paris. Not near the university. What they have will be here.'

'Find it?' Marguerite felt her mind sway. 'Find it how?' She wanted her father to be still, to stop. She wished her sister finally dead. At rest. She yearned for the tranquillity of convention.

'O God, grant that no flame of guilt lay waste the souls of thy servants.'

Who is it? Who's there?

8

Happiness, a new idea in Christendom, began to take hold in the thirteenth century.

Perhaps it was a lone Turkish jingler at the town gates. Or a renegade musician plucking a psaltery with a goose quill at the hour of mass.

Soon it was a troupe of flute players, accordionists, tumblers, actors and dancing bears making their camp on the wild fringes of town. So the idea of happiness spread. In Beauvais, behind high walls, pleasure gardens came to life with topiary beasts, gushing fountains and ornamental trees. Through chinks in those walls, boys spied on lovers, bright and foolish, in love with love, and the notion of happiness could not be contained.

A restlessness of spirit burgeoned in coloured breads; parakeet stalls; mechanical dragons; magicians with mirrors, boxes and scarves; glaziers dazzled by colour; pilgrims dizzied by spires; boys with wounded kites; old men with skittering dice; girls who sweetened their breath with wild honey; crowned and drooling Fools; Mayday poles, green-garlanded; feasts of twelve to one hundred and twenty courses; glorious peacocks, roasted and refeathered, their claws and beaks painted with gold; life-size elephants born of pastry; and galloping hobbyhorses, no mere toys but ushers, rather, of festive marvels to come. So the notion of *contemptus mundi*, official ideology of a Church now in trouble, began to falter.

Yet do not mistake happiness for merry liberality. In Beauvais in 1284 there were nine hangings, three public draggings and two live burials. In court, a man convicted of the theft of a falcon was ordered to surrender six ounces of meat to the beak of said falcon, from his own breast or head.

There was, too, a fever for angels.

If the Fourth Lateran Council of 1215 had found that bread and wine could be transfigured, in the hands of the supplicating priest, into the living body of Christ, what other incarnations might yet be among us? What other acts of faith might yet be generative of fact? What, after all, was the power of the heart?

In every blade of grass, an angel. At the birth of every child, an angel. An angel to spin each planet; an angel to cast each star trembling into the night.

As the bell for matins tolled, just before first light on the Friday morning Christina would fail to wake, did an angel take a single perilous step?

Thomas Aquinas, writing in 1264, the year of Christina's birth, would have overruled the question. Angels, he pronounced, were incorporeal creatures who only assumed bodies, including wings, in times of mortal need. Moreover, to assume a body with ears, nose, mouth and all the parts a human is heir to, was not, Thomas was clear, to take on a body's vital functions or its passions. Angels, he would have us know, are without anger, lust or bodily joy. While Augustine, several centuries earlier, permitted angels 'a sensitive faculty', that is to say, a means of perception through the senses, Thomas could not agree.

Furthermore, while some, including the theologian Dionysius, claimed for demons – those fallen relations of angels – the power of perverted phantasy, and therefore, by implication, the power of elevated phantasy for angels, Thomas again is sure: 'The angel has no imagination.' The angel was officially, in 1284, a being of pure reason and will, and angelic will, if it need be said, was a will without appetite or desire.

Yet while Thomas, chief among the scholastics, was clear

about the nature of angels, and above all about the essential incorporeality of angels, the Church knew that seeing was indeed believing if the faithful were to remain convinced. If Christianity were to compete with happiness.

'There is a difficulty,' l'Ymagier once replied to the bishop himself.

'There is no difficulty.'

'Am I to understand that the angel's body will have hands and feet and hair? Its wings, I gather, will be capable of flight?'

The bishop had paused, looking up from his knuckles, suddenly no longer bored. He sensed a peculiar stubbornness in the artisan who stood before him. A resistance behind the man's words. Perhaps a carefully veiled passion for cosmology. 'I say nothing, Monsieur l'Ymagier. I merely ask you this. If a hissing swan on the Avelon river is capable of flight, do you think an angel of His glorious ranks might not also demonstrate some aptitude?'

So l'Ymagier carved the stuff of heaven. He worked in ash, oak and white birch – timber lifted from the forest floor of Beauvais. He laid his hands on the coolness of marble and granite, and felt for the seams of life within. He imagined the uprush of thermals in terracotta and clay.

Yet how was ether made matter? How could the body of an angel be rendered mortal? Should it be covered? Was its nakedness not beautiful? An angel was not, after all, born into the original sin of scripture. Yet to deliver a naked angel to the bishop would be an affront even he dared not attempt. He wished he had the courage – not merely to risk the raw energy of muscle and bone; not only to hew the longing of flesh – but to carve in stone life-force itself.

Blasphemy. Without doubt.

Yet might not that which bridged two bodies also bridge two worlds, the mortal and the divine?

41

The question was futile, for there was no reputation that could survive the charge.

He occupied himself with the dream of wings. He cast the wings of apocalypse outspread in the uplift of God's unending breath. He lifted tentative wings from raw matter and sent them, shuddering, into flight. He laboured over the broken wing of an angel, eternally falling from a rung on Jacob's ladder.

Yet each time he was frustrated by technicality. How should the drapery fall? Should the wings push through, like arms through sleeves? Or should they tremble beneath, a brooding potential for flight?

And too the question of construction. Are the wings of angels taut and segmented, like those of the bat scurrying at twilight, or gauzy as the wings of a bee? He contemplated all, including diverse wings on the ankles, like those of the pagan gods, until it occurred to him to change the dimensions of the angel himself. A stronger frame alone could support the demand of wings. So he altered trunk and sternum. He deformed clavicle and neck. And his angels grew to monstrosity.

This dream of wings was l'Ymagier's final and most painful struggle to believe – to see heaven in the Holy and Apostolic Church, to see God in Thomas's static Creation.

But pain is initiatory. After dumping the gutted swan at the door of the bishop's palace, l'Ymagier gave himself to the singing materiality of stone; to the animate grain of wood. He mocked the Church's covert distaste for the world with an egregious delight in all its detail. His serpents, his apples, his grinning demons and fork-tailed mermaids, his burgeoning Trees of Life and *memento mori* – all rendered the hereafter, by comparison, a pallid dream.

His celebrity grew. He was known in Paris and beyond

for his effigies of the noble dead and for his wildly decorative work in pleasure gardens. It was said he'd sculpted a fountain-head for an anonymous patron, a pink marble bouquet of gushing phalluses; that the locals could hardly keep the thing in buffalo's milk. It was said, too, that a crowd in Lombardy had tried, one after another, to break off a minor prince's dead finger, a usual sought-after relic; that they'd been amazed when it had at last come away – wax flesh and knuckle – in a small boy's hands. The child had dropped it, terrified, and run.

L'Ymagier had a talent for bringing things to life.

So the Church found him unavoidably indispensable. It could not afford not to employ him. Yet he did not make it easy. He did not mask his contempt. While every other crafts-man in the Île-de-France converged on Beauvais in the hope of employment, he made the chapter request his services. He spoke his mind. He appeared bemused by the hierarchy of halo shapes and the designation of colours for robes. He laughed at a prelate's argument that the ox was more sacred than the ass. And he made the bishop himself wait. For fifteen years he made him wait.

It didn't take the bishop that long, of course, to realize that he was dealing with a one-time Arabist, a university heretic, a radical Avicennan who'd only just escaped the authorities at Paris all those years ago. L'Ymagier had flaunted it. What else was that old allegation – 'Fear of the Angel' – but a bold snub of a reference to the Tenth Angel controversy? The bishop still remembered the stink of the swan. His servants had refused to touch it. They'd feared the words, scrawled in blood, they could not read.

Of course he'd sent for the records. He'd read the lengthy transcripts of the tribunal at Paris, often observed by Aquinas himself – still master of theology in that year and not yet struck mute by the fearful will of God. He'd located the relevant testimony. In 1259, a twenty-one-year-old student called Giles of Beauvais had confessed himself an Avicennan.

The testimony was flagrant. He condemned their adoption of Aquinas's own translations of Aristotle over those of Avicenna. ('And the man without a word of Greek,' he was reported to have said to a fellow student.) He went on to assert the existence and power of the outlawed Tenth Angel. He admitted a belief in Avicenna's twofold soul – the *intellectus passivus* and the *intellectus possibilitus*; that is to say, the temporal mortal persona, or character, of a man, and what Avicenna described as the eternal, envisioning mind within each of us.

When generously encouraged to admit confusion, to say that he had merely mistaken Avicenna's twofold soul for Aristotle's doctrine of the practical and theoretical intelligences – that he meant nothing more than this, that the Avicennan translation had, of course, been poor – he refused to yield.

Instead, unbelievably, he elaborated. While the mortal persona would die, he dared to remind those gathered that the *intellectus possibilitus* was, of its self, immortal because it participated in the stuff of Creation – through communion with the Tenth Angel – whether we were aware or not.

He admitted he spoke in full knowledge of William of Auvergne's express injunctions against such outlandish Arabianism. 'But what are such injunctions?' he dared. 'In the interests of truth and knowledge, this university flouts even the papal ban on studies of Aristotle, for where would we be otherwise?'

He informed the university authorities, including Thomas, that the *intellectus possibilitus* alone could 'achieve' salvation, not solely through the grace of Our Father, but through an ardent desire for the angel from whom it had emanated and with whom it was intimately bound. (It was duly noted that the heretic espoused emanationism against the express instruction of the Fourth Lateran Council.) Furthermore, Giles of Beauvais confessed that he did indeed 'deplore' the Church's 'erasure' of the *alam al-mithal*, or the Imaginal World, as he termed it.

The interest of the tribunal was unexpectedly whetted. Would the student care to explain the gravity of their so-called offence – this ostensible conspiracy – of which they and the Church Fathers stood accused?

He hedged. He said he did not believe a group of men as learned and informed as they were in need of explanation. He was in over his head.

Turning over the cracked and confidential papers of testament, the bishop knew Giles of Beauvais had been given little choice but to continue. His speech began tentatively: 'There is a creative cause that moves the universe.' He was prompted. Twice. He asked for the question to be repeated. They toyed with him, naturally. Yet had he confined himself to embarrassing generalities, he would have been permitted to slip the noose of his interrogator. It was the way of these things, the bishop reflected. Heresy could not be tolerated, but a heretic's righteousness would never be drawn where it might, more usefully, spend itself. The student-fool, however, grew bolder.

'Desire moves all. By this I mean an inner necessity not merely to be but to become. It moves planets. It moves the angelic ranks. It moves the feeble soul of man. It is a faculty of the heart which carries all life towards that which is not yet realized in it. We evolve, the cosmos evolves, even the angels evolve, in longing.

'What is hitherto innate is lifted from the fabric of reality by the act of ardent imagining; by the force of the desiring mind. And the metamorphosis, quiet or large, happens firstly on this plain of the Imaginal World, the intermediate world between matter and spirit of which Avicenna speaks.

'It is a real place. A peninsula between worlds. It is also man's only bridge to his own deification.'

He had, the bishop observed, helpfully walked into a trap of his own making.

'Giles of Beauvais, do you believe Christ was born the Son of God?'

The copyist's oblique stroke marked his silence.

'You will answer the question. Giles of Beauvais, do you believe Jesus Christ was born the Son of God?'

'No.'

'What is it you believe?'

'I have stated what I believe.'

'Be very clear. Many of us here are gum-toothed old men, are we not? Our minds fail us. You do not believe Christ was born the Son of God. Is that correct?'

Again. The stylus stroke.

'It is a straightforward question.'

'And I have answered it.'

'Then you will expand. For the third time, do you, Giles of Beauvais, believe Christ was born the Son of God?'

'I believe he became the Son of God.'

Even the bishop, twenty-five years later, in the quiet of his rooms, felt the blood in his temples flare.

'Then you cannot believe that man's hopeful redemption lies in the grace of the miracle of the Holy Incarnation.'

'No.'

'Tell us, Giles of Beauvais. Wherein lies our salvation?'

'I believe we are saved by Christ.'

'You contradict yourself.'

'I believe we are saved by the example of Christ's becoming.'

'Not by His sacrifice on the Cross; not by the grace of God at our moment of death?'

'No.'

'Do you not believe, as your Arab did, that Jesus Christ was in fact Christos-Angelos, a "deified" or "angelicized" man and not Our Lord incarnate?'

'With respect, Avicenna was not Arabian, but Persian. He was born in the province of Bukhara. Arabic was his second language.'

'Answer the question. Is it true you believe Christ to have been a deified, or an angelicized, man?'

'It is true.'

'Might we each then become a Son of God? Might you, Giles of Beauvais, become the Son of God?'

It was too dangerous, even for the impetuous likes of Giles of Beauvais. He started to panic. The bishop could hear him losing control of his argument. 'The question is specious. You yourselves have read Avicenna. In fact, you must avow he was all you read until –' He would regret his haste.

'Until . . .'

'Until you realized the implications.'

'Which you will now delineate on our behalf.'

Despair made him reckless. 'You realized it is within the reach of mortal man to contact the divine, himself, within, on the plain of the *alam al-mithal*, the Imaginal World.'

'Please, Giles. Speak plainly. Do.'

The sarcasm aroused the young man. His tone grew peevish. He was – the bishop smiled – an angry child after all. 'I tell you only what you know already. Avicenna was your trusted authority until you suddenly understood the dangerous import of his philosophy: that Christians need no longer passively await the grace of salvation; that the Church might no longer be sole mediator between man and God; that the apparently base elements of this world of matter would no longer merit our contempt, but rather our attention; that its details are, potentially, the language, the very syllables, of divine revelation; that revelation is forever unfolding, uncontainable by Church or scripture; that God is not above His Creation but indivisible from it; that each of us, whether we know it or not, renews Creation moment by moment; that each of us therefore might yet discover our innate divinity – might yet say "I am God" even as we humbly know we are no more, and perhaps no less, than a mote of dust in the unstoppable light.'

Amazingly, the tribunal had laughed. The bishop could hardly credit it. The records indicated that the assembly had to be reminded of the solemnity of the proceedings.

Paris. This was Paris, the bishop recalled. Gathered here was the intellectual elite of Christendom. Who among them would dare register more than urbane amusement? Who among them had the moral rectitude?

Yet there had to have been a certain confusion. The authorities would have been thrown from the grooves of habit and precedent. And this failure of readiness must have been Giles of Beauvais's single stroke of luck.

In the bishop's experience, heretics who had admitted much less, who had been far less coherent in their testimonies, had been sentenced to torture, to unspeakable privation. Hadn't Pope Innocent's bull provided unambiguous guidance? Giles of Beauvais, however, was sentenced only to lock-up within the university walls. Furthermore, when he escaped three months later, he was neither pursued nor excommunicated. The bishop suspected Aquinas had, privately, been impressed. He himself found the man's pride repugnant.

Which did nothing to diminish the threat of secularity in his own diocese. The faithful grew increasingly distracted. There was little choice but to co-opt the heretic's singular talent in the employ of scripture. There was no choice but to bargain for his services; to flatter his monstrous pride; to puff

48

on the fire of his vanity. There was no choice, quite simply, because l'Ymagier gave him no choice. He had made the bishop ask. No other imaginator in the service of the Church was his equal. And the bishop's cathedral could have no rival.

The bishop was tall, strongly built. He came from peasant stock in Picardy. As a boy, the yoke on his back had been as easy as a thought in the mind of another. He had tough hands, an effortless stamina, also an agility in the material world rarely seen in clerics. He understood the value of land, and the power of a Church that could afford to use land merely in the display of vaulted space.

As for faith, it was an abstraction he could appreciate in others but would fail to know in himself, a failure he would guard even from his confessor. He understood loyalty. It would serve. He understood Church law and hierarchy as a necessary expression of that loyalty. And because of his secret failure of faith, his concern for its tenets, not surprisingly, would grow and grow. At the age of only thirty, William of Grez – the son of a peasant farmer famed for his cabbages (the active ingredient in a local hangover remedy) – became bishop of Beauvais.

This much he knew: he would not have indulged the young Giles of Beauvais in the manner of Aquinas. This he also knew: had he been a one-time Arabist and heretic, he would have answered the prelate when approached by the chapter; he would not have drawn a bishop's attention. He would not have made a bishop wait.

Now the daughter of l'Ymagier, it would seem, was dead. Healthy one day. Cold as clay the next. There were rumours in Beauvais. The bishop was not unaware, nor could he repress a wan smile.

It was Father Joseph who'd found it difficult to contain his emotions.

Summoned before His Grace, the old man was peremptorily informed that he, Father Joseph, would offer up a requiem mass for his deceased parishioner Christina at the new cathedral of St Pierre. Her 'bier right' was to be invoked. She was to be given all rites; the Offices of the Dead were to be performed in full. All trade in the town was to be suspended for the day. The family, especially the father, were under no circumstances to feel alone in their grief. Did Father Joseph understand? Under no circumstances. Regarding the mass itself, the diocese, he was told, would spare no expense.

Bewildered, Father Joseph faltered to his knees and kissed the bishop's gold-stitched hem.

9

Even as matter is frozen light, so is time past a memory of a future awaiting release.

Look again at the bishop's rising cathedral in 1284. Here, space, typically the absence of anything, becomes a dizzying force in itself, a vast longing, a rogue wave of light caught between those great expanses of translucent surface. Even then, between the cathedral's striving ribs and vaults, in its vertiginous invocation of light, lay the phantom architecture of Fermilab, a sixteen-storey 'Research Lab on the Energy Frontier', conceived by a man who was both physicist and sculptor; an American inspired by a visit to the cathedral at Beauvais.

Here at Fermilab, in a hinterland that lies far beyond the secular faith of Chicago's soaring skyline, physicists chase, among other things, the elusive 'God particle', or, more humbly perhaps, the principle that will mediate the mysterious indeterminacy of the microscopic realm with the bricks and mortar of the macroscopic world; a principle that will reconcile the ephemera of quanta, leptons and quarks with the mass of big bangs, beetroot and the bodies of great-uncles.

Thirty feet beneath the prairie, beams of protons and anti-protons are fired around a vast particle accelerator, a ring four miles in circumference. Every year, thousands of students come, pilgrims, to observe for themselves the winking reality of the world's underface; to follow in faith the movement of particles, insubstantial as the trajectories of angels.

Giant magnets force the two beams to collide. The magnets

must be kept cold, −267 degrees Celsius. Cold beyond imagining. In one second a proton can speed around that ring 50,000 times. In ten seconds it will have travelled two million miles. In the debris of the collisions, particles are born that have not been known to the universe since the time of the Big Bang. Some of these particles will exist for less than a billionth of a billionth of a second. Yet finally, fleetingly, they are observed: dancing filaments of light on a phosphor screen, more transient than a dream.

Imagine. You stand on the threshold of the Energy Frontier. In the distance you see it. Twin concrete towers, like praying hands, spanned by a two-hundred-foot wall of glass and a vast atrium. (Twin towers, in crumbling chalk, spanned by a mighty rose of a window.) Walk in. Across the broad, light-filled foyer (through the transept). You see two young girls watching an elevator door open and close, open and close. A fault. No one is pushing the buttons. They giggle nervously to each other.

It's a late Sunday afternoon, and the place is dead. You step inside the elevator, and the girls squeeze in beside you as you push the button for the fourteenth floor – in reality, the thirteenth. Odd that even a world-class research lab pays its respect to superstition.

You stare at the ceiling, uncomfortable in the company of children who observe you so openly. The ceiling is simulated stained glass. Plastic, but vaguely funereal none the less. You watch the numbers overhead come to life, one by one. Rise up.

They tell you their father works here. He's promised them a treat because it's a Sunday and they're getting bored. He hasn't forgotten. You too approach his lab. You hesitate at the door, then walk in.

For though you might not know it yet, you are the privileged Observer. You enter at will.

★

52

During his tribunal at Paris, Giles of Beauvais argued – passion-ately? ridiculously? – for the 'desiring mind' as a physical force within Creation.

Wishful thinking? Overblown mysticism?

Try this. For Giles of Beauvais's 'desiring mind' or 'acts of ardent imagining' read quantum theory's 'Observer Effect'.

The Observer Effect refers to the elusive subatomic inter-action that somehow lifts reality out of virtuality, or 'event' from a smear of quantum probabilities. It is triggered, osten-sibly, by the act of measurement – or, more simply put, by the act of observation.

The Observer is, for all intents and purposes, the same as the measuring device: a microscope, let's say, or a tracking chamber in a particle detector. Here quantum flux meets the solid world and is instantaneously flat-packed into reality.

That's the story – and also the least unsettling, philo-sophically, of our options.

Yet why should the location of newborn reality be the microscope or the core of the tracking chamber? What is unique, in the material sense, about either of these locations or indeed any measuring device? We might just as easily point to, say, the computer processor where data is first uploaded or the computer screen, where particle showers are first glimpsed in delicate tracks of phosphorescence.

For that matter, why the computer screen and not the Observer's own retina, where light alchemizes into meaning at the back of the seeing eye? Could this not be where quantum flux gives way to the unquestionably real?

Mystery yields only to greater mystery.

Move on, from the eye of the Observer (yours, for instance) to the mind of the Observer (yours again), a reality as physical as any other. Think of the initiatory light of the concentrated mind; of a mind that cannot be separated, fundamentally, from the stuff of the world it beholds. For what is the quickfire of thought but a residue of an incalculable light that is fifteen billion years old? Can such a heat be left out of the equation?

Listen. 'There is mind in every electron.' Listen. 'The action of consciousness has the physical consequence of determining the subsequent states of a system in a manner that corresponds to the concept of *will*.' And even: 'If the observer is emotionally involved in the outcome of the experiment and particularly wants one result to come out rather than another, there may be a corresponding shift in the probability distribution.'

It sounds like madness. Or magic.

Back in the Sunday quiet of the lab, you're watching something pulsing, alive, in an assistant's hand. You squint. He takes it into his other hand as he adjusts a dial. A frog. An ordinary frog here in a place of boosters, injectors and superconducting magnets. Surprising, but not entirely unfamiliar. For within the frog that once danced in the trick hollow of l'Ymagier's loaf of bread is the green memory of this, this other frog, alive now and, understandably, jumpy.

The assistant places it gently in a metal cylinder and tells you, as he does so, that they're using a magnetic field of sixteen tesla. 'That's a million times more powerful than the earth's field.' His boss turns around. No, your eyes do not deceive you. It is l'Ymagier – in cargo trousers and rolled-up shirtsleeves. He sees you for the first time: a seemingly casual observer with a pamphlet and map in one hand. A visitor on the self-guided tour for off-season visitors. He smiles an apology for his overexcited children. 'Poor frog,' he says. 'They never tire of this one.'

L'Ymagier adjusts the apparatus. His hands fly over a computer keyboard. His assistant commentates. 'It's simple really. We distort the electron orbits in the frog's atoms. That generates a tiny electric current which generates a magnetic field in the opposite direction from the main magnet. The repulsive force pushes them apart, and the frog, as you can see, gets caught in the middle.' And suddenly you do see: the confused frog is suspended in mid-air, six feet off the ground.

The girls clap, and you find yourself wanting to do likewise. L'Ymagier shines, like a child himself.

'Do me now,' cries the elder girl. 'Me now, Dad. I want to float, too.'

'I've told you, Tina. You're too big.'

'But I *want* to!' As if this changes everything.

And, somewhere, perhaps it does.

IO

In the Chapel of the Holy Sepulchre, laid out upon her bier, Christina is cold. Were you to lift her hand from her breast, you'd feel the dead weight of her waxen fingers. You'd see her nails are blue. It's true, the chapel, one of eight which radiate off the choir, is chill with evening dew, for the cathedral of St Pierre is still without even temporary doors.

Given the bishop's interest in the girl, the priests have chased out the pilgrims who routinely bed down for the night on the stone flags in the choir – the nave has yet to be built. Tonight, some will sleep in open graves under the summer sky. Others will steal into vineyards and crush grapes in their sleep.

As recently as Thursday, Christina herself walked through the cathedral. She scanned the heights for the speck of her father, reckless in the scaffolding, a zealot with a chisel. She found, as usual, not only pilgrims, but also children playing ball, a couple courting, townsmen exercising their dogs, a falconer training bird to glove, gossiping women, and an array of miscellaneous merchant stalls that rivalled the daily market. She loved the careless hubbub of it all. She loved the sight of her father swinging madly from a harness on high.

He was putting the final touches on the choir's central keystone: a cluster of nine angelic heads. Three groups of three running around the edge of the stone. A design commissioned by the bishop himself.

The hair shone in a glory of gold leaf. Each mouth was open in praise. No, l'Ymagier had been told, there could be, would be, no tenth. ('In the very centre,' he'd proposed. 'To make the best possible use of the space.') A tenth angel would ruin not only the harmony of the bishop's composition, but also l'Ymagier's own chances of future employment on the Île-de-France. Was that abundantly clear?

Far below, Christina called as she did at the end of every day. L'Ymagier's supper was ready.

As she walked back up the centre aisle, the approaching solitude of Sunday evening and the profound loneliness of the chapel would have been unimaginable in the afternoon din of saddle makers, soap boilers, glaziers, glovers, tongue scrapers, tooth pullers, ear pickers, cheese sellers, wool combers, crystal gazers, relic traders, moneychangers, diviners casting entrails and barber-surgeons bleeding clients according to their charts. 'Disaster,' they might have said to her had she stopped to listen. Dis-aster. Literally, trouble in the stars.

How might a girl of twenty unfix the action of the stars?

By moving beyond her sphere.

This is the wisdom, for soothsayers are as suspicious of change as the rest of us. They know very well that it comes at a cost.

I remember rain. Heavy, though it hardly lasted. And me marking the tree with the hive. The drip of branches. Water running down the bridge of my nose. Something just ahead. A muddy shoulder, a flash of white arm behind a dead trunk, a pair of suspicious eyes.

It is true. I had a young girl's weakness for abandoned things. Was I not reared on my father's solitary grief? Did I not already understand the frost and fire of a spirit blasted by loss? Outcast, outlaw, wood demon, wandering player. That first day, I didn't know what you were.

Rain, yes. Wood anemones underfoot. Something ahead, then nothing. You, like some trick of the light, and Marguerite, a lifetime before, calling, calling. I didn't turn back. I outran her easily. Past the quarry, up the hill, through the vineyards and into the wood.

Then a flash of heat through the core of me. And suddenly the hive, as if I'd been led.

L'Ymagier tested the effigy in his arms. Quite light. Surprisingly light. Athalie would have no trouble.

Hers was the door with the small painting over the lintel: an unblinking eye in the middle of a flaming heart. The old sign – the rebel sign – of ecstatic contemplation. In the town she was thought a gypsy, a necromancer. She allowed it. Relied on it even.

On the Saturday she'd found her old friend on her doorstep. 'I know, Giles. I heard. I am so sorry.'

'Don't be,' he said. His voice was strange. From within, her grown son, Ahmed, watched through a wall of white muslin as l'Ymagier pressed Athalie's hand in his. 'Don't be.'

She felt the back of her neck go cold, but she said, 'Come in, Giles. You are welcome. Ahmed, it's Monsieur l'Ymagier.'

Inside, everywhere, the necessary evidence of her trade. Jars of mumia, a youth potion made from the boiled fat of the dead – noblemen, mostly, who'd wanted to escape the bite of the worm. In a mortar on the table, pulverized diadochos, a powder to evoke forms of the deceased when sprinkled into water. On shelves overhead, diverse phials – *venena sterilitatis*, abortion drinks – and rows of sinciput candles made from the worms of the grave, candles to cast unholy visions.

There were, too, in a large chest, holy relics from questionable sources. 'In truth,' she'd once laughed, 'they conceal the volumes my father left me.'

He has seen the wares. A piece of shinbone from the leg of St Vitalis. A shoulder blade of St Affia. A molar of John the Baptist. A rib of St Sophia. A phial of the Blessed Virgin's milk. And, Athalie's latest and greatest find, a Holy Foreskin of the Infant Christ. 'The bishop himself couldn't resist a visit. Would you believe? And your master mason. He knows I am Egyptian

– you masons and your folly for sun gods and phalluses. You fool no one. He stared at it as if it were a piece of the cock of Osiris himself.' She laughed, then remembered herself. 'Giles, forgive me.'

'There's no need.'

'You grieve and I smile.'

'I do not grieve. Not as you think.'

'It's true then.'

'What is true?'

'I hear talk.'

'Of?'

'Of a young woman, full of life, who dies in her sleep. Of a father who refuses the physic, who scorns his priest's offices, who shows no grief. People will poke at a mystery as they will a loose tooth. I worry for you.'

'I confess I do as well.' L'Ymagier smiled, shyly. 'I'm watched, it would seem. There are shadows outside the atelier.'

'Are you guilty?'

'Of what?'

'Of too much love, perhaps?'

'It's possible.'

'Why are you here, Giles?'

'My daughter isn't dead.'

'A moment, please.' Athalie motioned to her son. There was a ripple of muslin, a sliding of a bolt, and they were alone. She seated herself on the battered trunk that held her father's books. 'All right. She is not dead.'

'They will bury her.'

'A problem. I see that.'

'You humour me.'

'You credit me with too much interest, Giles. Don't misunderstand me. I am sorry for your daughter, dead or alive, and I am sorry for you. We have long been fond, have we not, and, yes, I make my living by tawdry magic. But you know me for the fraud I am. Everything else is the meditation of a lifetime. I cannot stop a funeral.'

'You and Ahmed are the only citizens of Beauvais who will not be in that cathedral on Monday morning.'

'There are the monks, too. And the leper, Yvain. Did you know I once knew his mother, and she swore to me she did not copulate during her menses? For her sake, I think I will one day help him to take his own cruel life. He can almost bear the priests no longer.'

'Athalie.' He stopped her. 'Athalie, you must help me.'

'Ah, Giles,' she sighed. 'I feared as much.'

Marguerite raised her hand to the nail in the beam. The wreath of her mother's hair was missing.

As the wife of l'Ymagier lay in bed, burning up with sickness, the physic had told him that her hair must be cut; that it depleted the only reserves of energy that remained to her. As it slid to the floor in thick, coppery streams, her two small daughters gathered it, like spun wool, from the floor. Then they sat at the table, plaiting it with gold thread into a wreath for her to see when she was well again.

When the priests came, l'Ymagier held her. He noticed again the length of her fingers, the openness of her palms, the rough skin at her elbow, the pretty arch of her feet. He checked the details of her, as if she'd only just come new into the world. He ran his fingers over her shorn head. He touched the soft-ness of her earlobes. He opened her eyes and tried to name for himself the blue of her eyes, but he couldn't find the word. He couldn't find the word, and still he'd let the priests take her.

She'd had no peace from the time she fell sick, and when she was taken from the house, his peace went with her.

'I can't remember the colour of your mother's eyes,' he said, looking now at the far wall where the nail jutted from the beam.

Marguerite stared at him. 'Blue. She had blue eyes.' Why did he always pretend he couldn't remember? Why did he not say something instead about the wreath? Sometimes red, sometimes yellow, depending on the brightness of the hour. Twelve years it had hung in the one place, all the life of her that remained to them: her hair still changing its colour in the sun.

'Mother's wreath,' she made herself say. 'It's not on the wall.'

He didn't look up.

'Where is it? It's not on its nail.' She refused to conspire.

He heaved himself out of his chair. 'Before first light, Marguerite. Yes? You will go before first light. You have not forgotten?'

She would never be the one to make her father speak straight and clear. She would never be the one to understand his meaning. 'No,' she said. 'I have not forgotten.' First her sister, now her father – both slipping beyond her. And with each went the safe and solid world.

Athalie had been clear: 'The derelict lodge on the edge of the wood. Do you know it?'

'The ashmen's old place?' He'd come upon it once, looking for a good piece of felled oak.

'Exactly. There is nowhere else. When do they come for her?'

'Tomorrow evening. Before the curfew.'

'Then you must get the carving out of your house and to the lodge before that. Before they come.'

'I need more time to work. There are details.'

'You're not thinking, Giles. What if they search your atelier?'

'On what grounds?'

'When has a priest needed grounds?'

He scowled. 'Christina is all the evidence they're after.'

'Hope to God you're right, or all is lost.' She closed her eyes, concentrating. 'Daybreak, then, on Monday. Before the bell rings for matins. Before the town stirs. If you leave it any later, if you insist on perfection, Giles, someone will see you, no matter how quietly you go.'

'You worry too much.'

'And you are too confident. I swear it will be your downfall.'

'Perhaps. But it will not be my daughter's. The carving will be in the lodge before daybreak on Monday. What then?'

'I'll go for it as the bell tolls for her, as the congregation gathers. I'll avoid town. I'll take the cart track by the river.'

'And you won't . . .'

'I won't . . . ?'

'Have second thoughts?'

'Tenth thoughts, Giles, yes. Second thoughts, no.'

'Because I would understand if –'

'You fool yourself, Giles. You would not understand. How could you? Even so, it is as I've said. Ahmed and I will wait with the carving outside this side chapel you describe. We will be there before they break the bread at her mass. You are sure there are no doors? No keys to keep us out when the moment arrives?'

'None.'

'Then why do you frown?'

'You will think of something?'

'I've told you. It will come to me. There is time yet.' She folded her arms across her breast. 'It is the best – it is the only – assurance I can give.'

'I'm grateful. Don't think I'm not. And it is all I can do to get the carving right by Monday morning. But, Athalie, I beg you. Don't let me coax you into merely saying what I need to hear. I know I have taken advantage of a better nature than mine. I know you must be afraid of drawing attention. I know Ahmed is wary. Yet even so I'm asking you: Can I depend on you?'

'You will have to, Giles.' Beneath the smile, her face was stoical. 'You can depend on no one else.'

II

By night, outside, Marguerite watches her father, a dark mass against the translucent horn of the atelier windows. In the next room her sister will neither wake up nor die.

Marguerite wants mealtimes and three bowls. She wants 'spoons face down to keep out the devil', and the words to be nothing more than her mother's old saying, and her mother's before her. She wants fresh air and old women nodding to her again at market. She wants the unbroken peace of the scriptorium. She wants to be telling Christina the tales of the world she lifts from the pages of Brother Vincent's books.

By day, she tests the door of her father's atelier. She presses her face to the crack where the fit is bad and smells the sweetness of chipped wood from within. It makes her uneasy. Sometimes she observes his hands, nicked by an urgent determination she can't explain.

She follows him through town. He stops at the lodge, by the cathedral's west wall. He speaks to the master mason. Pleasantries. Condolences, she assumes. Her father has always remained aloof from the lodge – no time, he claimed, for passwords, allegories, demiurges and secret handgrips. Yet she sees it is the older man, the master mason, who is uneasy with her father, and not the other way around. He surveys Giles of Beauvais like he might a magician's sleeve, as if to say, What will come next? Finally, at the sign of the eye in the flaming heart, she watches her father disappear into the gypsy's house.

★

She wakes before first light on Monday morning. In the yard behind the house, where the hides are scraped, the tanner's dog barks at no one. It is the day of her sister's burial, and the whole world is suddenly false: the jaundiced moon; the absent stars; the blank-faced earth, careless of Christina's return to it.

Marguerite? Are you asleep?

She has no choice. She pulls on her gown, tunic and clogs, runs across town and over the muddy footbridge, her heart – and a heavy key – banging at her chest. St Germer lies on the other side of the Avelon. As she approaches, light spreads furtively from the east. She has never seen the grounds of the monastery so still. Only a thin breath of mist clings to the place, like the expelled dreams of the men who sleep within.

She passes Christina's bees. The gloves and wicker veil are where she herself left them on Friday. She remembers the monk in the rabbit pen waving to her, mistaking her for her sister because old men see only youth.

The bees are neglected. There are too many stray in the air.

She avoids the kitchen, her usual entrance. Jerome may be there, sweeping out the grates. She slips off her clogs and enters by way of the common room. At the back is the door that opens on to the corridor. At the end of that corridor, the scriptorium.

The common room is empty. The morning light edges across benches and the scattering of woolsacks. It settles, here and there, into the impressions of bodies departed. Marguerite feels as insubstantial, or would were it not for the key around her neck. It beats out a reminder of the day; of where she is; of what she is about to do. In the whole of the monastery, only the scriptorium door is locked.

Is it for this that her father persuaded Brother Bernard to allow her to work here all those months ago? To be his eyes? To steal a heretical volume? Was he in touch with radicals in Paris? With Aquinas dead, there had been yet more unrest. Her father said as much himself. And as a free mason, he travels at will. He's one of the elite. He can gain entry even to the university if he chooses.

But why now? Why has he insisted on the volume this morning of all days?

Will she be cast out of the scriptorium now that suspicion gathers around her father? Will even tomorrow be too late? Already in the town it is known that the bishop watches him. Father Joseph fools no one: a requiem mass for a girl who kept bees, for a girl whose father tolerated the clergy at best?

Only the bishop would have the authority. And what does the bishop know? What does he await? Will her dead sister indeed sit up on her bier and point a cold finger at their father?

The key stutters in the lock and turns.

She locates the volume, or rather a single fragment of it, with relative ease. It is as her father remembered: uterine vellum. Beautiful to hold. *Risala fi'l – Mala'ika*. And below it, in Latin: *Epistle on the Angels*. Avicenna.

Her heart lurches. Footsteps. In the corridor. The first to rise for matins. She slips the epistle back into the cage, covers it with other illicit works, and crouches behind.

Until the steps recede. Back down the corridor.

She has now only to negotiate the common room. Her body does not so much relax as slacken. A sudden indifference.

For life has ceased to mean. The fear that comes only with a sense of urgency, of necessity, is, for Marguerite, draining away.

She lifts the lid, reaches for her father's prize a second time, fits the lock and replaces the key for the cage in the hole in the masonry. She walks through the scriptorium, past Brother Vincent's desk, back up the corridor, and through the common room once more. She carries the volume lightly under her arm. She can hear Jerome at the kitchen grates. She no longer cares. She is a page turner. She goes unnoticed in the world.

12

When she arrives home, there's little time. She runs out the front door, through the alley, behind the house and into the courtyard. She rattles the door of the atelier, and it opens unexpectedly.

'Father?' The room is empty. Swept bare. The carving horse has been returned to its corner. And he's gone.

She runs back into the house, the volume still in her hand. She wants only to be rid of it. Yet where would her father have her hide it? Surely it must be hidden? Already it is hot. She wipes her face, smoothes her hair and covers her head in a wimple.

Her scalp itches below it as she walks. In the meagre shade, dogs thump their tails. L'Ymagier is nowhere in sight. She presses the stolen volume to her breast. Her fingers sweat against the vellum.

She does not know that he is already with Christina, watchful as her sister is borne on a litter from the side chapel to the choir. Nor does she know that he carries a white lily to Christina's bier which will serve as a token of their love for her. He will lay it upon his daughter's breast. He will close her hands upon its thick stem. No detail, no stagecraft, has been overlooked. For he has carved and painted even the lily's wooden-bloomed likeness – a flower as finely hewn as the wooden hands that clasp it. Does he not have a talent for bringing things to life?

At Bartot the wine merchant's house, Marguerite stops abruptly. Everything is unreal. Her sister is holding her breath, her father is gone, and monks are running amok in the topiary, their faces transformed oddly by expression. Several wave their arms. Three or four hold long muslin nets. One climbs an apple tree.

Marguerite looks up. Christina's bees are swarming. How many hives did she keep? They cluster now, trembling masses on heavy branches.

But the voice of the single bell drowns their hum. It sounds in her intestines.

She moves on. Past the burial ground and the communal grave, open now. A flash of winding sheets, soiled and rotting.

Marguerite? Are you asleep?

She crouches in the empty street and is sick.

When she spots him at the top of the cathedral steps, she feels no relief, no gladdening of her heart. Did he not leave her, alone and anxious, on the morning of her sister's funeral? Did he not insist she put herself at risk today of all days? Does he not forget that she, *she*, is alive?

It is time. He smiles at the sight of her with the volume under her arm. They walk in together, seemingly as one.

A sea of cathedral light rolls over her as they move up the centre aisle. People nod, row upon row tossed back upon her: dozens of pilgrims, many barefoot; the tanner and grumpy Marthe who scrapes the hides; the woman who keeps the bathhouse; the oneiromancer from the arcade. Row after row. The young physic who pronounced Christina dead; the prosperous shoemaker; François, the crucifix and knife maker, and his eight sharp-eyed children; Roland the smiling embalmer; masons from the lodge; Bartot the wine merchant, unaware of the monks in his topiary; three of her father's patrons and their families; a legion of nuns; at the front, perhaps a dozen hired *pleurants* in their wide grey hoods.

She cannot know that you also are here. Both outside the scene and in it. Don't turn around.

The bishop has spared no expense. There are six three-pound beeswax tapers on the altar and one to be borne by each of the four acolytes. There are four more by her bier.

Far above, the vaults of the choir seem to rest on a flood of morning light. Marguerite is dizzy. L'Ymagier steadies her, his hand on the small of her back. He tries to relieve her of the volume she carries, but her arm does not relent. 'My psalter,' she lies.

The *pleurants* groan under their grey hoods. In the sacristy, behind the screen, the priests mumble the exorcism of the water and salt. 'That there may be banished from the place in which thou hast been sprinkled every kind of hallucination. Let no spirit of pestilence or baleful breath abide therein. Let all the snares of the enemy who lieth in wait for us be driven forth . . . In nomine Patris, et Filii, et Spiritus Sancti.'

At last, belatedly, Marguerite makes herself look.

Her sister rests on the litter that will bear her away. Her bier is draped by the linen of the winding sheet. In the vast light of the day, her hair is ablaze.

She faces east, the direction of paradise, so that her soul will find its way. Her body is covered only by the vigil-cloth, for one goes naked to the grave, in humility.

Someone, Marguerite notices, has folded her hands across her breast, upon which she seems to clasp a lily. Something flares within her – Christina hated lilies.

Does no one know her? She liked fireweed. She has freckles on her back. A red birthmark on the curve of her hip. The lines on her hands are clear and deep. Her eyes are blue. They used to catch the sun like a wolf's – she and Christina once saw a wolf stretched out on the tanner's rack, its head intact and its eyes still looking. The soles of her feet were always dirty. Each night Marguerite would tell her she couldn't get into bed until she washed her feet.

She was greedy for wild strawberries, for festival mayhem, for Marguerite's tales, for their father's love. She'd pull faces whenever a priest went past, to make l'Ymagier laugh. She would even do Father Joseph's fretful walk.

Her temper was quick to spark, yet she was eternally patient with wounded things: the three-legged dog who foraged in the streets; the old parakeet seller who was both mad and deaf; the dancing bear cub whose nose oozed blood where it had been pierced by the red-hot hoop.

She cried all day when they found the aborted baby in the river.

Acolytes light the tapers on the altar. Try as you will, Marguerite thinks, you will not make a penitent of my sister. Wasn't her body open? They say so in town. *Janua diaboli.* Gate of the devil. Her sister's womb. 'You're hurting me,' Christina had mumbled to the night, but she was laughing in her sleep – surely she was laughing? – and there were no bruises, no marks.

Her sister has hair like their mother's. Sometimes red, sometimes yellow. Always changing with the light.

The soles of her feet are tough as resin.

Her laugh was like a summer downpour, sudden and easy.

And Marguerite can't remember enough. Already, she realizes, she cannot remember exactly the sound of her own sister's voice.

A stone hit me in the chest, hard. I squinted into the dripping trees, and this time I saw you – crouching on the balls of your feet. You thought I'd run, that I'd abandon the hive.

The wood was steaming. You reached for another stone. I moved towards you. You stood, took aim. 'Are you human?' I said, and the sound of my voice stopped your arm.

'Lord have mercy, Christ have mercy.'

The priests intone the Kyrie eleison. In the sanctuary, Father Joseph lifts the evergreen branch, dips it in the font and sprinkles the altar, himself and the acolytes with holy water. He dips it again, moves towards the bier and sprinkles the body of Christina.

Inches from you, I reached out and wrapped your fist in mine and its stone in my fingers. I held your hand, and your eyes, still black with suspicion, filled. 'Don't hurt me,' I said. 'Do you understand?'

'Brethren, we will not have you ignorant concerning them that are asleep, that you be not sorrowful, for if we believe that Jesus died and rose again, even so them that have slept through Jesus. For this we say unto you is the word of the Lord, that we who are alive, who remain unto the coming of the Lord, shall not prevent them who have slept.'

Marguerite punishes her own hopes. She tells herself, My sister died in her sleep. Though she was not ill. Though she did not soak the sheets with fever and urine, like our mother as she lay dying. Though she talked – of everything – only hours before. How she was hungry, how they should go outside to watch the lightning, how bears will try to make love to women because they mate on two legs, not four. She said all this. Yet this is my sister's funeral mass.

Marguerite hears shuffling behind her. She can feel the breathy expectation of the congregation, hot at her neck. She wants to shout, 'Leave us be! Do you think she will sit up and talk for you?'

Yet, in truth, it is her father she mistrusts above all. She observes him now as he bows his head. She thinks at him: You keep only yourself alive. Yourself and no one else. You threw your voice and I almost believed she talked in her sleep. You filled your lungs; I woke and thought I heard her breathing. You dreamed she was dreaming, and I thought, yes, of course, sleep heals. Sleep is restorative. Her lungs, her heart, need only rest to recover. As she lay in our bed, I whispered to her, 'You're out of the woods, Christina. You're out of the woods.' Yet she never came out of the woods, Father. Deceiver. Ymagier.

From the threshold, Athalie watches. She and her son wait like thieves outside the Chapel of the Holy Sepulchre. They listen through the doorless portal, just out of view.

'You will have to wait for the last Gospel,' l'Ymagier instructed her. 'The priest will kiss the Holy Book and, vested only in a black cope, he will come down from the altar and move to the bier. He will position himself at her feet. Yes? He will be attended by his deacon. A sub-deacon will hold the processional cross. On either side of him, you'll see an acolyte bearing a candle. He will read over her in a loud voice. That will be the final contact. It must be after. Some time after they have returned to the altar. You will have to choose your moment. And it must be a commotion, Athalie. Not an interruption. Not a distraction. It must be a *commotion* at the far end of the choir. The priests must come down from the altar. They must walk towards the main portals. Every mourner in that cathedral must turn around to see.'

'You believe in my magic after all,' she smiled.

'In merciful forgiveness look down, O Lord, upon the soul of Christina, thy servant, for whom we offer up to thee the

71

sacrifice of praise and the Holy Offering which we do humbly lay at thy feet, in atonement for her transgressions.'

It was like a wild root. When I took it in my mouth, I sucked as I had once sucked at my mother's nipple, drawing you to life. After-wards, you pressed me to you, so hard I thought you'd crush me.

That's how it was. A wild root, and my mouth, my maidenhead, the bloom of you. A fragile pairing.

In a lifetime each of us will cry some 1,850,000 tears. That's sixty-five litres. Six to ten buckets full. Each tear is in itself nothing – water, salt, a little sugar and antiseptic. Yet, in Beauvais, no one has yet cried a tear for Christina.

Stay where you are. Bow your head. Even if noticed, you will not be remembered. Those gathered here are not so much mourners as spectators who hold their breath. For in 1284, the new aesthetic of death has almost upstaged the thing itself.

The twelve hired *pleurants* move soundlessly in their grey hoods and cloaks. They are faceless, eyeless. Each takes up a position by a soaring pillar, and their moans, belly-deep, rise up, making of everything an emptiness. Marguerite looks up. The vaults are midnight blue, and fecund with golden stars that draw everything silently, inexorably, towards resurrection.

The nuns stare at her back. She knows they do. Sister Paul is among them. She does not dare turn around.

They are waiting for the sign, the sign that Christina is to make through the grace of God. The sign that will point to Giles of Beauvais, Ymagier.

Who killed his daughter by enchantment.

Or, who made of his house a demon's portal.

Or, who sucked her breath from her lips as she slept.

Marguerite wants to soar, high as the cathedral keystone,

flapping her arms like the black wings of an avenging angel. She wants to roar, 'Have you eyes? She is cold! Her corpse will not sing for you!'

Instead she murmurs the responses.

. . .

'And with thy spirit.'

. . .

'We lift them up to the Lord.'

. . .

'It is meet and just.'

First, it is a shadow from behind, only dimly sensed as it spills through the cathedral's main portals. Then, high overhead, it is a strange pitch, just audible over the sonorous grief of the *pleurants*.

Father Joseph looks up, squinting at the blot that slips and slides against the brightness of stained glass – yet another dark spot on his patchy vision. He blinks. He wipes his eyes. But that sound, that sound. A drone. An urgent hum. His spine tenses. He silences the *pleurants* and trains his ear on the unknown. What terrible chant is this?

The congregation, too, clenches in readiness. The drone descends, louder and louder, until it takes form, a sudden storm cloud in the sanctuary, a cloud that bears the frenzy of 20,000 bees.

The sub-deacon waves the processional cross, trying to chase the dark mass from the altar. Father Joseph retrieves the evergreen bough and raises it, a feeble weapon against insurgency. An acolyte runs from the altar, genuflecting wildly. Another shakes the censer in an effort to smoke out the colony, but he only disperses it, so that thousands of bees fly like bright sparks among the mourners.

Several land on Christina's face. Children and old folk wail as bees become trapped in clothing and sting soft flesh. Two nuns, awaiting revelation, faint.

Marguerite wants to run to her sister and brush away the bees that crawl over her face, but l'Ymagier reaches for her hand and stops her. She turns to protest but the words don't come. For he alone, she realizes, is contained.

And afterwards you reached into the hollow, high into the top of the comb, and, scooping honey in your hands, you fed me.

13

The mourners clamber into the blank daylight, swatting bees. 'Ite missa est,' Father Joseph intones. 'Go, the mass is over.' Only the nuns remember to pause at the kissing board for Christ's bleeding feet.

Christina's body is brushed of bees and carried on the litter back into the shelter of the chapel. The sacristan apologizes and informs l'Ymagier that only when all is quiet again, only when the congregation has calmed itself, will the pallbearers enter from the side and bear her litter out of the chapel, through the choir and out of the main portals. Only then, he explains, will the burial procession begin. The elderly man nods sagely at the measure of his own words and guides l'Ymagier out of the choir and into the morning light.

Suddenly l'Ymagier understands: Athalie has won the confidence of the sacristan. There is a connection there, something he, l'Ymagier, can only guess at. The sacristan's brief smile says as much as they step together through St Pierre's broad portal. For in all this uproar has Christina not been left alone in the darkness of the chapel? Is there not more than enough time for Athalie and Ahmed to gather up his daughter and leave the effigy in her place?

He breathes deeply. Athalie has been true to her word.

L'Ymagier is the only principal mourner, for women and girls are not permitted to walk behind the body of the deceased. He will follow his daughter's likeness through the town streets, accompanied by the priests, the *pleurants* and the men of

Beauvais. They will circle back to the open grave. Marguerite will remain on the cathedral steps.

Outside, people talk of the Sign of the Bees. Bees originated in paradise. They are creatures of sweetness and light. Didn't Christ eat honey at the end? An angry swarm in the sanctuary, what did it mean?

Marguerite stops listening. She watches François smear his youngest daughter's inflamed cheek with cool mud from the open grave. The child howls. A breeze rises over the morning heat. Marguerite can smell the old pilgrim from Toulouse, buried less than a fortnight ago.

She sits down on the dusty step, dazed.

Marguerite? Tell me about the men who can wrap themselves in their own ears.

She looks up. Athalie the gypsy is suddenly on the steps among the women. She stands too close. 'Marguerite,' she asks, 'where is your father?'

It is a stupid question. Marguerite points to the procession as it moves off just ahead. The sun is strong. Her eyes water. Only the last of the *pleurants* is still in sight, a mystery in a grey cloak and hood. A thirteenth figure, at the back of two lines of six. Pull the hood close. Don't turn around.

It is dark, suddenly quiet. Sometimes, in the absence of the world, I almost forget myself.

My name is Christina. I keep bees. My sister is Marguerite. She works in the scriptorium. My father is Giles of Beauvais. Ymagier. Free mason. He can bring even granite to life.

He has demons, it's true. Their faces trouble the masonry of the new cathedral. A goat that dances on its hind legs. A horned man. A griffin, its beak stuffed with grapes. A weeping devil, exorcized. Remember? 'And the devil wept, saying: "I leave thee, my fairest consort, whom long since I found and rested in thee; I forsake thee, my sure sister, my beloved in whom I was well pleased. What I shall do, I know not."' The Acts of Thomas. From the Apocrypha. Marguerite found it in the scriptorium and copied the tale when no one was looking. My mind wanders.

'It is a good likeness?' Athalie had asked.

'You don't know my work?' L'Ymagier had smiled.

'And the hair?' There was no time for banter.

'Faded, but it will serve. In the morning light, and raised high on the litter –'

'It must not be heavy, this body. We can use the barrow on the cart track, but remember, Giles, at the cathedral itself, we will have only our arms.'

'Wood then, not stone. There was an ash tree down behind Tibideau's slaughterhouse last month. It's in my studio, already cured and roughed. It will be manageable.'

'The derelict camp on the edge of the wood. Do you know it?'

'The ashmen's old lodge?'

'There.'

It is disrespectful for a pallbearer to look at the body as he raises the litter to his shoulders. Moreover, it is bad luck. L'Ymagier is well aware.

High above the *pleurants'* grey hoods, the hair of his dead wife lifts on the breeze.

Marguerite hears Marthe whispering to the bathhouse woman. The priests watch her father.

'Every action has magic at its source, and the entire life of the practical man is a bewitchment.' That's what he used to say.

Of course they watch him. Of course he's suspected.

She suspects him herself, of what she can't say.

Beneath her, on the cathedral step, the volume. She sits on it to hide it.

She wants to go back to the days when she could love him for turning a white rose red; when the stories he told them by candlelight with the shadows of his hands seemed the entire world.

You lived rough, without even words most of the time. When I told you my name, it was useless birdsong to your ears. But you would breathe deeply of me. Your nostrils were wide.

We ran at the sight of anyone, laughing as we went. Others seemed so slow, so stupid on their feet: charcoal burners, bark pullers, pig herds, ashmen. They knew us only by the skirmish of our passing and the hair on the backs of their necks. Both of us, of a middle nature.

The stench from the communal grave marks the end of the procession. In the distance l'Ymagier can see Marguerite, solitary on the cathedral's highest step. Below her, women in black drift like ash.

Soon, soon, he thinks, they will be three again. In no time Christina will be safe at Athalie's. In a few days, perhaps less, he and Marguerite will leave for Paris. On the road they will overtake Ahmed in his tumbledown caravan, with Christina its hidden cargo. Ahmed will take them as far as the outskirts of Paris. If the Church should blacklist him from working, and it is likely it will, he will sell the Avicennan volume, priceless though it is, to the underground at the university. He will if he must.

The ritual at the grave is familiar. How is it twelve years? Twelve years since he buried his wife in the mud of a wet October. He watches carefully as each of the pallbearers at the front raises a blind hand to ease the vigil-cloth over the face. The purple-and-gold tissue flutters for a moment, then falls, covering the wooden likeness of his daughter.

The litter is lowered to the ground. The mourners bow their heads as Father Joseph chants the song of death. The four bearers bend and take hold of the wide flaps of the winding sheet, letting them fall over the body. The moment has come. L'Ymagier bows his head too. Each bearer takes in his hand a length of the sheet's linen bindings. One man, the sexton, nods to the other three, and the wooden form of his daughter is raised up, free of the litter, and wound for the grave.

To touch the body is forbidden.

You spun me round and round under that oak tree till I was giddy. When you let go, I fell hard.

We were not happy again. You watched me. You asked half questions. Your face clouded at my words, at my laughter. You listened for my footfall, impatient for it and of it. Sometimes, your pupils shrank to almost nothing.

'Who?' I'd demand. 'Who could there be?' You smelled me for the sweat of other men. You laid traps.

You understand me. The baiting. Other times, the pretence of ease.

'Gloria Patri, et Filio, et Spiritui Sancto.'

And for the first time, l'Ymagier is afraid.

Is it possible he vivifies his daughter's body with nothing more than the force of his own need? Is it possible that Athalie, even now, is bearing his daughter away in her barrow – dead in spite of him?

A breeze rises. Grit from the grave blows into his teeth as he mouths the responses.

It is all right. He will trust the voice within. He must. And Marguerite has found the volume. His ancient touchstone. Their assurance, come what may.

Ashman's son, I think you did not mean to kill me. Only the need of me.

How many nights ago was it that I jabbered to Marguerite in our bed? I thought, I can will myself free – from you, from the clobbering wood. I can will myself into the bright world again. But you found me even in my dreams. You climbed on top of me. Again, the weight of you. I'd missed you so. I touched your arms, your chest, but you wouldn't take your hands from my face, and even my heart faltered.

As Marguerite waits, she is aware of the coiling curiosity of the women of Beauvais. She wants to be gone from this place. She wants Christina dead and buried. She wants to spit the truth at them. 'There were no marks of any kind!'

But it is a truth of which she should have no knowledge. The semblance of innocence is all that protects her now in the world.

L'Ymagier watches the pallbearers move to the edge. He flinches, in spite of himself, as they lower the carving into the grave. He thinks of Marguerite. He sees in his mind's eye the volume under her arm. Soon, they will be safe.

He stares.

Through the corner of the winding sheet, something. A bare heel. A waxy foot. Separated toes. The half-moons of nails. The crookedness of her second toe.

My father is crying.
That is the sound of my father crying.

★

His shouts break the day. Marguerite stops running only when she reaches the sexton's hut, only as her father comes into view.

It is as they say. He is over Christina's body. He is stripping the winding sheet from her as if she is on fire. He is slapping her dead face, her dead arms. He is calling her name. He is shouting that, by the gore of Christ, her foot *did* move.

It is not possible. He is not possible.

She runs headlong. She pushes through the huddle of *pleurants* and priests.

She is not yet at the grave's edge, her feet are sinking in a mound of earth, she is about to denounce her father, to show everyone the stolen volume, to do anything that will make everything stop, when she beholds her dead sister sit up.

14

Stillness at the grave but for her.

She sucks at the air as if it can never fill her, as if it is only light or heat. She is naked. Thin. Dumb. Her face is the colour of meal. Her eyes blink and strain against the strangeness of light. Her nipples stand hard, as if she alone is cold this smothering day.

She retches, but there is nothing in her stomach to bring up. Her back is caked with mud. She sits in a pool of urine, scratching at her forearms and stares, horrified, as wax comes away in her hands. The arum lily that rested on her chest lies crumpled now between her thighs, its bright, sticky stamen an absurd obscenity.

Marguerite turns, dazed. Something is on her arm. At her arm. Someone is tapping her arm. A finger. A hand. You.

Pass it to her.

She stares, slow to realize. The stolen volume. You nod to the ground where it fell. She takes it, not meeting your eyes under the wide grey of your hood. She knows you know such a thing cannot belong to her.

She wants to run back, to the cool of the cathedral step; to François smearing his daughter's face with mud; to the dogs' thumping tails and the monks in the pleasure garden; and beyond all that, before it, to the tap-tap of Brother Vincent's nailless finger on the page about to be turned.

Perhaps she is about to speak, to make an excuse, but her sister falls back again, and there is a crack of flesh on flesh. Marguerite winces. You turn. L'Ymagier has hit his newly risen daughter. He is cursing her weakness for all to hear.

He remembers her nakedness. He demands an acolyte's alb. He asks for help as he struggles to get her on the litter. No one moves. He asks again. The stink of the churned grave is riotous in the heat.

He bends and hoists her clumsily into his arms. People are quick to step out of his way as he carries her past the grave and out of the burial ground, a perverse pietà. What can Marguerite do but follow? She does not lift her face as she walks. She does not meet anyone's eye. She knows her way by the gathering stream of boots and clogs.

There is no joy this marvellous day.

Athalie approaches them on the street, hot, bewildered. She is the only one who does. 'Giles, it wasn't there. I swear to you. Ahmed and I went with the barrow. The lodge was empty.'

He refuses to look at her. 'I left it there myself.'

'Someone must have found it.'

'Who? Who would want a likeness of my daughter? Who would trouble themselves with such a thing?'

'It wasn't there, Giles. I swear.'

'It had no legs, no feet. Do you think it walked?'

'You've had a shock, I know. But what could I do?'

'Stop the bees. Why disrupt the mass if there is no body to switch? Why not keep the damned queen in whatever phial you carried her in? If nothing had happened, I would at least have known that something was wrong.'

'I knew nothing of the bees, Giles – that had nothing to do with me. Yvain was to run in during the mass. Ahmed and I stood waiting with him at the door of the chapel, to give him courage. For still we were going to act, we were going to take her, with or without the carving to leave in her place. A risk, and perhaps a wrong-headed one, but I understood your despair. I told Yvain to enter by the main doors shouting for holy water for his sores, as if crazed with the pain. I told him to stay at the back and not to leave until the priests themselves came down from the sanctuary. I knew no one would remove him. They'd have to touch him first. And not one of your priests is your St Francis, no?

'Ahmed had a flat-bottomed boat waiting on the Avelon. We needed only a few minutes' confusion. A good head start. He'd left the caravan upriver. We were going to get word to you. But when the bees flew in, the chaos was too much – people were suddenly everywhere – and Yvain was terrified. Of the bees with his sores. Of the priests. Of the commotion. We had to get him out of there before his cries led everyone to us. So our moment was lost. Thank the heavens she was able to move her foot. This at least is what I've heard.'

L'Ymagier shifts the body of his daughter in his arms. 'You will excuse me, Athalie.' He starts to walk again. 'As you can see, my daughter is not well.'

I am not. My skin is like wax. See how it comes away.

15

The *Epistle on the Angels*. A volume smuggled eight centuries ago across the craggy peaks of northern Spain into France to be locked, finally, in the scriptorium of sleepy St Germer. A volume purchased at great expense only so that it might never be opened again.

L'Ymagier had guessed right.

Yet a controversy of angels? A heresy of the heavenly host?

Once upon a time metaphysics of course *was* physics. The richness of matter in the medieval universe was nothing other than an endless series of vibrations emanating from an original, divine energy. The angel was both the receiver and transmitter of this energy, and not merely a decorous messenger. Church wisdom decreed not one heaven, not two, not the seven of Ptolemy and popular song, but nine, each governed by its own lofty angel.

Avicenna went further. He believed there was a tenth sphere between the nine ordained orbits and our own lonely mortal sphere. This was the clime of the Tenth Angel, the divine guide to whom we were intimately bound and for whom we could not but long.

Which was the problem. The embarrassment. All this desire.

Not surprising then that the Church Fathers ushered in the static universe. Here, as we well know, angels do not yearn. They do not evolve. They are eternal. They act on God's will. They may on occasion mediate on our behalf. Or advise from time to time on points of knowledge, especially in the domains of justice and ethics. They do not seek relationship. They do not deal in personal revelation or the stuff of private epiphanies.

They also have no balls. Literally.

As for the force of universal desire, it will be erased again and again with the ease with which whole texts were once erased from wax-covered tablets in the scriptoria of monasteries. Listen. 'Love,' spake the mystic, that scientist of the heart, 'is closer to the lover than is his jugular vein.' Ancient words. Words with a pulse. Scrape, rub, blow and they're gone. Like that. 'Thou wert I, but dark was my heart.' Scrape, rub, blow and the Tenth Angel never was.

Scrape. Rub. Blow.

Trailing behind her father, behind the body of a sister who has come back to life, Marguerite feels herself only in the necessity of each step. Onlookers gather in the street and in doorways. She hears them above her on the scaffolding by the west wall.

She tries to assume the face of a girl whose sister is merely unwell, whose sister has fainted and needs fresh air. Nothing is changed. She will buy meat at the market again without feeling her neck go hot. She will make confession without stumbling over her words. She will go tomorrow to the scriptorium. Soon perhaps she will even marry. Perhaps here, now, he looks at her. Perhaps he will tell her that it was pity for her troubles this day that moved him first.

She dares, fleetingly, to take in the faces. They look past her, at her sister's body, at its state of collapse, at the ragged tail of Christina's hair drawing a vague line in the dust.

She remembers the contraband under her tunic. *Risala fi'l – Mala'ika*. And below it, in smaller letters: *Epistle on the Angels*. That's what her father wanted. So badly he insisted she steal it this day of all days. Did he know their world would turn upside down? Is there rare wisdom between its covers? Or does someone at the university in Paris wait for the volume? Will he put even his family at risk for the sake of old passions?

She takes the volume from beneath her tunic as she walks. Suddenly she is past caring. The cover is sticky with the sweat of her stomach. She opens it to a random page. It's waxy and thick with time. She turns to another.

'Marguerite,' shouts l'Ymagier from ahead, 'keep up, I said!'

It is too late, she thinks. Don't you know? Already I have lost myself in the world. No magician's cloak for me, Father. No seven leaves of St John's wort needed here, for already I am invisible.

She stops in the middle of the street. She takes her time. Her sister can die all over again. The drama is not hers. She opens the volume once more. She turns over the first page and the second. She turns the third, the fourth. She has missed something. She starts again. The first page. The second. The third. The fourth. Page 5. Page 6. She is losing patience. She flips through the loosely bound sheaf.

She has opened hundreds of volumes in the scriptorium. She has turned thousands of pages. But this is a volume no longer. Through the thickness of the wax, she can see only the ghosts of words.

Does her father know some enchantment by which it may yet be read? Like the time he scattered nettle juice on words and they appeared, drop by drop, on the page. Is that the reason it is still kept in the scriptorium's cage? Or have the monks been at it with their knives and pumice stones? Is it preserved as nothing more than a mute testament to the authority and determination of the Mother Church?

One page after another: as blank, as smooth, as apparently untouched as the last.

16

Keep the hood up, though it is hot. And your head down. Lie low. Anonymity is your talent.

You will not see Marguerite. She will circle the cathedral, dazed, alone. She will return at last to the burial ground, where she will find the sexton already at work with the shovel. 'Your sister,' he'll tell her, 'might be the first in Beauvais to come back to life, but she sure as hell isn't the first to die.' He'll jump into the grave and sigh as he shifts corpses.

When his back is turned, Marguerite will let it slip from her hand.

And when her father says, 'Where is it, Marguerite?' she will say, 'I'm sorry, Father.' When he says, 'Enough. I will have it now,' she will show him her psalter. 'It is my psalter you saw at mass,' she will say. 'There was no volume. No fragment.' She will not say she was suspicious of its invisible words. Of the trouble they could yet cause. Had they not had enough already? She will repeat, 'There was nothing.'

Follow l'Ymagier. Up ahead. Christina is slack in his arms. The strain cannot be easy in the swelter of the day. Already he has been to his home. Others are there before him. They stand by his water trough and toe the earth. They lean against the door of his atelier, arms folded across broad chests. They press their faces to the horn of his windows. They have rubble in their hands, lifted no doubt from the pile outside the masons' lodge. They have shards of glass too, cast-offs from the glaziers' yard. One with a thick sunburnt neck pisses against the door.

L'Ymagier has no choice but to shift her weight in his arms and turn back towards town.

He walks in the direction of St Pierre, and passes it. He is slowing down, yet he does not stop. At the fringes of town he passes Yvain the leper's hovel and the tumblers' makeshift camp. At last, at the edge of Beauvais, in a warren of houses that teeter against the town wall, he stops at the sign of the eye in the flaming heart. Ahmed opens the door.

'My mother is not here,' he says.

'I will wait if I may. You see –'

'You cannot stay.' He looks at Christina. 'This is no place.'

'Perhaps for only a day or two. Till we can go elsewhere. It's not safe for her –'

'You forget yourself, Monsieur l'Ymagier. You forget how things are for my mother and me.' He draws himself in, changes his course. 'It is all I can say. We have done all we can.'

'I am sorry to ask. I am afraid for her. Do you understand? If there were anywhere else –'

'I will tell my mother you came, Monsieur l'Ymagier.' His eyes narrow. 'I will tell her that you are grateful for her help.'

You think your eyes play tricks.

It is l'Ymagier, at another door. We have been here before.

He is doubled up now with the strain. He beats the knocker with difficulty. No one. He hammers with his fist. For he, who once bore a rotting swan to the door of a bishop, now stands before that same door, his newly risen daughter a dead weight in his arms.

The door opens.

'I have come to ask for the Church's asylum.' L'Ymagier looks the man in the eye. 'For my daughter. Not for myself.'

If the bishop is surprised, he does not show it. 'She will

not be denied.' He dismisses the serving nun with a brief nod.

'There is nowhere else,' says l'Ymagier.

'Evidently.'

'She needs to be kept warm.'

'She will be seen to. You have my assurance.'

'She needs quiet.'

'Is that all?'

'What else is there?'

'No terms? No conditions?'

L'Ymagier looks up, measures his thoughts and smiles. 'Another time perhaps.' He passes Christina, not to the attendant the bishop is about to summon, but into the arms of the bishop himself. Then he turns to go.

'A moment, Monsieur l'Ymagier. I don't think you understand. There won't be another time.'

'You have my daughter.'

'Precisely. I have your daughter.'

'I have another. Marguerite. I'm going to find her now.'

'Nor will she lack.'

'I don't understand.'

'But you do, Monsieur l'Ymagier. I feel sure you do. Your services to the Mother Church are now complete. You are no longer required.'

Does l'Ymagier suppress something? A smile? An oath? 'Be that as it may, Your Grace, I cannot simply disappear. Surely we have had marvel enough this day.'

'Indeed, you will find you can disappear, Monsieur l'Ymagier, for you are finished here already.'

'Marguerite and I will be back, just as soon as I can make provision –'

'Forget Beauvais, Monsieur l'Ymagier. That is my strong advice.'

L'Ymagier frowns in an act of apparent contemplation.

'Very difficult, Your Grace, given I was born here. That my daughters were born here. That my wife is buried here.'

The bishop sighs. 'I regret to say that you have an unhappy habit of not recognizing grace when it is given you. You truly do not seem to understand, and you, I gather, a well-educated man. Why, if I'm not mistaken, I believe the tribunal at Paris commended your scholarship, if not your heresy, all those years ago.'

L'Ymagier feels the heat rise in his face.

' "Fear of the Angel". Yes, as I recall, that was the charge dropped at my door, along with – that's right – a rotting swan. Goodness. How you like to perform, Monsieur l'Ymagier. My poor serving nun Françoise never recovered from the shock.

'Naturally, you assumed I wouldn't take seriously, or even remember, what I couldn't understand, for who would have expected word of the politics at Paris to reach a backwater like Beauvais? An understandable mistake even for – no, especially for – an educated man. Yet, in spite of your considerable learning, I see I will have to make myself perfectly clear.

'You will forget Beauvais. You will disappear, even as I have said you will. For there is worse. There are privations . . .' He regards l'Ymagier. He observes the soiled garments, the flickering eyes, the panic that bubbles below the intelligence. 'Do not berate yourself. You have been foolish, perhaps. Proud, undoubtedly. But wherever you walked, you would have found yourself here at my door. There is a Will, you see.'

He shifts the young woman in his arms, then calls inside. He looks once more at l'Ymagier. There is a hushed query from the other side of the door – a member of the bishop's retinue. He cocks an ear to his right. 'No,' he says. 'No need. He is gone.'

★

You see the door close. You see Christina disappear behind it. Giles of Beauvais turns around, a man unlike the one who arrived at that door. He is without magic. He is without celebrity. He is without daughters, wife, family, a home, a town. He looks up. He does not expect to see you standing there, a stranger under a cloak and hood. He does not expect to see anyone, for he understands now. It is true. Already he is gone.

Through the wavering haze of heat, he peers at you, suspicious, as if you might be in the bishop's employ. A spy masquerading as a *pleurant*.

'Weep for me if you will,' he says. 'You'll be alone.'

Say nothing.

He draws closer, studying you studying him. He lowers his voice. 'Are you from the university? I have nothing. There is nothing. I cannot help.' He hesitates, moving on only reluctantly, as if there is something more yet to be said.

You watch the dark line of him recede and finally disappear, as if into a ripple of the day's relentless heat. And from this same ripple, from this same dizzying moment, something – someone – emerges, gathering form and mass as he approaches. For in the bright flux of eye, mind and world, realities tangle.

Giles Carver is walking back towards you.

Dr Giles Carver of River Forest, Illinois.

Digital Time

I

You read his face. High colour. A lean line of a mouth. Eyes like lodestones. He's looking at the sky – ahead, behind. He's smelling the air for rain.

'Every day,' he begins. 'I don't get it.' A woman laden with groceries eases past you on the sidewalk. 'I get off the train at Oak Park. The River Forest stop makes more sense, but after work I like the walk. I buy a paper outside the station and hang a right on to Oak Park Avenue. By Erie Street, you're behind me. Where'd you come from? No idea. Sometimes I cut over to Forest instead and head home through the gardens. I used to take my daughters there years ago – they liked the wild flowers. But by the time I hit Erie, you're behind me, same as usual.'

He looks up – wonders if that was a drop of rain he felt. 'Coincidence? Okay. I leave the station and stick to North Boulevard instead. But by the time I turn from Harlem on to Lake, you're there. We pass William. Monroe. Jackson. Lathrop. I turn up Lathrop, only because I don't live there. Then it's Quick Street. The tennis club. The public library, where my younger daughter – never mind. I turn to look once, maybe twice, and, sure enough, you're still there. Listen. If someone at the university has put you up to this, you're wasting your time.'

His eyes water in the glare of the day. He wonders if he's said too much. He didn't mention the phone calls. He tells himself he shouldn't have mentioned his daughters. At the same time he's aware of the absurdity of the situation as it unfolds in front of Something's Brewing on Oak Park Avenue: Dr Giles Carver, a middle-aged professional, is talking to a complete stranger like *they* are after him.

He knows his mind can tip into paranoia. Jen used to point it out. Didn't his final days in the department give him reason enough? But he wants it said. 'I don't care who's asking. Faculty. Fringe element. M-theory acolyte. There's no key to any universe on my chain. Got it?'

His face is rimmed with sweat. He squints at the shadow of your face. Is he waiting for an apology? A demand? He turns and walks on, a Milky Way wrapper flapping from the sole of his shoe.

Words move through you, catalysing the moment. 'You can't leave her there.'

Giles Carver stops short. 'What did you say?'

'Your daughter.'

'What do you know about my daughter?'

'You can't leave her there.'

He stares, bewildered.

The rain comes at last. A downpour in an Indian summer. Commuters, on the home stretch, dive for doors and bus shelters. They huddle for cover under awnings and newspapers. Across the street someone darts out of a shop to save a table of second-hand paperbacks. In a moment, he'll walk on, lost to his thoughts, to whatever it is he won't say out loud.

Don't lose him.

You nod at the streaming window of Something's Brewing.

He blinks like someone coming up for air. 'Why not?' he says.

Inside, he shakes himself off. There's a spree of rain. Two women at a neighbouring table look up, pained. He grabs a booth. Flings down his coat. 'Mine's a double espresso,' he calls to you.

You understand. You're soaked through. In here, he thinks, you'll drop the hood and take off your jacket. He's telling himself that things at last will begin to make sense.

You stand at the counter, dripping. The kid behind the counter is telling a customer how Calista Flockhart came in once. How she ordered a fruit infusion. How that had to be her carbs for the week: one fruit *infusion*. How a teaspoon of honey would have made her cry.

No, he couldn't remember whether it was persimmon and vanilla, or ginseng, raspberry and elderflower. Maybe she wanted to look at Hemingway's old house. Or the Frank Lloyd Wright stuff. Maybe, right now, she's starting a retro trend in prairie architecture among famous people.

'Can I get some service over here?' you ask. People don't always seem to notice you.

At last, the kid behind the counter is pouring the coffees, punching the register and taking your money. He's explaining something about stamps and loyalty cards as a cellphone goes off.

'Of course it's me – who else were you expecting on your old dad's phone? No, sweetheart, I'm not sure where she's got to . . .' Carver's voice is light, easy, but when you turn to look, he's staring at the ceiling, his face strained. He remembers his surroundings, turns to the wall. 'Of course I haven't left you there. No, listen, Christina. I keep saying. No one's *left* you anywhere . . . Well, what does Bishop say?'

You cross to the table and lower the tray.

'I'm just asking, Christina. I'm just asking if he had anything new to say. Maybe something about medication? No, of course he's not God. I'm merely . . . Well, don't worry about them . . . Again? As in again today? Well, who authorized that?' He pushes his hand through the wet thickness of his hair. 'What sort of questions?'

He meets your eyes briefly.

'Okay. Christina. Christina? Listen to me. Listen. I'm coming now. Are you listening? Yes, right now.' He reaches for his coat, sliding one arm awkwardly in. 'No . . . Like I said, ladybug, I don't know where Maggie is but . . . Christina, listen. I'm leaving now.' He glances at his watch. 'It's six fifteen. I should be with you by seven. Quarter past at the latest. Do you have a clock in your room? Good. So I'll be there soon.' He shuts his eyes, like he's making a wish. 'The video's yours for the choosing on the way home. Anything but *Dr Zhivago* again.' He forces a laugh. 'A benign dictator? *Me*? Are you sure we're talking about the same guy here?' He winces – he's just said the wrong thing. 'That's what I said, didn't I? Okay . . . Yup. Bye . . . Bye, ladybug.'

He flips his phone shut. 'Have to be somewhere.' He slides out of the booth. Studies you for a moment. 'See you around.'

By 9 p.m. he'll be home. He'll throw the keys on the kitchen table. He'll walk from room to room, pulling blinds and curtains. He'll peel off the damp skin of his coat. Finally, he'll hit the button on the answering machine. One message. From 6.10. Just before she tried his cellphone.

Maggie? Dad? It's me. Will you pick up? Are you there?

He'll play it again. He'll listen to every pause, to every hesitation in her voice. He'll hear the final beat of frustration. Are you *there*? He'll listen as if his daughter is speaking to him from whatever place it is that passes for the Beyond these days.

2

We begin again.

It was a phone call in the middle of the night. Her heart stopped before she could say hello.

Maggie had woken too. Had gone to the top of the stairs to listen and found her sister moments later on the kitchen floor, a woman's faraway voice insisting that she please hang up and try her call again.

Forget an ambulance, he said. Maple Avenue was five minutes in the car. Less that time of night if he ran the reds.

They got her on to the back seat. Maggie crouched over her sister's slack face. She positioned her head. She cleared her airway. She pinched her nostrils and covered her blue lips with her own. Then she blew into her chest like she'd learned to do in the Girl Scouts years ago on a Saturday afternoon. (Blow. Blow. Blow. Turn to the chest. Watch for movement. Blow. Blow. Blow.)

And suddenly she was no longer in the car, passing William Street and Bonnie Brae, all the houses asleep. Suddenly she was standing next to Tina, in front of Mills Brothers' window, where they stood every Christmas to see Snow White laid out, pale and beautiful on her bier, and the dwarves, gathered round her, sighing and weeping diamante tears and sighing and blowing silent noses in an endless, automated cycle of loss. And it's hard to leave, to walk on, past this moving drama, past this scene without close, as long as Snow White's breast moves (up and down, up and down, up and down) below her high-necked, gauzy gown; as long as there is the terrible tease of life we know as hope.

He noticed his feet were still bare as he hit the gas.

Outside Emergency, he left the car running and told Maggie to stay where she was. 'Stop crying, Maggie. Do you hear me? I do *not* want to hear you crying.' He took Christina into his arms again. How many years since he'd last held her? He swore at someone running towards him with a wheelchair. Ignored shouts from reception and headed for a corridor marked AUTHORIZED PERSONNEL ONLY. Flung back a curtain. Passed her into the surprised arms of a bleary-eyed MD. 'She's not breathing,' he said. 'My daughter's not breathing.'

It was just ten minutes since she'd run for the phone. Ten minutes since the night had turned inside out.

What are the wild electrics of the heart?

The crucial spark is struck at its very core. A signal is relayed from the power cable of the sinus node to the atria to the second node. The first of five. Together, a smooth wave of energy spreading across the membrane of the heart. The ventricles contracting. The heart relaxing. A heartbeat.

Sixty to a hundred of them a minute for most of us. Though of course your heart can race. Or miss a beat. There are, too, palpitations, flutters and the occasional poundings. Extra heartbeats are commonly noticed just before going to sleep, when resting quietly or when changing positions. This is the conventional wisdom. The beat of a healthy heart is regular. It does not vary to any significant extent. Disease, malfunction and ageing arise from stress on an otherwise orderly system.

The human heart an orderly system? Don't believe it.

Chaoticians examining beat-by-beat analyses of the human

heart have found, on the contrary, 'a surprisingly erratic pattern' in the heart rate of healthy subjects – a pattern formerly dismissed as mere 'noise' in the quest for physiological order. A healthy heartbeat, it turns out, shows unexpectedly random dynamics. Health, it seems, is the natural ability of the heart to adapt to disorder; youth, the body's ease with complexity. With fluctuations. Perturbations. Chaos.

When you reach equilibrium, you're dead.

And Christina?

She was not yet awake as her feet hit the carpet that night. Nor did she wake as she opened her bedroom door, flew down the corridor, down the stairs and lifted the receiver of the kitchen phone, breathless with panic.

Her records indicate a history of parasomnia dating approximately from a death in her immediate family. As a child Christina experienced bed-wetting and sleeptalking. In her teens, sleepwalking. More recently, attacks of breathlessness and panic during sleep. Sometimes, the sensation of a weight on her chest in deep sleep – or, in sleep-lab jargon, the incubus. A Latin leftover of a word.

Picture it again. Five electrical pulses from the heart of the heart. Yet instead of one smooth wave of energy, there is a signalling blockage in the electrical pathway of a single cardiovascular cell. One cell falls out of rhythm. Neighbouring cells cease to act as one. Asynchronous riot spreads, cell to cell. The rhythm section of the heart is thrown.

Arrhythmia. And Maggie lifting the slab of her sister's cheek from the cold of the kitchen linoleum.

Yet what of youth? What of health? What of her heart's natural ability to adapt to chaos, to complexity? Certainly, late that Friday night, the heart of Christina Carver failed. It lost strength and force. Perhaps a single cell did lie, like a terrible secret within, congenitally flawed. A bud of disorder.

Or did her heart strain towards something? Did it beat, not faster and faster, but higher and higher, yearning towards something other as Christina moved through the sleepscape of the night?

What, after all, is the cardiology of Transport?

Hush. She is sleeping. There, below the plastic cloud of the oxygen mask. It is not yet clear how far she has travelled.

Voices.

Please understand. Sometimes a person in this condition is not entirely unconscious but is unable to respond to external stimuli. A stupor, medically speaking, is something less than a coma. A persistent vegetative state is clearly something more. A coma, it's worth pointing out, is a fairly generalized term that refers to a deep state of unconsciousness. That she is suffering from 'decreased consciousness' is all that can be confirmed at this point.

Yes. As you can see. She will not wake up.

It is impossible at this time to comment on the quality of any eventual recovery. Or whether it will happen in a day or a year.

Let's not get ahead of ourselves.

The EEG results indicate that a seizure was not the cause of collapse; electrical activity in the brain is registering normal. You will be glad to hear that an eye examination has not revealed any swelling at the back of the eye, which means increased intracranial pressure is not an immediate concern. So there is no need for a tap, at least at this point. Rest assured, her ICP will be monitored at all times.

Her cardiovascular function is also, of course, being monitored. A stress-EKG would be a sensible precaution upon any eventual recovery, though, for obvious reasons, it is not feasible now. They will, however, run a routine test for electrolyte irregularities – sometimes associated with cardiac arrhythmia.

Sorry. A failure in the electrical signalling system of the heart. Precise cause unknown, though sudden physical stress or emotional arousal has been implicated. It is little consolation, but it is a fortunate few who experience a faint or a coma rather than sudden death.

You need to know that Christina may have suffered a loss of blood flow or a diminished blood flow to the brain. Brain cells are extremely sensitive to oxygen deprivation; they can begin to die within five minutes. Cerebral hypoxia may lead to temporary and/or permanent damage. It is difficult to say more at this point.

Fortunately, she did not aspirate upon collapse, and her breathing seems to have stabilized. The probe you will have noticed on her finger will allow staff to monitor her oxygen levels. For the time being, they'll keep her on the 24 per cent – a low delivery – mask. They might switch to a pair of nasal prongs in the morning.

There are no noticeable abnormalities of the skin or limbs. And you should be neither alarmed nor unduly hopeful should her body move spontaneously. It is possible, for example, that she will start to shake or make jerking movements. Patients in her condition have even been known to sit up. It is possible that her eyes may move abnormally. She may even open her eyes as if suddenly awake. Bear in mind it is unlikely, in any such instance, that she will be awake. You may need to close her eyes for her, or you may ask a nurse to do so if you prefer.

Christina is moved to a private room. From the window, in the far distance, one can just see the green haze of the forest preserve. Come morning, Maggie will bring relics to her bedside in two plastic bags.

An old snapshot of their mother. The print on the white border says NOVEMBER 1979, but it is summertime – she's wearing a halter top – so the film must have sat in the camera for months. She is turning into the wind, her long hair catching in her sudden smile. There is a blur of birds and architecture behind her. On the back, in ballpoint, it says, 'Paris, Jardin du Luxembourg (where Hemingway gunned down pigeons for his din-din!).' Their dad's writing. The pressure of it comes through to the other side.

Her nightgown too. The one she wore before she lost her own smell to the toxins of the chemo. Their father helped them wrap it in Mills Brothers' tissue paper and cellophane before their neighbour, Mrs Ingram, came to take her clothes away.

An old cassette of music from the 70s with 'Honey' by Bobby Goldsboro. Their mom had always sung along, not very well – one of her favourite songs, she'd tell them with her big, big smile. And as children, Maggie and Christina had loved the way the chorus of angels burst into song as Honey died.

French for Beginners. A twelve-week course. She is on week three and Tina is on week two.

Her new burgundy fishnet stockings, still pristine in their package.

Her garnet ring. Their father found it only the day before in the drum of the washing machine.

Her big spiral sketchpad with her studies. Loads of them, Maggie realizes. Page after page. Some in chalks, some in pastels. Wild hyacinth. Trout lily. Golden alexander. Woodland sunflowers. A white lady's slipper. A bumblebee on a stalk of sweet joe pyeweed. A wood thrush. A great blue heron. A crested flycatcher. A hummingbird drinking from a cup of wild columbine.

She's a volunteer in Thatcher Woods, less than half a mile from their house; part of a small team that catalogues native flora and fauna. They meet at weekends at the edge of the woods, though, more often than not, Christina heads out on her own.

Near the end of the pad: a charcoal drawing of a group of oak trees on the river bank. The oldest ones in the wood, each over three feet round. And in the sketch, a canopy of new leaves. It must have been May? June? At the base of the trunks, there's a surge of sweetgrass and spangled light. In the background, a trace of the West Line and the smudge of the railway bridge.

But this is not another nature study for the museum's catalogue. Here, her sister is after something more: the gravitas of the ancient trunks; the tangled energy of their branches; maybe what their mother used to call the spirit of the place.

The sketch is still unfinished. There's a figure. Someone coming down the embankment. A vague half shape only.

3

When he arrives back at the house – to sleep, to wash, to wake Maggie so she can take his place at the hospital – when he arrives back at the house, he slips off the surgeon's slippers someone offered him in the night, walks into the kitchen, eases the receiver from the hook and dials *69.

The last number has been blocked. Again.

Other nights, he's caught the call on the first few rings, on the phone by his bed. Since June, four or five calls in all. But always the click in his ear. When the girls asked, what else was there to say? 'Just another crank call.'

He phones Ameritech. Says he wants a call traced.

'I'm sorry, sir. That's not a service we offer our residential customers.'

'It's important. I –'

'Have you been the victim of abusive calls, sir?'

'No –'

'Could your request relate, for example, to a judicial issue?'

'Like what?'

'Like the breakdown of the terms of a current restraining order.'

'No.'

'If you can inform us of the number, sir, we can arrange for that number to be blocked.'

'That's what I'm trying to tell you. *That*'s the problem. I don't know the number.'

'How can I help you, sir?'

He hangs up.

He goes to Maggie's room. He coaxes her from sleep. He reminds her Christina must not be alone when she wakes up.

The day of that first late-night call, he'd met Nat for coffee. June sunshine. Cappuccinos and biscotti at Starbucks. The first time they'd seen each other in more than a year. He'd had to stop himself from kissing her cheek as she arrived – she would have thought him false. Of course she would have.

He'd grabbed the big table in the middle of the window, though, sitting there with her, he felt strangely conspicuous, as if he were the view for passers-by and not the other way around. She seemed bemused, her eyes wide, searching, over the white rim of her cup. He asked her how she was. She shrugged in that French way of hers. He crunched away on the biscotti, his mouth always full when he went to speak. She sat very straight in her chair, elegant, braced from the start. And though he'd wanted to apologize, though he'd asked her there expressly to apologize, even after he'd left it too late, he never managed the words. He smiled, at the table mostly. He played with his cuffs. He found himself flirting happily with the waitress. He never found a way to begin.

When she first arrived in the department in 1990, there was the usual flutter of interest in a new face. She was half French-Canadian, half Egyptian. His boss had lured her, just as she'd started to publish, from McGill with a low-rung salary and a temporary visa. She spoke with a French accent. Was Muslim, someone said, but who really knew anyone's private world in that place? He remembered noticing her heavily pregnant the following year. Was embarrassed when she saw him staring at her.

He knew something of her research on $E_8 \times E_8$ strings, one of the five rival string theories. But mostly, he knew her only to see her. Dark hair. Dark eyes. A generous mouth.

When was that student-staff picnic? '92? '93? She had Aarif with her, balanced on her hip most of the day. Just another single working mom, he heard her joke modestly. No, she said, no family in Chicago. Everyone was back in Montreal. Yes, she admitted, sometimes it did make her feel unmoored in the world.

He brushed her shoulder, accidentally. Somewhere between the chicken jambalaya and the potato salad. A sudden voltage. Maybe he said, Excuse me. Or smiled an apology.

Jen was failing. His girl. Still with her big tail of honey hair, in spite of the chemo. Still reading every old novel she could because she'd die, she said, if she died without reading *The Rainbow* or *The Buccaneers* or *Bleak House*.

He never could bear the joke.

In bed at nights, sweating against her stack of pillows, she popped morphine pills and turned pages, awake often for the first time in the whole of the day. 'Giles, where's the pencil?' she'd whisper as he slept, her hand rooting under the covers. She scribbled notes in the margins. 'I hope she's <u>not</u> going to India with him. Don't ever go to India with a man who secretly hopes you might fail your exams.' 'Yes, DHL gets wordy, of course he does, but you've come too far now to stop.' He was to keep her books so that one day her daughters might turn the pages and find her talking to them. So her voice would always be there for them.

He wasn't about to tell her that he'd been suspended from teaching. He never mentioned the disciplinary hearing.

It was Nathalie, a woman he'd never even spoken to, who knocked on his office door one day, saying he could tell her to mind her own business. She got him a top-notch legal adviser from the union. She organized student testimonials. She offered to speak at the tribunal on his behalf. One day, in the staff cafeteria, she grabbed his palm, squinted at it and, laughing, assured him things would work out. 'Your career line shoots right up your hand, straight as an arrow. This is just a setback.'

'You're joking.'

'About your career?'

'About reading palms.'

'My aunt from Cairo taught me every summer. I used to work street corners in Old Montreal.'

He looked at her.

'I was *good*. How do you think I paid my tuition?'

There were things about Nathalie Haddad he'd never know.

By '93 there was infighting in the strings camp. Fewer positions. Less of the brash confidence of the early days. Because the theory was starting to look less like a theory and more like a five-headed monster. And what does she do while everyone's arguing whose head is first for the chop? She takes up the cause of the department's heretic. Someone who kept coming up with eleven dimensions when everyone else was counting ten.

Yet he let her do it. His own life was imploding. Jen weighed just seventy-two pounds.

'What are you doing?' he shouted at her one day when she wouldn't take another sip of her Ensure. 'Trying to *kill* yourself, for Christ's sake?'

The world was bursting its banks. Space-time itself was bending and twisting. Its coordinates were blurring. Where was his wife's funny, dirty laugh? Where was her lap for Maggie's sleeping head in the car? Where was the rise of her nipple for his mouth? Where would the light of her eyes *go*?

He left the department at the end of that academic year. He and Nat spoke once or twice afterwards. He can't remember if he ever asked after her. If he ever asked how things were for her, really.

★

Five years later, they alight from the same commuter train at Geneva. They're a few feet from one another in the cab line. They're both on their way to Wilson Hall. She's hardly changed – still hasn't lost her accent. She's one of a number of physicists being briefed at Fermilab on the new plans for the Tevatron accelerator. Run II, they're calling it. He's got work in the lab. The shuttle's late. They agree to share a cab. They each appear casual. He wonders, fleetingly, if he should sit up front with the driver. Instead, he gets the door for her, walks round to the other side, and slides on to the back seat.

There's a moment or two of silence. Then filler.

Predictably, she's struggling to get her contract renewed again. Says she'd rather be in Montreal, but it's not as easy as you think it's going to be to make the move back. He nods. Mentions a name, an idea or two. She asks after him. He says, yup, he's well. Not that the old conundrum isn't still keeping him awake at nights. Nothing new there.

The cab driver takes in the rear-view, fleetingly interested. He imagines Dr Giles Carver is talking relationships. It's what they *don't* say, he'll tell his wife later, that tells you the most. The driver's smug. His own mid-life crisis is comfortably past: a mother of two who bartended downtown at Sly Al's, showing more than her roots.

Would he be interested if he knew that Carver was in fact referring to one of the physical world's most stubborn mysteries? How to make gravity *fit*. How to make sense of it in the world of the very small as well as the very big – because there's no escaping the fact that the very big is always, first and finally, made of the very small. If we can describe the speed and location of a cannonball at any one moment, we should be able to do likewise with one of its electrons.

Only we can't. The electron eludes us every time.

Giles Carver is still trying to figure out how to translate supergravity's non-linear language, Einstein's difficult legacy, into orthodox quantum-speak. How to complete the puzzle of quantum-think. How to find himself a place, holding fast to gravity's elusive coat-tails, in the fold of meaning.

She nods. Smiles. Turns to look out the window as they pull at last into Fermilab's west entrance, the cab scooting below the high, bright arches of the *Broken Symmetry* sculpture. The silence turns to calm. Her arm is warm against his. They both know this is where they begin.

Two years together, on and off. Then last summer – was that the last time? – he's out of control. He can't help himself. He's telling her to fuck off, to just fuck off out of his life.

The day was stifling. He'd assumed the girls were too old to be interested in a Sunday walk with their old dad – but they said, sure, why not? It was too hot not to go for ice cream. They hadn't been to Petersen's in ages. Great, Nat said. He hustled everyone out the door, remembering his keys only at the last minute, as usual. Maybe afterwards, he said, they could stretch out in the shade of Austin Gardens.

Most of the way, the sidewalk wasn't wide enough for four abreast, but Nat understood. Anyway, in front of the girls, out of respect for them and Jen's memory, he wouldn't show her partiality. He walked with the girls. She walked behind, pretending to window-shop along the way. And the girls pretended not to notice she was no longer with them.

('I want to *marry* Christina.' He'd said that once. One night, apparently, as they slipped drunkenly, happily, off to sleep in his bed, after sex. He was dewy-eyed as he mumbled it, she said, like a sixteen-year-old boy in love. She'd laughed. She didn't make it into anything, and he'd liked her for that.)

In the ice-cream parlour, it was her treat, she said. She took the order. Black Walnut for him. Blue Moon for Christina. Cookies 'n' Cream for Maggie. Tradition, he said, and the girls beamed.

At the booth, when she arrived with the four double-scoop cones in a tray, he was next to Christina, squeezing her knee; teasing her out of an approaching mood. She sat down next to Maggie, who sat twisting the rings on her fingers. The air conditioner rattled above their heads, but there was a breeze at least.

They were halfway through their ice creams when he asked her what time she had to catch her train.

'Giles, I only just got here.'

'I think we're all a little tired today, aren't we, girls?' He looked at her. 'The weather,' he said with a shrug.

'You invited me over. I booked Aarif's babysitter until this evening. So we could spend some time.'

'I know. But I didn't count on the day being so muggy.'

'I feel fine. The air conditioning's revived me. What about you, Maggie?'

'There's a three o'clock train on Sundays, Nat.'

'Can I talk to you?'

'You're talking to me. Isn't Nat talking to me, girls?'

Christina and Maggie stared at the table.

'We used to go to Austin Gardens with Jen,' he said quietly. 'It's sort of our special place.' Both girls looked up briefly and smiled, quiescent, the old family romance flickering to life. 'I'll walk you to the door.'

By the time they got to the door, she was pale with the strain and, seeing her like that, put upon, he started shouting. He knew what he was doing even as he did it, but he couldn't stop himself.

Christina and Maggie could only have heard it all. The whole restaurant heard it all. But when he returned to the table, smiling, embarrassed – 'Whoops!' he joked – both were concentrating on their cones.

'Good ice creams?' he tried, sliding into the booth.

'Delectable,' said Maggie, still keen in those days to flex her burgeoning vocab.

'Are we going to the gardens soon?' asked Christina. But it wasn't a question in search of an answer.

Under the table, she stretched out her legs and rested her feet on the seat next to Maggie. Maggie pulled out a library book and spread it flat on the Formica table. Neither told him off, like they did when he barked at the parking-lot guy the week before. Neither said, how could he speak to anyone like that, let alone Nat? Instead, the three of them sank deeper into the cracked red leather of the booth, sighing, letting formalities go, as if they, together, had summoned the torpor of the day.

He lies in his bed now, trying to catch a few hours of sleep, the blinds shut against the daze of light. But his mind is racing.

Could it have been Nat on the phone? Did the disastrous coffee date in June heap insult on injury?

It's absurd. He knows it is.

Yet he can't chase the question from his head.

And there are others.

In the final days at the university, colleagues he'd worked with for years wouldn't look him in the eye. But that was the least of it. His funding had already been curtailed. No self-respecting postgrad wanted to work with him. And, yes, he kept himself aloof where he might have more usefully played dead. He alienated people. Made a few enemies probably. It's what happens.

After the hearing, and the highly conditional offer of

continued employment, he quit. It made little difference. Effectively, he'd already been cast into the hinterland.

So there were those who were less than thrilled when he landed on his feet in a matter of months. At Fermilab. With a grant. A hefty grant.

But God, that was eight years ago now. Enough time surely for anyone to grab hold of new grudges. If someone wanted to harass him, why now?

He thinks back to his early exchanges with Ed Witten. To the M-theory stuff.

Wasn't there a landmark conference at Cambridge only last month? The very first to catch the public eye. Wasn't he himself footnoted in at least a dozen of the M-theory papers? Hadn't he just started to shine unforgivably in Witten's reflected glory?

Giles Carver needs answers. He will have answers.

And he'll grasp at them as long as his daughter lies silent as a riddle in a hospital bed.

4

It was December '94. Edward Witten contacted him out of the blue. He was going to be in town for a few days. A family visit to Chicago over the holidays. Is that what he'd said? They'd agreed to meet late one frosty morning in the lobby of the Sears Tower next to Calder's spiralling *Universe*.

Witten must have been in his mid-forties then, about the same age Carver was now. Carver was then thirty-six. Recently widowed. Still sick and restless with grief at night, alone in their bed. Suddenly a single parent of two small girls. Newly outcast from the university, and still a stranger in Fermilab's community. When Witten's call came through, it was as if someone had thrown him a lifeline. *Someone* was talking to him, someone was interested, and that someone was Edward Witten.

Carver arrived first. He and Witten had never formally met, but he didn't doubt that he'd know him right away. You saw his eyebrows coming first – intent writ large on his face. Carver remembered them from a U of M conference in '81.

Witten had been one of the plenary speakers. There'd been a blizzard at the time; winds of eighty miles per hour whipping the rooftop of the lecture hall. Drifts were amassing at the windows. The overhead lights sizzled. Then died. For a minute or two the room was cast into complete darkness. Witten's microphone failed. Naturally soft spoken, he made a joke that only the front rows heard. Who wants a roomful of high-energy physicists when you'd pay double-time for just one electrician with a pager? Somewhere a back-up generator kicked in. The lecture continued.

Everyone arrived for the meal that night, dazed by snow. Yet within minutes, the whole room was talking about Witten's simpler proof of the positive mass conjecture. Even to Carver, then a postgraduate, a humble initiate, Witten had seemed like a man with some kind of tongue of fire. He seemed able to speak everyone's language, and, in the climate of the day, that constituted a minor miracle.

As a boy, Giles Carver had juggled: apples, oranges, golf balls, ping-pong balls. He did magic too. Sleights of hand mostly with coconut shells and balls of red foam. To his surprise, he discovered in the eighth grade that algebra was like the balls and coconut shells; that its equations asked only to be arranged and rearranged until the unknown appeared – always there, both obscured and revealed by the terms of the known. As he grew older, he was drawn to the algebra of an invisible world; to the search for deep principles.

He chose Stanford for a BSc in physics in the end, because everyone knew that only actors got less work than mathematicians. Then it was the École Normale Supérieure for master's work in '78 and '79 under Joel Scherk.

Scherk's version of supergravity was the first in which Giles glimpsed the possibility of a multidimensional universe. Of extra dimensions that might lie hidden in the three we know so well – undreamed-of spaces that lie curled up or crunched down in what we see only as length, breadth and depth.

Of course string theory also depended on a multidimensional space. Ten in its case. But the maths of supergravity predicted an *eleventh* dimension: a dimension that was infinitely long but only a tiny distance across – a trillionth of a millimetre maximum. Closer to you now than the clothes on your body. Yet because of it, one could harness, on paper anyway, the force that had eluded the quantum world so far – gravity.

Carver couldn't resist.

He met Jen in Paris. Discovered her sitting on a bench in the Jardin du Luxembourg, ignoring her Hemingway novel, her face turned like a sunflower to the noonday sky. In time, she joined him in Stanford, in a crummy apartment that overlooked a gas station and truck stop. He was starting his postgrad. She was teaching night classes – literature, literacy, composition.

He found Jack Conroy's office at the end of a remote, unswept corridor in a building far beyond the science block. He introduced himself by saying he'd worked with Scherk in Paris. He was young, gung-ho. He said, Throw it all at me: the crazy dualities, the broken symmetries, the tease of the graviton.

'Okay,' said Conroy, leaning back in an oversized La-Z-Boy recliner. 'This is supergravity. I've got no fellowships or bursaries or stipends. The best I can do is get you some undergrad teaching. Kids who want to hear that Einstein was a mystic and that Bell's theorem means we're all actually telepathic. This is Californ-i-a, remember. And would you mind losing the lab coat? The things give me the creeps. My therapist says it's got something to do with an unresolved fear of priests.'

Carver got up, shook his hand, made to go.

'And one other thing . . .' The springs of the La-Z-Boy creaked. 'This is the only time you'll hear me say this. A good theory's more than just a good theory. It's more than a hunch. It's more than an educated guess. A good theory is one that's caught reality by the jugular. If *you're* any good, you'll know it first and prove it second. So roll up your sleeves, Giles Carver.'

Giles Carver *was* good, which is why he was also trouble. To himself as much as anyone else.

Edward Witten would have known his reputation. Yet perhaps, too, he had recognized something oddly familiar in Carver's research. Didn't they share, after all, a quiet passion for pure mathematics, for its symbolic language, for its uncanny magic? Certainly Witten had noticed something, for he was travelling out of his own very comfortable camp to meet a colleague who'd almost been thrown to the wolves.

In the Sears Tower lobby, Carver spotted him coming in from Wacker Drive, stamping the slush off his boots. He introduced himself. They shook hands. They strolled over to the Calder sculpture and looked thirty feet up to its animate spheres, to its bright moving parts, like a couple of kids gazing at the kinetics of Creation. Then they hopped the elevator to the Skydeck, climbing 1,300 feet in just under a minute, their ears popping.

It was a clear, cold day. Not a breath of a wind off the river. Below them, the fabled towers of the city exhaled long sighs of steam. Their coup de grâce flourishes – gilded minarets, neoclassical cupolas, bright arrows of glass – flashed in the late-morning light. Carver pointed out Michigan, Indiana, Wisconsin. You could see forty, maybe even fifty, miles. 'Like infinity at your windshield,' said Witten, and, for a few minutes, each was lost to the view.

Then Witten said he was hungry. Could they pass on the slide show? He never bothered with breakfast, despite his wife's blandishments, and now he was peckish. They ordered sandwiches from the deli on the restaurant level. Witten grabbed a souvenir ballpoint and a wedge of napkins.

They talked noncompact global symmetries and massless spin -1 fields. Witten reached for his glasses and passed Carver the pen. Carver said, 'Okay. Here goes,' and started to sketch the latest solitonic solutions to various supergravity theories. 'I don't know what you've heard, but it's not pie in the sky.'

In fact, he said, he and others in the field had already shown that if one of the eleven dimensions was a circle its two edges could conceivably come together to form a kind of tube. 'Or, in other words' – he grinned – 'something that could be *mistaken* for a string if you happened to be working in your – with respect – more meagre ten-dimensional continuum. And, even though we were ignored by just about everyone at the time, there's no denying that certain of the supergravity symmetries do carry over to string theory. *With* gravity in tow.'

Carver picked up the pen again, and his hand flew over napkin after napkin. The mathematics of the eleventh dimension was at his fingertips, literally.

He pieced the fragments into a panoramic vision, hauling over the neighbouring table so it wouldn't be interrupted. Then he sat back, and even he had to draw breath. The old equations still looked astonishingly elegant.

'But you didn't come here,' he said, 'to get reports from the outback.'

Witten hesitated. 'I've got a hunch.'

Carver looked at the table, smiled. 'And I've got a hunch you've got more than a hunch.'

Witten started talking. Sometimes he'd consider the food on his plate: pick up a half of sandwich and put it down again, forgetting to eat. Finally he said, 'It's like this. What if the five competing string theories are just part of one bigger theory? It sounds crazy, I know.'

'Word has it that I'm used to crazy.'

'What if I've got another theory – it's not strings or supergravity. Call it whatever you like. Pick a letter.'

'What?'

'Any letter.'

'M.'

'Okay, like I say, this theory, this M-theory, is not super-gravity, and it's not strings either. But it has your eleven-dimensional supergravity, and all five string theories are among its possible low-energy manifestations.'

Carver whistled low.

'But of course there's a catch, and the catch is strong coupling. You need to start with the Type IIA string and increase its coupling constant from a value much less than one to a value much greater than one. As the constant gets larger, your eleventh dimension becomes visible. And as the value increases, the dimension grows and things, for lack of a better phrase, "take life".'

'Take life how exactly?'

'Well, what we know as simple strings, they stretch and . . . and combine and sweep . . . A one-dimensional string stretches into something that looks like a ribbon which stretches into a cylinder of sorts which in turn stretches into a membrane. When the Type IIA description, or any one of the five theories, breaks down because a coupling parameter becomes too large, another description takes over.'

Carver rubbed his temple.

'And the math works. It all works. With electromagnetism, with the strong and weak nuclears, *and* with gravity.'

'So you're saying all five are merely different manifestations of . . .'

'Of one underlying and, frankly, still mysterious theory. I think we're looking at *one* dynamic structure of the physical world. A matrix. Maybe some kind of vast membrane after all. A membrane to which our world is tied.'

'Paul Dirac. 1962.'

'Only he couldn't get the equations to pan out. Do you know Townsend's stuff? At Cambridge. He went back to Dirac. I've seen the work. They've got it this time. They've discovered the membrane mathematically. On paper, it's stunning. And I've got an idea for demonstrating how the extra dimension, that all-important eleventh, could shrink into a segment of a line. So you get two ten-dimensional universes, like this' – he started drawing – 'each at an end of the line of the eleventh dimension. But they're not discrete. The two universes "communicate" with each other by . . . Are you ready?'

'Gravity,' breathed Carver.

'Exactly.'

'God.'

'Thanks,' he murmured, wiping his glasses, 'but my wife still says, if only I could put up a shelf.' He looked up, smiled, looked down again.

'What kind of Planck energy do you think we're talking about?'

'Far less than that at which gravity has been expected to become strong.' Witten passed him his jottings on the napkin. Circled a figure.

Carver leaned back in his chair. Wiped his mouth with the back of his hand. 'Get the road map, honey. We could be gone for a while.'

'At least.'

'So what are we looking at? What are you seeing?'

'A kind of multiverse of universes, I suppose. Coexistent worlds. Worlds strung on a thread.'

Carver nodded slowly, meeting Witten's eye. Then, 'There's just one problem.'

'Go on.'

'The M of M-theory.'

Witten smiled.

'What does it stand for?'

'Membrane?' Witten mused, as if trying out a new book title.

'Not too catchy.'

'Matrix . . .' Witten tried again.

'What about Multiverse?' Carver picked a gherkin off his plate and snapped it in two between his teeth. 'Better yet . . . Mystery.'

Witten laughed. 'Wait. It's coming . . .' He smiled, waggling his considerable eyebrows like a quack conjuror. '*Magic*. M is for Magic.'

Carver grabbed the salt and pepper shakers and reached for a neighbouring pair. He cast one, two, three, then four into the air, juggling them in a trickling cascade until the manager of the deli emerged and confiscated all four.

They tried to clink cardboard cups, cold coffee sloshing over the rims. The waitress stared. They could only have looked ridiculous. Yet there was the sense of something unfolding, there, against the skyline of a crystalline winter's day. And for a moment, no more, each went quiet, lost in his own thoughts; suspended in the space-time dream of the 103rd storey.

That couldn't have been long before Witten's now famous M-theory paper at the University of Southern California in '95. Carver had seen the abstract. 'The richer theory, which has as limiting cases the five string theories studied in the last generation, has come to be called *M*-theory, where *M* stands for magic, mystery, membrane or matrix, according to taste.' He'd laughed. And had silently toasted Ed Witten with the stale coffee on his desk.

That day in '94, Witten had seemed to him as open-minded as a kid. Carver's enfant terrible reputation hadn't fazed him. Not at all. In fact, they'd made a damned good double act. And the exchanges had continued, by letter, by email.

The conference in Cambridge last month was huge. Already

it was spawning a generation of M-theory zealots. So was that who was behind the phone calls? Some fervent postgrad looking for a father figure?

No. Too easy.

Something was going on.

After all, his association with Witten had armed him with clout, hadn't it? Who didn't want a piece of M-theory these days? The Web was a good measure of just how far it had travelled. There was new madness every day. Travel in eleven dimensions just steps away. Japanese teleport large objects across miles. M-theory's living cosmos: the new Neo-platonism.

Then there was *The West Wing* furore. In a ratings-winner of an episode some TV character up and reports the discovery of the Grand Unified Theory at Fermilab. The so-called Theory of Everything. It's H. G. Wells and *The War of the Worlds*, twenty-first-century-style.

The switchboard at Fermilab is jammed the next day. Reporters line the steps of Wilson Hall. Not because they've confused a TV show with the real thing, but because there's allegedly been a Fermilab leak at the highest level. The particular *West Wing* episode is a double bluff, they claim. A carefully negotiated bit of spin to ensure the Everything story, by its nature uncontainable, is dismissed as TV sophistry.

More media turned up for the *West Wing* story than for the discovery of the top quark in '95.

As if there could be a shred of experimental data. To find a string itself, and not just the ghostly trace of one, they'd need an accelerator the size of the Milky Way.

Irrelevant, apparently. Doubletalk. Fermilab had reality's number.

Paranoia, after all, is only a surplus of logic – as Carver sometimes comforts himself.

One cock-eyed journalist ran with the story: 'Dark Matters: the Universe Rattling in Fermilab's Closet'. His byline went coast to coast. Fermilab's Office of Public Affairs could barely cope. It was fiction hurdling the real.

In the days when Giles Carver could still tell which was which.

5

When he returns to the hospital, Christina's feet are uncovered, and there are wedges of pink sponge between her
toes.

Maggie is at the foot of the bed. She has a bottle of nail
polish in one hand and a brush in the other. The sight of her
there, bending awkwardly over her sister, takes him aback.
'What you up to, Maggiekins?'

She turns, trying to look casual. 'The nurse suggested it.'
She hadn't wanted to. She couldn't tell the nurse. She can't
say it now. She is afraid of her sister's comatose body.

He looks away. 'Is there a vase somewhere in here?'

'By the sink. Sssh, Dad. I'm concentrating.' Summer Fireweed. She found it in the drug store in the hospital lobby.
Only it's going everywhere now. She can't make her fingers
work.

He runs the water, unwraps the large arum lily from its
tissue paper and places it in the vase. She glances back over
her shoulder. She doesn't remind him that Tina never liked
lilies. He places the vase on the bedside table, next to the
snapshot of their mother. 'Have you been talking to her,
Maggiekins?'

She blows on her sister's toes, her face darkening. 'No . . .'

'Only I'm sure she'd –'

'No one's sure, Dad.' She looks up. 'Not even you.'

'She's going to wake up, Maggie.'

'I wish you wouldn't say it like that.'

'Like what?'

'Like there's no problem, really. Like Tina might not be gone already.' Her eyes are filling.

'For God's sake, Maggie. What if she can hear you?'

'I don't think she can.'

'The doctors said to keep –'

'She barely hears me when I try to wake her if she oversleeps. So I can't believe she's going to hear me now.'

He sinks into the chair by the bed and leans back, contemplating the blank of the ceiling. 'Sweetheart, I could really use a coffee from the cafeteria. Maybe a Danish. You could get yourself something to eat while you're at it.'

She closes the bottle and turns to him. 'What are you going to talk to her about?'

'I'm allowed to talk to her, aren't I?'

She sighs, exasperated. 'Don't play hard done by, Dad. You always do that. I'm just saying I can't pretend for you, okay?'

'Pretend what?' He passes her his wallet and winks. 'Maggie?'

She meets his eyes begrudgingly.

'Either you're with me . . .'

She half smiles, in spite of herself.

'. . . or you're *with* me. Which is it?'

She rolls her eyes. 'I'm with you.' She picks up the paperback she's been reading. *Jane Eyre*. 'When haven't I been?' She's at the bit where Rochester calls 'Jane! Jane! Jane!' and, miraculously, Jane hears him across the miles. She'd rather let the story go now – she's not in the mood any more – but she can never not finish one of her mother's old books. In case she turns over a page and finds one of her scribbled messages. 'Okay. One coffee, black, and one Danish.'

In its original form, enchantment was magic by language – literally, conjuring with words.

Take the standard medieval case of possession. Here, the priest needed a command of Latin, of course, some garbled Greek, and a secret lexicon that might, forgivably, be mistaken for gibberish: 'Amara Tonta Tyra post hos firabis ficalir: Elypolis starras poly polyque lique linarras buccabor uel bartin vel Titram celi massis Metumbor o priczoni Jordan Ciriacus Valentinus.'

Or, more reasonably, perhaps: 'In nomine Patris, et Filii, et Spiritus Sancti. By the power of the Lord, may the Cross + (here the priest crosses himself) and the passion of Christ + be a medicine for me. May the five wounds of the Lord be my medicine +. May the Virgin Mary aid and defend me from every malign demon and from every malign spirit, amen. + A + G + L + A + Tetragrammaton + alpha + O.'

Meaning?

Once upon a time, words did more than mean.

Giles Carver takes his sleeping daughter's hand in his. He bows his head, covers his face with one hand, and tries to pray to something he can't believe in. 'Please. Please let –' A food cart rattles past in the corridor. There is a quick knock at the door before it opens. 'Coffee? Tea?'

He shakes his head. The door closes again. Through the window's open vents, he can hear people in the parking lot below. A new baby is crying – its first time in the open air.

He strokes his daughter's forehead. 'Sssh,' he says. 'Sssh,' as if she is upset. 'Everything is going to be okay.'

Promise? Her eight-year-old voice. Slightly nasal. She hasn't yet had her adenoids removed.

Promise.

When are you going to take us to your work again and make the frog fly?

We'll see.

Is Maggie already in bed?

Not yet.

Then why do I have to go to sleep? I'm older.

You're not feeling well, ladybug.

But I can stay up longer than her when I get better.

We'll see.

Tell me some secret words.

You don't listen to the ones I tell you.

Is that why you tell Maggie?

Maggie needs some too.

But you don't give her my ones?

Would they be secret if I did?

Tell me.

I don't know any more tonight.

Yes you do.

Okay, okay. Close your eyes. Closed? Right, now not a word.

Not a word.

That was three.

Oops.

That was one.

. . .

. . .

. . .

'I never . . . saw a moor,
I never saw the sea;
Yet know I how the heather looks,
And what a wave must be.'

I never saw . . .

A moor. I never . . .

Saw the sea.

Yet know I how the . . .

There's a girl at school called Heather. She –
How the heather looks. Your go.
And what a wave must be.
Very good, ladybug.
I won't remember. I never do in the morning.
That's because they're secret words.
What do they mean?
You'll know as soon as you're asleep.
Really?
Really.
Night, Daddy.
Night, my baby.

Alone in the cafeteria, her midday breakfast still untouched, Maggie withdraws the bookmark from her book and turns it over. She copied the number in small, neat numbers before wiping all trace of it from the palm of her sister's hand. When she discovered it that morning, painting Christina's nails, the number was already faint.

What is it? The number of a friend from school she met on the bus? The number of some take-out place, quickly scribbled? The number of one of the other forest preserve volunteers? Tina was out there just yesterday afternoon.

Has it faded as a matter of course? Did Christina herself try to wash it away, last night before bed? Or was a nurse simply indiscriminate as she sponge-bathed her sister's body late last night, before they moved her into the private room?

Maggie opens her father's wallet, fishes in the change pocket for a quarter, then walks to the payphone on the opposite side of the cafeteria. She picks up the receiver, punches the buttons and waits.

No answering machine. No voicemail. No answer.

6

The payphone rings and rings. A few passersby glance that way, but no one stops. It's Saturday lunchtime in the metropolis. Labor Day weekend. Everyone has somewhere they want to be. A trumpeter with a prosthetic arm is playing 'Fly Me to the Moon'. He squeezes his eyes against the ringing of the phone but he doesn't miss a beat.

The shoeshine kid, on the other hand, is hardly aware. He's sizing up his prey. Tourists today. The heat means too many are in sandals and sneakers, but he's not giving up. Brits are good. They get off the plane at O'Hare and think they've walked into a movie. He's not even halfway through the patter before they're nodding. Cos they're thinking: shoe brush in the jacket pocket or handgun? Shoe brush? Handgun? He likes Canadians the best. They know he's ripping them off, but they're too PC to turn down an inner-city kid on the make.

Keep walking.

The walls on either side of you are vast, opaque. They ripple and curve, on and on, as if deep space has suddenly solidified into Plexiglas. You're in the terminal at Madison and Canal. You walk past the ringing phone and into the public washroom.

You are not an abstraction. You need to go.

As you enter, two of the sinks turn on by themselves and, momentarily, you're spooked.

By the time Maggie replaces the receiver, you're heading across the concourse. You've got your ticket. The West Line. That's the one. Follow your instincts.

The train's at the platform already. In the distance you hear the lonely call of another, beautiful above the din of brakes and steel doors. Yours is a double-decker. Climb on. There's a single row of seats only. The feeling is vaguely claustrophobic despite the long, cigar-shaped windows; despite the fact that you're the first to board. You take the stairs to the upper level. The strip lighting flickers. The seat creaks as you slide across the blue-grey vinyl.

Maggie arrives for her Saturday shift. She works at the River Forest Public Library Saturday afternoons, and sometimes on Sundays. She and Christina are saving for their trip to France, though Christina keeps giving her money away to new causes: Save Chicago's Birds or, last time, the Campaign for Dark Skies. 'Starlight,' she insisted to Maggie. 'Of course it's important.'

Maggie does not tell Mrs McFarland, the senior librarian, that they rushed Christina to the hospital in the middle of the night. She does not tell anyone that her sister will not wake up.

Mrs McFarland would cluck in her Scottish way. She'd cluck as if the sky were falling but (sigh), 'Of course, it cannae be helped.' She'd send Maggie home so that, later, she could whisper to Miss Slack and Helen, the other weekend assistant, 'Och aye, I sent the poor wee girl home.'

But home is not home with her sister gone from it.

In the stark days of early spring, Christina cleared the last pocked patches of snow by the big bay window, dug up dead grass with a spade, and scattered streams of sunflower seeds over the new bed. Later, in the backyard, she strung bright teacups from bare branches to cheer up the view.

Sometimes at night when Maggie is sleeping Christina creeps into her room and slides folded sketches under her

131

sister's pillow: their street after the first snow, the footsteps of the paperboy ghostly on the lawns; a still life of pears rotting in the kitchen fruit bowl; the crab-apple tree in the backyard in a froth of blossom.

She sings out of tune as she cooks, and burns herself often. She feeds the neighbourhood strays on the back porch. She leaves holes in the toothpaste tube, crumbs in the honey jar, honey on the morning headlines, runs in Maggie's tights and scraps of paper under fridge magnets saying 'I borrowed $4.84 from change in assorted coat pockets' or 'Let's make a really BIG dinner tonight, okay?'

In the gardens each spring she'll pick the wild hyacinths you're not allowed to pick and curse herself as soon as they're in her hand. She knows the stars by name. She smears her face in body glitter when she's feeling low.

She is eternally hopeful about the Reader's Digest Sweepstakes. She walks under ladders because she refuses to be afraid. When their father is brooding and silent, she sits with him.

The circulation desk is unusually quiet. It's a blazing summer's day. Outside the asphalt is melting, and, up and down the streets of River Forest, homeowners are watering their lawns with a collective will that could be mistaken for moral urgency. Old people, walking their dogs, pit their wills against sprinkler systems, as wide fans of water hit the sidewalk and retreat, hit and retreat. Goth teenagers loiter in the sprawling shade of oaks and maples, at the edge of civilization where Thatcher Woods begins. Kids are on bikes, skateboards, scooters, roller skates, rollerblades and hopscotch squares. They're behind home-made lemonade stands and in treehouses. They're high in mid-air above skipping ropes. They're turning into mermaids under the stagnating tides of plastic pools.

The good weather's holding.

Which means Maggie has a few minutes, maybe more, to return to *Jane Eyre*. Less than fifty pages to go, and still no note from her mother. She reads the scene again.

All the house was still; for I believe all, except St John and myself, were now retired to rest. The one candle was dying out: the room was full of moonlight. My heart beat thick and fast: I heard its throb. Suddenly it stood still to an inexpressible feeling that thrilled it through, and passed at once to my head and extremities. The feeling was not like an electric shock, but it was quite as sharp, as strange, as startling: it acted on my senses as if their utmost activity hitherto had been but torpor, from which they were now summoned and forced to wake. They rose expectant: eye and ear waited while the flesh quivered on my bones.

'What have you heard? What do you see?' asked St John. I saw nothing, but I heard a voice somewhere cry –

'Jane! Jane! Jane!' – nothing more.

'O God! What is it?' I gasped.

I might have said, 'Where is it?' for it did not seem in the room, nor in the house, nor in the garden; it did not come out of the air, nor from under the earth, nor from overhead. I had heard it – where, or whence, for ever impossible to know! And it was the voice of a human being – a known, loved, well-remembered voice –

Maggie stops. She just about trusted Jane and her account of events till now. How can she hear Rochester? In the movie, doesn't she just fall asleep over her Hindustani books and dream his forlorn call?

Maggie likes realism. Until last night, it served her well.

As she stamps the purple return date in a boy's *The Philosopher's Stone*, she wonders if she's betraying Christina by not insisting, like their dad, that her sister will wake up; if she's being disloyal by refusing to pretend that Christina can hear them, across the forested terrain of deep sleep.

(Tina! Tina! Tina!)

Later, after she's signed the time-sheet, she'll make for the payphone in the library's foyer. Once again she'll dial the number she copied on to her bookmark. She'll ease herself out of Mrs McFarland's line of sight. She'll hang up only when the ringing cuts out; when the one-armed trumpeter crosses to the payphone, lifts the receiver and drops it down again.

No reply.

The West Line rolls on. From Chicago to Kedzie. From Oak Park to River Forest, Giles Carver's station each morning. You know the route. Some days you slip into the same compartment, like an ordinary commuter. Other days you fall into step behind him at the end of the working day.

Now through the green blur of late summer, the train takes you over the river, past Maywood and into Melrose Park Station. You rub the back of your neck. You can't quite relax.

Onward. Bellwood. Berkeley. Elmhurst.

At Villa Park, children are in tears at the bottom of the stairs because their mother won't allow them to sit on the train's upper deck. You still have the space to yourself. No distractions. You'll know it when you see it. Or him. Or her.

Imagine.

Through the window, wasteland. A disused quarry. Smokestacks. The behemoths of water towers. Chicago is thinning out. The architectural might of Oak Park and River Forest has given way to faded frame houses and dirt yards that back on to the West Line. An old black man, sitting on a buckling lawn-chair, looks up and meets your eye.

You keep your things on your lap: jacket (too hot for the

day) and a light knapsack. Contents: a bottle of water, your cellphone, a Metra timetable, your guide to Chicago, and a disposable camera in case. In case of what, it's hard to say.

YOU ARE BEING WATCHED

A police surveillance sign at one of the stations. You smile. You appreciate irony when you see it. After all, it's you who's doing the watching.

Wheaton. College Avenue. Winfield. At West Chicago, the rail yard. Finally, Geneva station.

You've reached the end of the line. All passengers to disembark.

You scan the platform. Nothing. No one recognizable. No one who strikes you. You feel vaguely foolish. Like you've lost the plot.

You cross to the opposite platform. The next train back is already in the station. You hit the DOOR OPEN button. You hear voices on the upper deck. You stick to the lower, near the back. Your appetite for the view is gone.

The train pulls out of the station, almost empty. You let your head rest against the window, and in no time it seems the brakes are sounding for West Chicago station. Did you doze off?

Four rail workers get on. They're still in their jeans and yellow safety jackets, in spite of the heat. Each grabs a seat to himself and spreads out. Two bang all the windows in the compartment open.

Three rows in front of you, you see him. It's the blue ballpoint on the broad back of his jacket that catches your eye. Just above the seam of the yoke. Below one of the silver reflective strips. 'Angel'.

The A is drawn with the heavy lines and flourish of a Gothic letter. A nickname. Something a girlfriend might have written

135

with a smile, literally when his back was turned. 'What are you up to?' he would have asked with a laugh.

Station after station dissolves behind you into the day's heat. At River Forest you alight. Thatcher Station. Angel's already on the platform, stripping off his jacket. As you make for the exit to the street, you see him hurdle a security barrier. Then he heads off up the track, following the line north into the woods.

7

It was a provocative study. In 1982, neurophysiologist Dr Jacobo Grinberg asked couples to participate in an experiment that would explore the neurology of love.

Picture it. Each couple is seated in the lab, face to face – a conventional means of heightening empathy. They are not permitted to speak or touch. Observe how the pupils of each dilate at the sight of the loved one. Consider the force of the shared gaze. Remember the sweetness of lashes.

Twenty minutes later and the time's up. The subjects are moved into separate Faraday cages – screen rooms which shield against conventional forms of communication such as radio waves. Here, each is wired up with EEG sensors that will map the electrical activity in the brain.

Now the test. A stimulus is applied to one of the subjects – a bright light or a mildly painful shock. So quick, it is over as soon as it is felt. Yet the pattern given off by that person's brain in response to the light or the shock is mirrored instantly by the other person's brain pattern. Even though his or her mate has not been subjected to the stimulus. Even though he or she has no knowledge of the stimulus applied in the other screen room.

In one out of four cases, the minority certainly – yet a figure that demands attention, outstripping, as it does, the random probability stats.

Perhaps, too, it suggests that Jane *does* suddenly know Rochester's anguish; that it is not merely a febrile imagination at work; that she does, in some sense of the word, hear him.

Interestingly, Grinberg notes that this meeting of minds does not diminish even when, like Jane and Rochester, loved ones are some distance apart. Like ancient notions of 'contagious' or 'sympathetic' magic, Grinberg's 'transferred potential' suggests that substances, once joined together, continue to influence one another, even when those substances are physically separated.

Relatedness, it seems, does not end.

Talk to me, Maggie.
    I would if you could hear me.
    The nurse parted my hair in the middle.
    I'll fix it.
    My brush is in the –
    Bedside cupboard. I know. I put it there.
    You sound low.
    There. That's better.
    Talk to me.
    I don't know what to say.
    Dad says I'm going to get better.
    Yes.
    You don't believe it.
    Nobody knows, Tina.
    What day is it?
    Saturday. Saturday night.
    Were you at the library today?
    This afternoon.
    And?
The usual. Helen complained and complained about the heat and how we can't have a fan even at the circulation desk, and Mrs McFarland said what she always says: how her Uncle Jimmy had had his head blown off in the war –
    And nobody heard him complain.

Exactly. Then she and Miss Slack started swapping tragedies again. Today it was the girl who went with her boyfriend last week to the Dairy Queen in Spring Grove. Or maybe it was Silver Lake. Anyway, she had a Brownie Earthquake. He had a Peanut Buster Parfait. He kissed her goodnight. Ten minutes later, she's dead.

Peanut allergy.

The trace on his lips was enough.

See? There's always someone worse off.

Then Miss Slack started on about the woman in her home-town in Indiana who sent her son out to the root cellar to get potatoes for supper. He was taking his time so she asked her daughter to go. When her daughter didn't come back she sent her husband.

Oh no.

All three dead. Gas released by rotting vegetables. Blocked ventilation.

God. It's like the one she told you last week.

Which one?

About the couple with the baby who moved into their new house and asphyxiated themselves by redecorating with exterior house paint by mistake.

. . .

What's wrong, Maggie?

Nothing.

You're crying.

No.

Yes you are. Don't stop talking to me, Maggie. Do you hear?

Visiting hours are nearly over. Dad will be here soon to pick me up.

Talk to me, Maggie.

What was that number on your hand?

What number?

You wrote a number on your hand. I found it on you yesterday. I tried calling – twice – but no one answered.

I don't remember.

Is it the same person who phoned last night? Did you hear a voice on the other end before you collapsed?

No.

No, it isn't the same person? Or no, you didn't hear a voice?

Just no.

Why is it a secret?

Maggie?

Tell me.

Maggie?

I'm here, Tina.

Talk to me, Maggie.

I'm talking to you. I am. Just stay with me, Tina. Just stay.

8

'Transport' is not a notion with which we are especially comfortable. In its raw form, stripped of the sentiment of paper valentines and celluloid love, it is hardly recognizable. It does not seem to us a natural development of, say, happiness or gladness of heart. Nor do the expert witnesses reassure:

'a sudden or gradual though always involuntary process'

'characterized by a loss of normal muscle tone, a fall in body temperature and depressed respiration'

'which may seize the subject abruptly when in a normal state of consciousness'

'leading to psychic disturbance or invasions from the subliminal region'.

As for the condition sometimes termed 'rapture', the less said the better:

'a violent uprush'

'an uncontrollable expression of genius for the Absolute'

'which temporarily disorganizes and may lead to permanent damage of the nervous system'

'so, an accident, no matter how fertile the yield'.

On Sunday morning Giles Carver is informed by a medical team of three that his daughter has lost her senses. Her eye and verbal responses are almost nil. Her motor response is weak, though she is able to withdraw from pain, which, one of the team adds, is encouraging. Her Glasgow Coma Score, however, is only 7, an early indication which does, they are afraid to say, point to significant damage.

Carver is not afraid to say, How dare they presume? How dare they give up on his daughter? She is a girl of twenty. She has always been fit and well. She was not dragged from a car crash. She was not pulled out of the Chicago river. She ran for the phone in the middle of the night.

A member of the team will agree that, of course, every coma patient is unique. She will gently remind him that they are not giving up on her. She will pass him details of a counselling service for carers of persons with Acquired Brain Injury. Feelings of denial, she will add, are part of grieving, and his reaction is entirely understandable.

He knows it is futile to deny the charge of denial. He tells her to leave the room. He tells them all to leave. He has allowed them to doom-say at her bedside long enough. He refuses to not believe: that where there is life, there is presence.

Giles Carver cannot know that there are others like him, in hospitals everywhere; ordinary heretics (a civil servant, a piano tuner, a high-school German teacher) who would tell him that the comatose person is, contrary to appearances, exquisitely sensitive. That the mere touch of fingertips against fingertips has moved the sleeping loved one – beyond words. That the fluttering of his or her eyelids has signalled, not a chemical wash in the brain but a boundless flight of the spirit. So a young boy, left comatose after being hit by a car, communicates to his family that he is in the middle of a great heroic battle. A twenty-five-year-old man, a patient in an urban hospital, wakes from his coma and cries when he realizes that the nurses are unaware of the music he still hears.

These ordinary heretics believe that the comatose person can recognize, from the hands laid upon them, which nurses know they are alive and which believe them dead and gone. They would tell you that comatose people have communicated these things in the secret grammar of breath. In the stammered syllables of their hands. In time-lapsed messages of brow, cheeks and mouth. The loved one, the heretics would tell you, will make of his or her body a dowser by which you can find them.

Carver forgets the Glasgow Coma Score. He takes out the two books he has brought with him. All he could find yesterday at the local bookstores. He tells Christina about Coma Arousal Therapy. He strokes the palm of her hand. He tells her he's going to listen to her in new ways. That they're going to find a way through this.

He tells her that the first book says that her vital signs, such as her heart rate, can strengthen with touch and stimulation, especially from loved ones, even when there is no outward evidence of a reaction. He understands this. Not to fear. He won't fail her. He squeezes her hand.

He reads that his daughter may still enjoy emotional, sensual and intellectual pleasures at a level others may not understand; that she may, equally, feel pain, loneliness, fear and despair.

He won't allow it. 'You're not on your own. Do you understand, Christina? You're not on your own.' He scans the second book. The young nurse who comes in to check the ICP monitor watches his face darken.

The authors of this guide propose the use of a light source of at least 150 watts to achieve a pupillary reflex. Once the patient's eyes are fixed and open, they recommend the use of strobe or flashing lights. To be followed by the determined use of flash cards.

'Did you bring in a pair of shoes, Mr Carver, like the doctor asked?'

'I will tomorrow.'

The authors note that the banging of saucepans or the use of a loud whistle near the patient might trigger the startle response. Noises must be random. Remember, the brain is able to turn off continuous disturbances.

The nurse cleans her patient's mouth with a moistened sponge on a stick, pushing it past her gums and over her tongue. She takes a brush out of the bedside cupboard and smoothes the thick weight of Christina's hair, teasing out the knots as she goes. 'She's better off in shoes, really, as soon as possible.'

'I'm told Christina's not going anywhere.' Slapping, pinching, the use of stiff brushes or deep-pressure massage might help to stimulate the latent defence mechanism.

'Shoes that lace up are the best. In terms of support.'

'I understand.' He can't believe what he's reading. Vinegar, lemon juice or chilli on the tongue, and ammonia, garlic or rubbing alcohol under the nostrils can, in some patients, produce facial grimacing – a reliable indicator of rudimentary taste and smell responses.

'Otherwise, Mr Carver, in time, we could be looking at footdrop. You wouldn't want that, now, would you, and you'd be surprised how fast the muscles –'

He flings the book into the can in the far corner of the room. 'Medieval nonsense, ladybug. We don't need it.' Next they'll be advising burial alive – an effective aid to the stimulation of the choking reflex.

'That can's for clinical waste only, Mr Carver.'

He looks at her.

'If you walked over to the can, instead of throwing material into it from across the room, you would see it's clearly marked "Clinical Waste Only".'

'My daughter and I heard you the first time.'

'There's me thinking your daughter was playing possum.'

He gets to his feet. 'What?'

'Playing possum. You know. A bigger animal comes along.

The possum takes fright and bang, it falls down dead. Only it's not. It's in a coma. Maybe for a few minutes. Maybe for a few hours. I found one once with my mother under our front porch. We were digging dandelions.'

He stares.

'It's just what people say where I'm from.'

'And go to hell is just what people say where I'm from.'

He turns. Maggie is standing at the door, and he can see it on her face. She wishes she was someone else. She wishes she wasn't his daughter. But she only says, quietly, 'Last night, Dad. Christina was back.'

9

In the 1880s the house that stands at the corner of Thatcher Avenue and Chicago Avenue, on the edge of Thatcher Woods, was an institution devoted to the care and moral instruction of young men from broken homes. More than a century later, it is the home of orphaned and injured native animals before they are released back into the wild. Here you might see a blue-winged teal, its blue wing broken. Perhaps you will help to feed it on duckweed and snails from the river. In a cage opposite is a chipmunk, concussed in a fall from a tree, and a muskrat who got caught in the spokes of a boy's bike wheel on a woodland path.

In the clearing behind the nature centre, Angel sits on the wide spread of a solitary tree stump. He spent the night in the abandoned signalman's lodge, near the bridge. He does that sometimes, sleeps rough. His mouth grips a cigarette. His boot, still thick with the dust of yesterday's ballast, toes a clump of lovegrass. The day is bright. His eyes are trained on the leafy darkness of the trail ahead.

'Open the blinds, Maggie.'

'What?' Maggie is dropping her bags on a chair. She's letting the cold water run at the sink in Christina's room. She needs a long cool drink.

'Now. Open the blinds,' her father says. 'All the way.'

'Why?'

She turns. He is looming over her sister.

'She blinked. I saw her blink.'

'Are you sure?' She's twisting the pole to open the venetian blinds. She can't make it work quickly enough.

'Hurry.'

Then she's on the opposite side of the bed, in the sudden light, staring with him at her sister's face. 'Tina? Tina, it's me, Maggie. Can you hear me? Can you move your eyes?'

'That's right, sweetheart. Try. Try to open your eyes again.'

They wait one minute. Five minutes. Ten.

'Tina?'

They hover over her bed for half an hour.

Angel wonders what it must feel like to be on a family hike. Or a weekend picnic. He takes the double-time. On a long weekend he'll take any shift they throw at him.

He doesn't want to wonder. He doesn't want to be waiting here. A wide-open clearing. Behind a public place. On Labor Day weekend with families, young couples – everyone it seems – emerging from the woods. But not her.

It's all he can do not to bolt and run.

A lot of the time he takes red-zone work – work on a stretch of track they can't afford to shut down. Sometimes it's emergency repairs to the tie-rods, bolts or plates. Or ballast tamping on track beds they find sinking in the summer's heat. A few weeks ago it meant re-laying a section of conductor rail in a hurry before the morning rush hour. In the record-breaking rain last fall he was one of a team of four turning a landslide back into an embankment.

The other guys are always on the blower to the union, but him, he's saying, sure, okay, no problem. Who's my lookout?

That day, no lookout. He didn't see her coming.

It was a stone skipping on the river behind him. He turned. Got down on his haunches. Peered down through the screen of leaves and across the water's glassy surface.

147

'Four!' someone called to him from the opposite bank.

A girl with hair the colour of honey.

The next trackman, a guy called Malone, was at least five hundred yards up the line. Past the bridge. Angel threw down his jacket, spat out a piece of gum, then took the embankment in easy slipping strides.

When he landed at the water's edge, it seemed to be waiting for him: a gleaming oval of a stone. He bent down, got the feel of it in his hand, bounced it a few times against his palm, then let fly.

'Eight!' she called. 'Why do men always have to win?'

'I don't have to do anything.'

Why did he say that? She was joking. And now she was shrugging, turning to go. 'What are you drawing?' he called. She looked back over her shoulder. He pointed to the pad of paper under her arm.

'Things.'

He almost missed it. There was the distance, and her voice so reluctant. 'What kind of things?' He could hardly believe he was doing it, finding the words, drawing her back to the edge of the bank.

She stopped and turned. 'Thing things.'

'Fair enough.' Already he was forgetting the glare of metal and the dead weight of concrete. He was remembering the smell of fresh water. Of sweetgrass too – is that what he was getting on the breeze? Its vanilla scent. He must have trampled some underfoot. Somewhere too the trace of a fox – like a whiff of rancid red wine. 'If it's private, just say,' he called, and he buried his face in his T-shirt, wiping the smear of sweat and gravel dust from his face. The shirt still stank of mildew, from his night on the rotting floorboards of the lodge. Once, he'd boasted to his dad that he could live like a fox if he had to. Well, here, he'd said. You can skin and bone this rabbit before it goes stiff.

148

By her feet, lacy fronds of maidenhair.

'Wildlife,' she called suddenly. 'Mostly I draw wildlife.'

'That's good.' He reached for his smokes. 'Interesting, I mean.' He knew. If it hadn't been for the river between them – narrow enough here but steeply shelving – she would have retreated by now. He understood. 'I mean, that's a good thing to draw. Especially round here.'

'Do you know these woods?'

He felt a smile break across his face, the feeling strange. 'I half grew up around here.' He nodded to the woods, to the river, and, self-conscious suddenly, kicked a stone with the steel cap of his boot. It ricocheted off a nearby hickory tree and panicked a nest of tree swallows. She didn't know whether to stay or go. He could tell. She was jumping for a cluster of oak leaves, just beyond her reach.

He needed to say something else, to ask her another question. But instead he made a shield of his hand, straining skyward as he tracked the swallows' path. Anything to stop looking at her.

'Incubation', in its earliest and least remembered form, referred to the practice of sleeping in a consecrated place – for the purpose of dreaming oracular dreams or in the hope of attaining within oneself a new fullness of being. One appealed, not to a lofty deity or a transcendent power, but to the *genius loci*, the spirit of the place, who was kindled by the action of the human heart.

For spirit of the place, read also *incubus*.

Demonic molester and guardian attendant, the incubus had the capacity both to destroy and to heal. To beseech him was to die and to live again more fully. Medieval authorities, however, were less interested in the experience of supernatural love or seduction than in a positive identification. 'Between the moon and the earth,' writes Geoffrey of Monmouth, 'live spirits which we call incubi demons. These creatures, part men and part angels, assume mortal shapes and have intercourse with women.'

Notably, in the works of early Christian writers through to the thirteenth-century encyclopedists, the incubus is often equated – or confused – with the 'wild men' of the wood. This unhappy race was born of a time when the forest was suddenly the great 'Loneliness'; when townspeople were turning increasingly to cultivation for their survival and lived in fear of the encroaching wood. As time went on, wild men or wild people would haunt the public consciousness with an all-too-corporeal image of rabid desire and divine punishment.

The story of the wild man begins as a cautionary tale. He

abducts women and children who wander. He rapes the former and eats the latter. He has a thick pelt of hair, usually black. Only the face, palms and feet (and breasts of the woman) are bare. His elbows and knees are exposed, too, for hair will not grow on these areas of flex and wear. On his head the hair is long and tufted – sometimes filthy and matted with dirt and moss.

Because he has an innate understanding of wild beasts, he is a skilled hunter. He will eat all game completely raw. When meat (and succulent children) are scarce, he will scratch up roots from the ground, pluck berries where he may, and gnaw at verdure. He knows every season. He feels every shadow, every shaft of light, on the woodland floor. He can even assume the guises of animals.

The wild man is strong enough to uproot trees. When he gives vent to his rage and frustration, he sets up a mighty woodland din. He is by nature hyperactive, combative, noisy and 'fiery-complexioned', but he is also prone to bouts of silence, immobility and deep suspicion.

Though he is entirely wanton in his desires, he suffers no shame.

Though he has the body of a man, he is without a soul.

Though his strength is unrivalled, he shrinks from contact with humans.

He doesn't have the words.

Its juice is red, abundant, especially at the root. When injured, the stalk 'bleeds' like a person. A single broad notched leaf sheathes the new bud as it rises from the earth. The solitary bloom emerges white, immaculate. In spring sunshine, it might last a week; in rough winds as little as a day.

That first day he wanted to tell her this, but his own voice embarrassed him. 'Over there,' he called.

'What?'

'To your right . . . No, back a bit. Bloodroot. Those white ones. On the bank.'

'Oh –'

'Something for your book.'

She looked blank.

'For you to draw,' he shouted, louder than necessary.

She nodded, pushing her hair away from her smile.

He felt something catch light within him. 'The Indians used it. For dye and paint.'

'Really?'

She couldn't be more than twenty.

Young. Too young. And Malone would be wondering where he was.

Overhead, a train was clattering along the track, the 11.20, when – 'What?' He cocked his hand to his ear.

'Stay there,' she shouted again.

Something in his gut pulled sharp.

'I'm going upriver to the bridge.'

He had no words to call back. He wanted to run, to scramble back up the embankment. But the world was narrowing to the bright span of the river, to the shelter of the oaks, to shouting distance. And as she disappeared into the woods he felt something in himself clamber into being; life stumbling late from a hole into the warm earth of spring.

Love me, he felt everything in him say. *Love me.*

Then he was leaning against the hickory, peering now and again into the river, looking for shiners, for rainbow darters, to show her. It hardly seemed real. Sunlight flickered with the breeze. She sat cross-legged on the bank, careless of mud on her denim skirt, watching the sky, the trees, for birds. That's what she was supposed to be doing. Recording bird life today.

She had a pair of fold-up zoom binoculars. Which is how she first spotted him, she was saying, up there on the tracks. She didn't tell him about her last sketch – the fleeting shape of him moving down the embankment. She'd got the motion of him, his energy, but not his face, not the essence of him.

Did he know? At least a hundred million birds are killed each year across North America in collisions with skyscrapers. Think of it: one hundred million. *At least*. She's seen photographs showing large masses of birds circling certain buildings and battering the windows. Chicago is a death trap for birds – 50 per cent that hit are killed. They don't put that in the guidebooks, do they? They don't mention that on architecture tours. And glass is the worst. Had he heard that? She hadn't, until one of the other volunteers told her. Birds see the reflection of the trees or sky, so they think the forest or flight path continues. Or worse, they see their own image and mistake it for a rival bird they have to drive away. It's *the* major problem for the reintroduction of certain species like the peregrine falcon. Had he ever seen a peregrine falcon?

And starlight. What about starlight? Nobody cared. Not really. Even though it takes four whole years for the light from even the nearest star, not including the sun, to reach us. The Milky Way had never looked milky to her. Had it to him? Not even in the middle of the night outside a small cottage her father once rented for them on the wild shore of Lake Erie. The fact that she might never really see the Milky Way made her so angry. She was part of the Campaign for Dark Skies. For smart lights and sky-caps on street lights. For downshine. There are more than fifty million stars, she said. The sky should teem, like an ocean should teem.

And every single element here on Earth, every element heavier than hydrogen that is, originated inside a star. Did he know that? Sorry – her dad was a scientist. Everything that was anything began with a dying star: the calcium in our bones, the oxygen in our lungs, the iron in our blood.

'Bloodroot,' she said in his ear, as if only half remembering a detail from a long-ago time. A time, only earlier that day, when they were still strange to one another. And she could feel it too: his heart slamming at his chest.

Then, 'Don't hurt me,' she said, and he wanted to say the same but didn't know what it would mean even if he could say it. Breath. Blood beat. He was moving beyond knowing. 'Don't hurt me,' but her fingers were on the buttons of his fly. They were lifting him out, kindling him. Her head was bending low – her neck so white as her hair spilled away – and 'Oh.' She smiled, moved by him, moved as he yearned in her hands towards her.

Lips. Tongue. Mouth. The gift of being received.

He lifted her face, pressed her back to the trunk of the hickory. Her nose was in the musk of his chest, his armpit. His lips glanced over her neck, her shoulder, over the velvet of her nipple. Later, the marks of his fingers on her thighs, on her hip. And 'Lift me up with you' – that's what she was saying, her voice almost lost in her throat. 'Lift me up.'

II

The lid of the peephole slides back.

'Giles. What are you doing here?'

'Can I come in?'

The chain clatters and drops. The door opens. She smoothes her hair and pulls a shoulder strap back into place. 'How did you find –'

'You've left the South Loop. Boy, that was one great apartment.'

'Small. Extortionate. I'm on my way out.'

'Got a minute?'

'I'm picking Aarif up at school. Then I have to get groceries.'

'It's Sunday, Nat.'

'So?'

'No school.'

'Arabic lessons. After Sunday School at the mosque.'

He raises one eyebrow. 'Arabic?'

'His grandfather's language.'

'I just meant –'

'Another time maybe, eh?' She starts to close the door. But she stops, toeing the welcome mat, uncertain. 'Unless you're any good at carrying groceries.'

'Any good? Any *good*? You know me, Nat. I'm the goddamned best.'

She rolls her eyes, smiling. 'Still Giles.'

'And to think you once said you wouldn't change me for the world.'

'Thank God I realized I'd be better off with the world.'

He still loves the way she can't say her *th*s. He tries to see around the door. 'Is there someone here?'

'Someone?' She studies him. Laughs. 'Like a man, you mean?'

'Is there?'

'We had coffee two months ago. The first time in what? A year? Believe it or not, Giles, one Grande Whatever at Star-bucks doesn't give you the right.' She brushes a strand of hair out of her eyes. 'How did you find me?'

'You never said you were in Bridgeview, Nat.'

'I didn't. My point exactly.'

'Why Bridgeview?'

'It's a community. Aarif needs that.'

'What about you?'

'I'm easy, Giles. I don my *hijab* when I dust. I pull out my grandmother's rosary when the vampires of life descend.'

'I stand warned. On both counts.'

'Don't think I didn't notice that you avoided my question.'

'About?'

She sighs. 'Okay. We're out of here.'

She runs into the house for her keys and bag. He starts singing – 'It Don't Mean a Thing' – in his best Louis Armstrong voice. He sounds almost jaunty.

From inside: 'Amusing yourself out there?'

'No,' he calls back. 'On a good day I generally manage to save that for the shower.'

The old act. Yet, in these last few minutes, he's been out-performing even himself.

It wasn't her. On the phone. In the middle of the night. Of course it wasn't her. And the old sense of shame returns to him, as if he's lifted money from her bag when her head was turned.

She hasn't come.

Angel has waited for three and a half hours now, restless in the clearing, stared at, wondered about, and she hasn't come. Like the time only a few weeks ago when he'd cleaned and oiled the old signalling lanterns in the lodge and lit them, one by one, so they could picnic that night by more than flashlights and Duracell; so she'd be surprised by the glow of lantern-light in the woods.

That time, that night, she was supposed to go home, to get warm clothes, and then meet him back at the lodge. But she never came back.

She couldn't get out, she told him days later. Her sister, her father, both home unexpectedly. Their mother's favourite movie was on TV: *Dr Zhivago*. Lost love. They always watched it together. Her mother loved Omar Sharif, who was Egyptian, not Russian at all. Did he know that? She and her sister knew all the words to 'Somewhere, My Love'. Not from the movie, because the movie only uses the melody, but because their mother had it in an old songbook.

Gabbing away about a movie. She had no idea. Again.

She looked up, saw something in his face. Started talking faster. It was impossible, she said. They would have asked questions. And he was the one who didn't have a phone at home or even a cellphone. How were they supposed to do this if she couldn't even get him by phone?

'Do what exactly?' As if suddenly he didn't know her, as if she had imagined everything.

'*This*,' she said. 'Be together.'

'You think we're together?'

'I know we are.'

'I think you're "together" with a lot of people.'

'What's that supposed to mean?'

'I think you're together with that guy, for instance, that blond-guy-with-the-glasses volunteer you talk to a lot.'

'Jonathan?'

'I've *seen* you.'

'You've seen me what?'

'I've *seen* you with him. You light up around him.'

'I light up around a lot of people. I *love* you.'

'You touch him.'

'Did you hear me?'

'Seventeen times. You touched him seventeen times last Friday.'

'We were *working* together. We were a team.' She takes a step back. 'My God. You actually counted. You watched me from some bush or something and you counted.'

'I should have known. What kind of girl fucks at the back of a railway line? Maybe your brainy father could help me with that one. Maybe I'll get your dad on the horn and say, So, Mr Carver, tell me, what kind of girl – '

'My God. On the phone the other night.'

'What kind of girl, Mr – sorry – Dr Carver – '

'It was you, wasn't it?'

'Fucks a man she hardly knows against a tree?'

'Your mind goes into that crazy overdrive – '

'Or I'll walk up to your nice house and knock on its nice door – '

'Jesus.'

'And I'll say – '

'Listen to yourself. Just listen. No wonder you're so alone.'

He stopped, his eyes narrowing to something primitive. 'You've got it. I'm alone. On my own. I've got nobody. And you know what? I'm going to keep it that way.'

'Am I supposed to feel sorry for you?'

'You mean, instead of feeling sorry for yourself?'

'What are you talking about?'

'You go on about your mom dying, about seeing her waste

away, about feeling cheated. That's not cheated, Tina. That's just fucking bad luck.'

'Don't you dare talk –'

'*Cheated*, Tina, is having your mom run out on you and your dad when you're not even a year old because she's seventeen and she wanted to have you adopted, and so did her parents because you were keeping her from her high-school prom, but your dad said no because he's got no family, and he likes the idea of him and a son doing the great outdoors thing together. He likes the idea of being a moral force with his belt and its buckle, same as his dad was a moral force before him. Cheated, Tina, is then having your dad bail out, die, when you're twelve years old. Cheated is growing up in care, and "care" means getting tied to things – bedsteads, banisters – so you can't run away.'

'I don't get it,' she stammered. 'You're always talking about him. Your dad. About the two of you in the woods. Laying apples in the snow so you could watch deer together. About being in the lodge with him, him teaching you the hand signals. Why didn't you say something?'

'I'll tell you why. He started off as a trackman, same as me, right? He got promoted to signalman when a piece of concrete fell off a crane on to his leg. They handed him a promotion so he wouldn't go for compensation. Anyway, the leg never healed right. Never hit the floor running again, but signalman, it's practically a desk job. He got the certification stuff he needed. Bought himself a Thermos and a birdwatching book. And he was set. After a while he didn't even need the stick any more to walk. You wouldn't have known there was anything wrong with him unless he had to move in a hurry.

'He always worked the West Line – you could work just the one line in those days. So people had loyalties, traditions. They'd get to thinking they knew their bit of the line as well as the track of worn carpet in their own living rooms. But the thing is this. Your timing, from living alongside the track, starts to feel like some kind of sixth sense. It gets almost spooky, the way your body starts to know the timetable better than you do. So you get comfortable. Not lazy. But comfortable.

'Anyway, there were kids, about my age, messing around on the embankment on the other side. They got through a fence that was on its way down. So my old man crosses the track. He's done it a thousand times. Steps *over* the rails and sleepers. Doesn't step between the points. It's all second nature to him, right? Even in a hurry. Even with that twisted leg.

'I'm watching him from the other side, from the door of the lodge. I'm thinking about the really big Hershey's bar I get if I learn that day's hand signals on the page in the manual. He's standing on the embankment, trying to keep the kids at the seven-foot-minimum clearance while they argue with him. Because he knows a train's coming. High speed for those days. Eighty-five miles per hour. One of the kids has a pellet gun. The others are just mouthing off but, from the other side, I can see they're getting to him.

'He's got money problems. Gambling debts, someone told me later. So what? Everyone's got something, right? But the day before, I asked him for money to get a new pair of sneakers, because there's a big hole in the sole of one of the pair I had, and when I showed him his eyes started to fill up. Which scared me, I remember, cos I didn't even know then that adults cried, let alone a man and let alone your father. I didn't think there was anything scarier than the sight of him taking off his belt, but that day I wished it was the belt in his hand instead of his eyes filling up like that. Anyway, there are the kids and he's getting distracted and maybe he loses track of time. But he sees them off and starts to cross back.

'He must have thought he could make it. Either that, or he knew he couldn't. I don't know. He had a bit of insurance, and the company decided it was suicide, even though Metra said different in their own report. Maybe that was just Metra trying to help me out. Fuck knows.

'But the poor bastard did slip. I saw him. Saw him try to get his balance back, like you do. And you know how when you're falling, and almost righting yourself, and then falling again? You know how it feels like time is passing slower than it really is? Well, I felt like that too, like I was falling with him, for a long time. And I know he thought he was going to be on his feet again any moment. It was his track, after all. His territory.

'But the floorboards of the lodge are already humming through that hole in my sneakers and the tin coffee mugs on the shelf are starting to tremble like they always do, and I'm yelling at him, but already the horn's almost blowing him off the tracks, and I can't tell whether he's doing what you're supposed to do – raising his right arm clear over his head to tell the driver he knows the train's there – or whether his arm's flying up because he's falling down.

'He was stupid to be on that track – and that's the best-case scenario, right? But he didn't throw himself under or stand there waiting for the thing to flatten him. Guys I work with, when they find out, say to me, So what was it? Ice on the tracks? Rain? Wet leaves? A diesel leak? And usually I say, Yeah, one of those things, cos there are statistics.

'But the truth is, it wasn't any of those things. The truth is, the Metra report found that my old man slipped in cess. In toilet waste. The train that passed ten minutes before had evacuated its tank on its approach to the lodge, a few minutes before pulling into River Forest station.

'I don't tell people. They might be asking stupid questions, but it doesn't seem fair to leave them with that punchline. Or sometimes, if you make the mistake of saying too much, they think you're after sympathy or, worse, their girlfriend. But the real reason I tell as few people as possible is cos, when it comes down to it, I'm ashamed. My old man put up with shit in his lifetime and he died in shit at the end. "Start as you mean to go on." That's what he used to say to me.'

They were breathing. Just breathing. 'Look at me' – turning his cheek towards her. 'I'm sorry I didn't come back . . . I didn't *mean* not to come back.' Her arms round his neck. His arms, dead wood at his sides. 'Know that. Okay? Know that.'

Now, nowhere. He'd waited all morning and, again, she was nowhere.

'You're telling me only now, Giles?'

'Yes.'

'You come to my house. You joke with me on my doorstep. You walk with me to Aarif's school. You kick a ball around with a bunch of nine-year-olds in the playground. You wait, with what some might consider fortitude, while I scramble for back-to-school supplies at K-Mart. You sit on the bus and smile as Aarif sounds out every Arabic shop sign we pass, from Al-Omari Islamic Fashion to the Blueberry Hill Pancake House. And all the while your daughter is lying in a hospital in a coma?'

'I know. I don't know why I didn't say something . . .'

'What is it, Giles? What's going on?'

They are standing in the well-stocked Arab grocery section of a convenience store on Harlem Avenue, Bridgeview's main drag. Giles Carver stares at containers of hummus and 'Smoky Eggplant Mutabal'. He eyes vacuum-packed vine leaves, halal cheeses, packages of 'Islamically slaughtered' sliced meats, microwave kebabs – even halal pizza in cling film. Beyond the chiller section: red lentils. Falafel mix. Tabouli mix. Pitta bread. Bags of almonds still in their green husks. Majool dates. Jars of translucent honey. Fresh figs like small dark minarets.

'That's just it. I don't know what's going on, Nat. Nothing's making sense any more.'

Aarif is pleading with his mother to buy a special can of Turkish cookies. On the lid is a picture of a flash-toothed genie who holds one finger in the air.

'When did she go in?'

'Friday night. I got her there myself. In minutes. Maggie did mouth-to-mouth on the back seat.'

'Have they said anything?'

'Only that the tests indicate significant damage.'

'My God. Giles, I don't know what to say. I'm sorry – Aarif, I said *no*.'

'They're wrong.'

'They could be. They really could be.'

'They are.'

'I'm so sorry, Giles.'

By the olives, a heavily set woman adjusts her glasses and fixes him through the slot of her black burka. He looks away, back to Nathalie; to Aarif, who is scowling at him. 'She's going to be fine. She is.'

'Maggie. How's Maggie?'

'I don't know.' The woman is handling something labelled *zoater* and shaking her head, as his own mother might. At him, he feels sure. Not at the price of the zoater. 'Okay. Okay, I think.'

'Giles, look at me. Why are you here? Why aren't you at the hospital?'

As he opens his mouth, he feels himself empty – of words, of meaning, of logic. The truth is no good. How can he explain fast enough? He was crazy to have turned up at her door like he did. Crazy to be chasing a phone call. Crazy to have suspected her. A tied-up dog chasing its own tail. Only now, without it, without the chase, he feels he could start to break. He's got no clever words, no jokes, no bravado. There's only his tongue thick in his mouth; his shirt sticking to him; Nat's wary concern; Aarif wanting him to go away; and the tawdry genie on the cookie can promising one last wish.

'Nat, you have to help me.'

12

Marvel comes quietly, cloaked in the mundane.

It's the woman waking to the smell of smoke as fire spreads, miles away, through her brother's house. It's the sharp flash of recognition as a young man glimpses, in the ordinary hubbub, the stranger with whom he will share his life. It's a mother's dream of her baby, blue in the cold store, six months before he comes, stillborn, into the world.

Even the Church Fathers admitted the category of the marvellous – or *mirabilis*, as they knew it. For them, an irksome classification. A grey area.

Compare the marvel with its less troublesome metaphysical kin. In the thirteenth century, the miracle reflected the steady-handed authorship of the divine – truth made manifest. Similarly, magic or *magicus* demonstrated, with tell-tale showmanship, the desperate guile of the devil. The marvel, however, was of poor provenance and tended, therefore, towards ambiguity. It took shape in the merely mortal sphere. It seemed to lack the requisite supernatural chutzpah. Here, the clergy were typically surplus to requirements.

Yet, if less outwardly compelling, the marvel was also less easily contained than either the miraculous or the magical. It remained more elusive. More stubborn. And, if finally reducible in time, with the erosions of memory, to rationalization, anecdote, drinking tale or woman's lore, the marvel also rarely failed to leave behind a certain residual uncertainty. A discomfiting sense of possibility. Or, on bolder occasions, an appetite for wonder.

In an age of faith – spiritual or secular – awe is certainly helpful. Awe boosts ratings. Wonder, on the other hand, distracts. Wonder involves wondering. It takes us to the brink. It makes us think, imagine, beyond. It has a nose for gaps, for omissions.

Maggie is wondering. Now. There, in the hospital room.

Empty. Her sister's bed is empty.

She only went out for a cup of coffee.

Tina?

Her body moves on without her. It sets her cup of coffee down on the floor by her feet. It remembers the nurse's station down the hall. It turns to run for the door.

It stops short when she sees a waterfall of light on the air.

She lurches backward. Bumps into a metal frame. Tries to focus. Notices another frame on the other side of the bed – each like a movable rail on which you might hang coats. A pulley system with hooks. Christina is suspended above the bed on a broad sheepskin rug, her feet exposed; her hair dangling below her.

Maggie understands. She understands that she has mistaken one sight for another. Her sister's hair for a waterfall of light. She understands that the surprise of her sister not being where she left her has confused her. She knows this and, at the same time, she cannot *not* see the current of light slipping from her sister as she hovers four feet above her bed.

A nurse rushes in. 'I'm sorry. The hoist jammed, so we decided to work it higher, then it jammed again. Normally she'd be on an electronic mattress by now but they're all in use. The porters are coming just as soon as they can.'

Maggie can't speak.

'Did your father tell you? It's on her chart. Turning every four hours. To prevent bedsores.'

166

Doesn't she see? The gush of light is thinning now. It's drying up. Her hair is going dark, almost strand by strand. Energy is leaving her. Something's wrong. She feels she is about to cry. Her father has already told her. No unhappiness in front of Christina.

'Would you like a chair? Can I get you something?'

'No. Thank you.'

'What about your father? Can I call him for you?'

Not her father. Not now. 'I'm fine.' She needs the nurse to leave.

'The porters really will be here soon.'

The truth is, she doesn't want Christina to come down from her magic carpet. She is afraid that her sister's body – the body that shared baths and beds and a mother with her – will be different, that her sister will be a husk.

A stack of library books sits on her coffee table. He grabs a seat, scans the titles. Science? Philosophy? Eastern magic? The names on the covers mean nothing to him: Avicenna, al-Ghazzali, Yahya Suhrawardi, Ibn al-Arabi.

'One coffee, then I'm out of here,' he calls. 'Maggie'll be wondering where I am.'

She walks through from the kitchen, mugs steaming in her hands. He looks up, shaking his head. 'Your beach reading's getting worse, Nat.'

She laughs. 'My father's influence. Blame him.'

'That hardly seems fair.'

'He was a Sunni Muslim by birth but an old Sufi by inclination.'

'I see.' He doesn't.

'I'll tell you a story.' She joins him on the sofa, crossing her legs beneath her. 'My mother grew up in a Montreal neighbour-hood known as the Plateau. Catholic. Deeply working class.

Yet, at its heart, a proud boast of a church. Beautiful. Every morning she left for school early so she could take communion at Église St Jean Baptiste. She'd walk up rue Marie-Anne, chapel veil and bobby pins stuffed in her coat pocket, and, by quarter to eight, she'd cross boulevard St Laurent.

'Her first glimpse of my father was across the boulevard as he shut the bakery door behind him. He was just finishing the early shift. She was seventeen. He was almost thirty. She told me she noticed him because she felt you could read a man by his back, and in my father's back she immediately saw, not only his strength, but also his kindness in the world.

'At first they nodded to one another from their respective sides of St Laurent. If she were a little late, he'd wait for her across the street by the bakery door, tap his wrist and laugh – partly because it would make her blush and partly because the watch he pointed to was long gone, hawked at a pawnshop the day he got off the boat in Montreal.

'After a while, my father got bold. He'd finish a few minutes early so he could cross to her side of the street and pass her there instead. Now at least he could see the blue of her eyes and the small mole above her lips, and those things alone, he always said, were worth crossing the street for.

'When his French improved, he managed to tempt her to stop, to chat. About the weather. About the bread that morning. About the customers, who came from all over the Main. Eli Mandel, who came every morning to collect the tins of unbaked rolls for the Steakhouse ovens; who was growing thinner and thinner by the day because his wife was looking prettier and prettier. Monsieur Lafayette, the poet who swept floors in one of the garment factories on St Laurent and recited Rilke to the women at their machines. Miss Doyle, whose glass eye misted up in the rain or the snow, so she wept in equal measure for the poverty of the poet Monsieur Lafayette and for the glazed beauty of the almond croissants. The six Leblanc children, who would burst into the bakery on their way back from school and for whom my father made cinnamon pinwheels from the endcuts of pastry.

'My mother was still shy in those days. But she stood and she listened and she smiled. Especially at my father's terrible French. And she accepted his daily gift for the rest of that winter: a hot bun for each pocket, to keep her hands warm on her way to mass.

'After a few months, she agreed to a café au lait after mass, in the minutes before the school bell rang. He brought the bowls and the coffee himself, in an old army Thermos, and they sat on the bottom step of a different spiralling fire escape every day in a space he would clear of snow with his bare hands because he was saving for a pair of good leather gloves. Imagine. No gloves in a Montreal winter.

'But my mother, though always girlish, even now, is steelier than she looks. She only allowed herself to fall in love with my father when he told her one thing. Not that he was a graduate of Islamic sciences at al-Azhar, one of the world's oldest universities. Not that his ancestors had been *ulama*, travelling scholars and wise men. But that there were Sufis, himself included, he said, who were devoted, also, to Jesus.'

Giles Carver suppresses a smile. 'I'll have to remember that line.'

She slaps his leg. 'It was the loophole he needed. That same day, he ran like hell down St Laurent, almost got hit by a fish truck on St Dominique, shouted at kids on rue Coloniale, and landed finally on rue de Bullion. There, squeezed between brothels, he found a narrow apartment building and, in the darkness of a basement apartment, an old man who was known, alternatively, as a street philosopher, a vagrant and a Sufi *pir*.

'My father told him he needed to become a Sufi toute de suite. That it was his only hope of salvation. He told the master that he had always been a good student and that he learned fast, and the Sufi master said to him, "Well, in that case, you are not a good student. A good student learns only very slowly."

'My father felt something in him sink like a stone.

'"But unpromising as you are," pronounced the old man, "I will not turn you away."

'My father was so happy when he left the master that he lay down in the trampled snow of St Louis Square and made a snow angel, like he'd seen kids do that first long winter in Montreal. And, only years later, did he understand the meaning of what he had told my mother in that moment of sudden inspiration: that Jesus was an ideal Sufi because he had preached a gospel of love.'

'Have you found Jesus, Nat? Is this what you're trying to tell me?'

'I'm trying to tell you that I had long assumed that my parents were endearingly naïve in the way they looked at the world. Isn't that what people like you and I think of our parents? I'd assumed that their respective beliefs were little more than the products of a powerful cultural machinery. Roman Catholic in her case. Islamic in his. That both faiths were only thinly disguised forms of social control. And don't get me wrong. I'm not saying they're not. But I used to listen to my father talking about his days as a student at al-Azhar, and for me it might as well have been something out of the *Arabian Nights*. I felt very superior when I told him that the phrase "Islamic sciences" had to be one of the best oxymorons of all time.'

'Kids are brutal.'

'I was going to show him how it should be done. Physics at

McGill. I thrived. The department got me funding for postgrad work, research, the usual. My dad was very proud. Both my parents were.

'I moved here in 1990, after the offer came through. I'd always been really happy in Montreal, but the idea of an association with Fermilab was too tempting. That, and all the strings stuff that had come out of the department. Then Aarif was born two years later.'

'Yes.'

'With an enlarged heart.' She looks up. 'I never told you that.'

He looks at the coffee table. 'I wouldn't have told me anything.'

'It was a ventricular septal defect – a "hole in the heart" – not uncommon, but this hole was big. So he was very blue when he was born, and his heart was already enlarged under the massive pressure of trying to get the low-oxygen blood to his lungs. In many cases small holes repair themselves naturally, but this hole wasn't small. They told me that emergency surgery, on my tiny child, was the only option.

'It was unbearable. Just the idea of it. The risks were huge, and even if he survived that, there was all this evidence coming out at the time about anaesthetics used on newborns leading to brain damage. It seemed like the beginning of something that could go on for years; something I didn't have the stamina for. I couldn't stop crying.

'Aarif's father was heading for tenure-track at the university, not to mention a tenth-wedding anniversary. I never told you that either. It had all been a painful mistake, except for Aarif. So I wasn't surprised when he told me, on my answering machine, that he'd respect any decision I needed to make; that we had to remain civilized. I knew what that meant. We lost contact. My parents were with me for the birth, but my father couldn't stay indefinitely because the operation could be weeks away, and he just couldn't afford to keep the bakery shut.

'But back in Montreal, every couple of nights, he got his friends together: Muslim friends, French friends, Jewish friends, Portuguese, Greek, Irish. Men and women I'd grown up with. Monsieur Nasser. Monsieur Mahmoud. Monsieur et Madame Bellefleur. Mademoiselle Juneau, the niece of Madame Bellefleur. Monsieur Heschel. Monsieur Demetrious. Monsieur Gonsalves. Monsieur Rubenstein. *Le vieil et le jeune* Messieurs Broussard. Monsieur and Madame O'Grady. That's our neighbourhood, yes? *They* were where I'd grown up, something that had more to do with my parents' united charm than with any set of progressive politics.

'Anyway, sometimes in those nights after Aarif was born there'd be twenty or more squeezed into our small living room, the air thick with the smoke of all nations: with du Mauriers and Rothmans, with Gitanes and Camels, with roll-ups, cheroots, the occasional pipe, and I guess a bong here or a hookah there. Better than the Stanley Cup play-offs, he'd tell me on the phone. And, together, after exorcizing the pressures of the day with a good smoke, they'd pray for Aarif.

'The hole closed, Giles. Not in a year. Not in six months. It closed in twelve days. A hole they said was too big to close closed. I'm in the cardiologist's office, waiting to sign a consent form. A junior doctor comes in with Aarif's file, including that day's test results. The cardiologist tells her she's brought him the wrong child's file. Only she hasn't. He insists. But she hasn't.

'Later, my father told me that, when he prayed, he used to imagine the hole as the eye of Aarif's heart. It's the old mystic image of contemplation, of wisdom. If you can see the hole as more than a hole, Rami, it might surprise you. That's what he told himself. And, over and over again, he'd watch the eye of Aarif's heart close.

'I was grateful. Beyond words. To my mother, my father. To everyone in that smoke-filled upstairs room above the bakery. And yes, it made me wonder. But then your life takes over again. Some kind of normality returns.'

'Thank God.'

'Exactly. Thank God. I no longer had to think about it. Aarif and I had been released into the world. He was fine. And, after a year, maybe a year and a half, I finally stopped listening to him breathe at nights. Then, three years ago, I stumbled across something: the results of a 1988 study conducted by a cardiologist. Randolph Byrd. He was investigating the possible effects of intercessory prayer in a sample of coronary care unit patients. Over ten months. In the cases of almost four hundred patients. Some were prayed for by outside prayer groups; some were not. Nobody knew who was in which group. Not the doctors. Not the patients.'

'And?'

'Some of the results were certainly significant. The prayed-for patients were five times less likely to require antibiotics and three times less likely to develop pulmonary oedema – a complication involving fluid and swelling in the lungs. The prayed-for patients were less frequently intubated and ventil-ated. They had fewer cases of pneumonia and cardiac arrest.'

'Very *X-Files*.'

She smiles. Sips her coffee. 'In the end, though, the results were challenged, partly because no one could say that the control group, the group that hadn't been officially prayed for, were not being prayed for anyway. In fact, it's likely that many of them *were* being prayed for by miscellaneous loved ones. So the study, finally, yielded more questions than it answered.'

'With respect, Nat, this isn't exactly an offshoot of strings.'

'No.' She turned. Stared out the open window. 'But what if we do find, at Fermilab or at CERN, the experimental support we need – maybe a trace of your ghostly graviton? What if we do prove that *one* energy *is* the basis of all matter?'

'Stop. I'm going all tingly.'

'Giles, shut up for once. We know – or at least we think we know – that everything is a stream of particles emanating from a string or strings. But there's still "blur" or "smear" or "fuzziness", less fundamental mess than we once suspected *but* –'

' – but still a mess of waves. So we've still got the old question.'

'Of what collapses a probability wave into real life. And we're *still* ignoring it because the equations don't care whether we know why or not.'

'But you do.'

'Don't you – I mean, at the bottom of it all? What is it about the act of observation or measurement – '

'Or thought or will . . .' He smiles.

' – that yields an outcome? And, yes. Okay. I wasn't going to say it, but yes. Or thought or will – maybe. In any case, *if* the stuff of the world is only raw potential until *some* sort of act of consciousness kicks in and determines things, then isn't it also possible that deep prayer, essentially an act of the concentrated mind – '

' – collapses possibility into actuality?' He laughs. 'Nat, nobody will thank you for this.'

'I didn't say they would.'

'The faithful will think you're turning God into a gigavolt. The research community will think you're turning gigavolts into God.'

'But what if it *is* all the same thing? God, gigavolts. Spirit, energy. The Word, the Singularity. "In my Father's house are many mansions"; the many dimensions, eleven at last count, of M-theory. What if both versions are equally true?'

'But this idea of *willing* an outcome in the physical world . . .'

'"Will" is the wrong word. A good contemplative, of any faith, would tell you it's not about will; it's about attention. A sort of relaxed awareness that comes from looking inward.'

'And does what?'

'I'm going on too much.'

'And does what exactly?'

She stares into her mug. 'Makes manifest what was previously latent. Or virtual. Or implicit.'

'That's what we tell ourselves when we make a wish, Nat. We're back to the *Arabian Nights*.'

She turns her ear to the window; hears Aarif laughing in the yard with the boy from next door. 'There are always implicits in the explicit world, and you know it.'

'That's the point, Nat. I know it. I know it from hands-on experience in the lab.'

'You've got a slice of eleven dimensions in your lab? Giles, really. You should have said.'

'I know it mathematically.'

'A symbolic language.'

'That has made accurate predictions time and again.'

'As have many philosophies and works of art.'

'You *know* what I'm saying.'

'Do I? Maybe everything the physicist, the priest, the mathematician or the imam *knows* is always only a description – no, not even a description – a metaphor, and by that I mean a truly wonderful and revealing metaphor, for something we'll never hold in our hands.'

He drains his mug. Checks his watch. 'I have to go.' Through the open window, the wail of the late-afternoon *adhan*, the call to prayer, arises from the mosque's loudspeakers two streets away.

'I'm sorry. I'm keeping you.' She picks up his mug.

'You're doing this, Nat? This contemplation stuff?'

'No. I'm trying. That's all. Which is what tonight is about, partly. There are people from the mosque, from a local orthodox Sufi group, from a synagogue in Chicago, from the local Polish-Catholic church. We've also got one Quaker and two Buddhists coming tonight. I liaise with the spiritual director at the University of Chicago Hospitals. I usually have everyone here. We're given names.'

He stares at the carpet. He can't not risk it. 'Christina. Christina Grace Carver.'

It's on his way out of Bridgeview that he sees you.

He pulls up the handbrake and squints as you move on to the crosswalk. When it clicks. You're from the train. The West Line. In the same compartment, often, in the mornings; there on the platform at Oak Park at the end of the day. Behind him on Erie Street on his way home. Another commuter. Same neighbourhood. Why else –

Except, now you're here, in a random suburb, sixteen miles out of town, on a late Sunday afternoon at the same intersection.

As the light goes green, he watches the back of you disappear down a side street.

The car behind him honks.

He's not even sure he could describe you.

13

It was the eve of her birthday, her twentieth, just before midnight. He reached out and put his hands over her eyes. 'It feels faster if you don't look.' And in the window's smeared reflection, she smiled wide as the late-night train made its bone-juddering run at the ascent known to railmen as Angel's Flight. Thirty-five feet over the expressway, he pulled his hands away.

Far below, the Near West Side winked at her with the light of 50,000 lives. Bedside lamps. Porch lights. The bright bulbs of fridges opened for the late-hour snack. He wanted her to have that, the world unfolded. Greektown. Little Italy. The Congo, as they called it in his day. And there, fleetingly, where his finger smudged the window, Ashland, the street where he'd lived until his dad died, in a house at the back of the heaving, ramshackle Blue Line. Long before politicians started shouting, 'Renew the Blue.' In the days when you could go down to the Maxwell Street Market, the original one, that is, and get a set of hubcaps, a live blues tune and a prostitute all on the same Sunday afternoon. Beyond it: the lights of downtown, which could have been Mecca when he was growing up, that's how unreal all those towers seemed. 'If I'd heard of Mecca, I mean.'

She laughed.

'Good view?' he said.

She looked at him, eyes so bright he had to look away. The old shyness. But his heart kicked to life in his chest. He knew he could do this: make the world new for her. He felt things: the life in the current of a river, the vibrato of a bird call, the metabolic dimming of winter, the green charge of summer. He lived in the moment. He could net it when he wanted to.

The girl who sat beside him, nose to glass, wanted to see. She wanted to smell. She wanted to taste the world. And he wanted to hold it for her, live as a fish in his hands.

'Turn around,' she said, her eyes glinting. He was still in his safety jacket – they'd met at the terminal straight after his shift. He was on lates, all that week. He heard her unzip her bag; felt the point of a pen on his back. The impress of letters. 'Not until you get home,' she said.

He'd forgotten until the next morning when he was throwing his jacket into the locker at work. Angel. She'd written 'Angel'. With a fancy capital A. He didn't even try to get it off.

And he's angry now that it should have given him such pleasure. Angry that he's loitering by a payphone in the terminal at Madison and Canal, thinking *here*, she might try to reach him here. Wasn't it always their back-up plan if things went wrong?

An hour passes. Two. Angel crouches by the wall, sucking a cigarette, wondering where she is – who she's with.

Maggie is in a toilet cubicle. Her father will be on his way to the hospital by now. He said he would pick her up at 5:00, then return to spend the evening with Christina. She wishes she could lift her feet from the vinyl floor, pull them out of view, and become invisible to the world.

Because how can she explain? She saw the light of her sister go out. She watched light spill from her sister's body.

There is no paper in the dispenser. And her nose is still running. She reaches for her bag. Her hand pushes past the neglected *Jane Eyre*. It finds a remnant of tissue – and her bookmark, with the phone number on it, adrift at the bottom.

He's walking away across the concourse when he hears it – faint as the trill of a bird in winter.

He sprints back as Maggie crumples the bookmark in her hand and drops it, with the number, into a waste can by the hospital payphone. He picks up the receiver just as she is about to hang up for the third and final time.

'Hello?'

A voice. She shakes herself back into the world. 'Hello.'

Not Christina. After everything, not her.

Maggie doesn't know what to say. 'Who is this, please?'

'No one.' He's about to hang up. 'I was just passing.'

'It's about my sister . . .' She gambles.

He covers his other ear with his hand. 'Who am I talking to?'

'Maggie Carver.'

Something's wrong. 'What is it, Maggie?'

'Do you know who I am?'

He tries to sound casual. 'Sure. Is Tina there?'

'Did you phone our house last night? Was that you on the phone?'

'Maggie, is something wrong? Is that why you're calling?' A horn blows as a train enters the station. His father's arm flies up again. He can't hear himself think.

'If it was you, please don't phone us again.'

'Listen, Maggie. I was supposed to meet her – today, this morning – and she never came.'

'Never came where? I don't know who you are. She hasn't said anything about you.'

'I was here, waiting for her to call . . .'

'Where's "here"? What's that noise?'

179

He stops kicking the wall beside the phone. 'I need to know where she is, Maggie.'

She can't tell him where her sister is. The light of her sister went out.

'Maggie.'

The tears are coming back. 'I have to go now. I need a Kleenex.'

'Maggie, how did you get this number?'

She can't any more – she can't keep blowing on the world to keep it turning. 'I have to go now.'

'No –' He winces. He mustn't startle her. 'You still there?'

'I'm going now.'

'Where is she, Maggie?'

'We don't know you.'

'I need to see her.'

She thinks, Why talk like this? What are they talking about anyway? 'Because you love her?' She can hear her own voice. Flat. Dead.

And he tries to get them to stop: the pictures in his head. That volunteer she likes, his fingers. The dark centre of her, rich as a split fig. They're like flash cards in his head.

'Yes.' His voice is hoarse. 'Yes, because I love her.' He sounds suspicious even to himself.

But Maggie hardly hears. She's already saying, 'I shouldn't have called. I'm sorry.'

'Maggie?' He gets his wits back. 'Christina must have given you this number, right? She must have asked you to call me.' More words than he speaks in whole days sometimes.

'No. She didn't.' She looks up. Sees her father coming through the hospital's main doors. 'You don't understand –'

'Where is she, Maggie?'

Her father will ask her who she was phoning. If she says his cellphone, he'll check. He'll know she was lying.

'Just tell me where she is, okay?'

Her thoughts are slowing down in her ears, like they used to when she was little. Who will she say she is talking to? 'The library.'

'She's at the library?'

'I mean, St Thomas's.'

'Christ.'

She didn't mean to tell him. 'I have to go.' Her father winks at her on his way to the information desk.

'Can I see her?'

'I don't think so.' The woman at the desk smiles and fills out a visitor's pass for her father. 'She isn't awake.'

'Why not?'

'I can't talk –'

'Is she sedated?'

'*No.*' She wants out of this conversation. 'She *won't* wake up.' She can't bring herself to say the word 'coma'. Her father turns, clipping the pass to his lapel. As he walks back towards her, he stops.

'What's wrong, Maggie? I need to know what's wrong.'

His keys. She watches him feel his pockets; sees him look back to the desk. 'I mean, she can't. She can't wake up.'

'Why not? What are you saying?'

He's got them. Shirt pocket. She turns to the wall. 'Please don't phone us any more.'

'The room number. Maggie, I need a room number.'

Click. Dial tone.

14

You were in Bridgeview. Out of place. Out of time. No mere bystander.

Of course not.

At the information desk, Giles Carver asks to speak to the person responsible for security.

'It's a Sunday evening, sir.'

'Yes.'

'It's also Labor Day weekend.'

'Isn't that what pagers are for?'

Nathalie stacks the dinner dishes. 'I hadn't thought about it, sweetie pie. He might come again.'

'Tell him he can't.'

'We must be kind, Aarif. His daughter is very sick.'

'I don't like him. He likes you too much.'

'I thought you had fun playing soccer in the schoolyard.'

'He wouldn't give me the ball.'

'That's the point of soccer, Aarif. You have to get the ball. It was all of you and only one of him.'

'But if he comes over, it will be him and you, and only one of me.'

'It's always, always you and me. Now one game outside with Abdul and then bed.'

At 7:30 Angel arrives at the hospital. He finds an empty chair in the foyer. Visiting hours are till eight. He checked.

He sits, watching family and friends leave for the night. He studies middle-aged men for Christina's eyes, for the line of her mouth, for the colour of her hair in twenty-five years. Could that man be Giles Carver? Could the girl with the puffy eyes be Maggie?

'May I help you?' The woman at the information desk has noticed his boots, still thick with dust from Saturday's shift.

'I'm fine.' He nods. 'Thanks.'

He works out the cameras. One on the waiting area, one on the security desk where every visitor has to stop, and one trained on the main doors. The information desk, he estimates, should be just out of view.

By 8:05 he's the only person left in the waiting area.

Aarif is in bed, at last. Nathalie curls up on the sofa and reaches for a book before her guests arrive, skimming the blurb. An exploration of the philosophy of Avicenna, especially his *Philosophia Orientalis* – the lost text, known to us only through the commentaries. Stolen by Christian Crusaders from the library of Muhammad I of Granada – though they failed to take the kingdom. Stolen again by Spanish itinerants. Smuggled into France in the early thirteenth century in fragments – priceless contraband that was to ignite an underground battle between the Church and the University of Paris as each struggled to acquire the fragments before the other.

And the dangerous import of the Avicennan contraband? That man might, through acts of the imagination, co-create the world.

She looks up. Within minutes, her living room will be transformed by prayer mats, meditation cushions, prayer shawls, rosaries and small icons. She's expecting thirteen or fourteen people tonight. Some will sit in chairs with their eyes closed or their faces buried in their arms. Some will kneel. A few will move their lips as they pray. Some will face Mecca.

One or two will gaze up, as if they're seeing through her stucco ceiling into the vault of the world.

Giles Carver is shown into a small office full of monitors. 'The nerve centre, I guess,' he says, extending his hand to the head of security, who smells of the flame-grilled burgers he's just left behind.

Carver studies the twelve monitors. 'I work at Fermilab, Mr . . . Mr?'

'Ciacci.'

'I'll try to keep this short, Mr Ciacci. I work at Fermilab. I'm a physicist, and in my line of work, you can attract crackpots. There are people, for example, who will never understand that not every physicist is personally responsible for the atom bomb. Others will decide that you're part of some New World Order, that you *know* things.'

A wry smiles flickers across Mr Ciacci's face.

'It's ridiculous. I know it is. And I feel ridiculous telling you this now. But it *seems* I'm being followed – I'll spare you the details – and there have been phone calls, too, at odd times. None of it might be of any significance. But, as I was telling you a few minutes ago, my daughter's here at St Thomas's.'

Mr Ciacci turns to the console. 'You're looking for reassurance, Mr Carver. Okay. Let me reassure you. St Thomas's is monitored twenty-four, seven. Not only is everyone required to obtain a pass before passing through security, but we've got cameras trained on every public space and corridor. Take the foyer, for instance. There's the wide view of the waiting area for you. And if you like . . .' he presses a button on the console '. . . you can zoom in too. So look at that guy in the chair. The one in the reflective jacket. See him?'

'The back of him.'

'Well, here's the close-up. Right?'

Carver nods.

'Now look. There's something written on his jacket. See that? I can even highlight that area, like so . . . Right? And bingo! We can read the writing.'

Carver peers at the screen and smiles. 'Angel.'

Mr Ciacci returns to the wide view. 'We don't want to go troubling no angel, so perhaps we should draw a veil, as they say. If I can answer any other questions, Mr Carver, you know where to find me – Monday to Friday.'

Giles Carver returns to his daughter's room. He spends a few silent minutes with her and kisses her goodnight. On his way out, just after eight, with keys in hand, he glances at the guy in the jacket. Still there. Picking someone up as visiting hours finish, he supposes. Maybe his girlfriend. Maybe his wife. The idea of either strikes Giles Carver as some kind of novelty gift, an easy pleasure from the everyday world to which he no longer belongs. He sighs; walks over to the information desk; drops off his pass. He is just past the main doors when the woman from the desk comes running after him. 'Mr Carver!'

He stops, turns.

'Your keys!'

He slaps his head. 'I'm always doing that.'

'Nice to be consistent.'

'If only I was.'

'I'm sure you have your moments.'

'Precisely.'

She laughs. 'Safe home.'

'Thanks again.'

It's only as he gets into his car that he realizes what's been at the back of his mind since Mr Ciacci hit the zoom. The writing – on the jacket.

Hers.

Every day he sees it. Old notes on the fridge he can never bring himself to take down. (Let's make a really BIG dinner tonight, okay?)

He slams the car door. Runs back to the foyer.

'Mr Carver!'

Gone.

15

Emergency.

He grabs a number, takes a seat. The place is packed: with kids who have fallen out of treehouses and bunk beds; with Little Leaguers who've taken a ball to the head; with old people who've landed a piece of chicken bone in the throat at the family picnic.

Twenty minutes have passed and, so far, no one's come running.

To his left, a man who's more stomach than man sits down, heaving his dead leg on to the chair across from him. 'So what you in for?'

Suddenly the cigarettes in his pocket are all Angel can think of. 'You don't want to know.'

'Try me.'

He nods at his left hand, the one that's stuffed in his jacket pocket. 'Rabies.'

'Sheesh.'

'Yup.'

'Bad luck.'

'Yup.'

'Squirrel or something?'

'Or something.'

The guy sits for a moment, drumming his fingers on the armrest. Then, 'Hey, abracadabra! I think they just called my number.' He manoeuvres his leg on to the floor and drags himself into the distance.

Angel goes over the scene in his mind: the sudden jiggling

of car keys, the woman's heels tapping across the floor, and 'Mr Carver!' She was gone just long enough.

He pulls it from his pocket. Opens his hand. DATE: SUNDAY, SEPTEMBER 2, 2001. VISITOR: GILES CARVER. ACCESS TO: RM 212.

Hold on, baby. Hold on.

In a room above, two nurses undress her, unbuttoning her nightgown and easing it past her hips. They leave her on her side and wash her, front and back, with warm water, liquid soap and two facecloths. They dry her with a stiff white towel, the name of the hospital printed in large blue letters at its edge. They swab her mouth with water and mouthwash and moisten her lips with balm. One of them takes the brush from the bedside cupboard and smoothes the knots from the ends of her hair while the other squirts moisturizer into her hand, rubs it between her palms to warm it, and applies it to Christina's arms and legs, still brown with summer. 'They need to check her fluid levels,' she says. 'Her skin's getting dry.'

Her colleague checks the drip and the catheter bag. She grabs a pencil from her pocket and makes a note on the chart. Then, together, they turn Christina from her side on to her back and manoeuvre her pillows accordingly. They pull the nightdress back up over her hips – a sleeveless cotton one Maggie supplied – and they work the long line of miniature pearl buttons, one starting at the bottom and the other at the top.

'Pretty girl.'

'Yes.'

'Brown eyes?'

'That's what Jane said. After the eye test.'

'Christina?'

She nods. 'Twenty years old.'

They pull the white sheet and blanket over her, smoothing, tucking. They close the window blinds and dim the lights over her bed. 'Sweet dreams, Christina.' They hover a moment by the door. 'We're not far.'

By the time the emergency receptionist calls number 48, it's 9:45. 'Name?'

The one on the locker next to his at the railyard.

'Nature of problem?'

'Work injury,' he says through the perspex pane. 'My hand. I can't move it.'

She points to a room down the adjoining corridor where a nurse will take his details and assess the seriousness of the injury. He nods and heads up the corridor as patient 49 moves up to the window. He looks back once, then punches the button of what he has already determined, from the distance of his chair, is a small service elevator.

Come on, come on.

The door rattles back and he slides in.

If security is waiting for him on the next floor, he misheard the directions. He's got a dud ear. From too many years on the tracks.

He hits the button for the second floor. Waits for the door to close. Punches the DOOR CLOSE button, twice. The elevator grinds upward. Lights flash overhead. He's standing next to a mop, an empty bucket and a cleaner's cart. There are sprays, solvents, cloths and garbage bags, neatly tied. How long can the thing take between floors? There are only two, not including the basement. And 216 beds. He saw it on a poster.

The elevator lurches to a halt. His stomach does likewise. He presses his thumb to the DOOR OPEN button and holds it there, waiting.

Giles Carver sits at the kitchen table, his heated-up meat loaf – Maggie's speciality – cold on his plate. He's thinking. About

Maggie upstairs. About how she hasn't come down; about how she can stay in her room for hours at a time; how he should go up to her. And can't.

He's thinking about the way, when Christina was a toddler, Jen would try to get him to use that child harness every time he took her to the gardens. Because she was always disappearing. Into bushes. Under the jungle gym. Once she managed to climb into the back of the ice-cream truck.

At the time – it's hard to imagine now – they had to think twice about whether they wanted another baby. About whether they could manage another. About whether they could feel so close to another.

'I'll watch her, Jen. Really.' He can still hear himself telling her.

Angel breathes again. It's been three, maybe four, minutes – and security's nowhere. He strips off his jacket, grabs a new garbage bag and stuffs his jacket out of sight. He clips the visitor's pass to his shirt – he's noticed staff wear one of a similar size. Green not blue, but he guesses – hopes – the security screens are black and white. He pulls on a pair of cellophane gloves, grabs the cart and humps it, whining, into the corridor, and straight into the camera's path. 200. 202.

Her front room is warm with breath and the balmy evening. Already more than an hour has passed. Nathalie's eyes are closed. Her spine is straight against the wooden chair she pulled in from the kitchen when Alice, the Quaker woman, arrived. Inside her head, waves of warmth lap at her brow. She feels as relaxed, as well, as alert, as she does after loving sex. Joy overtakes her quietly. Breath by breath.

Past the nurse's station. 204. 206. No one calls out.

★

'Christina Grace Carver. Pray for her.' Fourteen voices.

208. 210. Nearly.

In the dark of the kitchen, he presses back tears with the palms of his hands. And it surprises him: her hand, so light on his shoulder. He didn't hear her on the stairs.
  'It's okay, Dad.'
  Maggie. Her face too white.

And Nathalie feels it. The furnace of the silent world.

212.

16

Under a blanket white as snow. A tube in her arm. Tubes up her nose. Electrodes stuck to her chest. A metal tab on one of her fingers.

'Christina?'

In a hundred-year sleep.

He takes her hand in his. Warm. He crouches by the bed and rubs her fingers across the stubble of his face, across his cracked lips. 'I'm here.' He presses his lips to her palm.

When he looks up: something. Her eyes pulsing beneath their lids. He's sure. He tries to smile. 'It's the bad shave, isn't it?'

Did her eyebrows lift?

'That's right. Talk to me, Tina. Talk to me.' Nothing.

He pulls up the bedside chair, reaches again for her hand; holds it next to his cheek. 'Try. Try to push through. Because you're going to. Because if anyone is made for this world, I swear it's you.'

A sound low in her throat. More than air in her windpipe. He knows it is. A fragment of her voice. 'I know you're here, Tina. I *know* it. I've been an asshole. I know that too. And you've held on – you're so stubborn, Tina Carver – you hold on when I want you to run screaming. When you should run screaming.' In the corridor outside, the slap of shoes.

He lowers his voice. 'But, what I'm trying to say, deep down, Tina, is I'm grateful – that you could still see me through all the shit. I am. I'm grateful.'

The strain again in her chest.

'And I love you. Which, before you start, isn't the same as me being grateful. I love you, right?'

Against his cheek: the slight pressure of her middle finger. As if she's discovered the tear. 'Me?' He wipes his face with the back of his hand. 'You gotta be kidding.'

He goes to the foot of the bed and untucks the blanket and sheet. He takes her foot and rubs it gently. He reaches under the covers and massages one calf, then the other.

Her eyebrows rise again, so fleeting he might have missed it.

Past her knees to her thighs. 'Beautiful. I never really told you that either. You're so beautiful, Tina. Your eyes, the way they flash. The way your laugh rises out of you like a . . . like a spring. The way you look at things. I mean, really look. I'll tell you something. That first day I saw you, I thought, How the hell am I ever going to look away again?'

The sound from the bottom of her throat.

'But all that said, I'm not going to lie to you . . . You still can't skip a stone for shit, Tina Carver.' He picks up her hand, runs her index finger over the sharp edges of his teeth; presses it to the hardness of his molars, like she does each time she explores him.

It's theirs. The dumb yearning of smell, skin, tongue and bite. The refusal to feel shame. Even when he's turned on her, when he's tried to shit with words all over what they have, she refuses to be ashamed. For them both, she refuses.

He lowers the blanket and sheet. Is surprised for a moment by the catheter tube between her legs. He runs his hand over the cotton of her nightgown, over the smooth rise of her stomach. He can feel the springiness of her pubic hair through the cotton. Maidenhair – their word for it. After the fern.

They'd arrest him if they found him. He's not stupid.

But after breath, water and food: touch. He knows this too.

His fingers are too big for the buttons. He's slow with them.

He can feel how sensitive she is; how every sensation is amplified, not deadened. He opens her nightgown as far as her belly button. He rubs the tip of his nose over the wide softness of her nipples. Like blossom, he always says.

Above them, electrodes, like sores on her chest. He can't bear it. He kisses her neck, her collarbone, her breastbone. More than anything, he wants to give her back to herself.

And he has life-force for them both. Even across the forest of deep sleep.

Her nipples rise. Small stamens. He bends down and sucks, humbled all over again by the fullness in his mouth. He unbuttons his jeans. Takes her hand. Wraps her fingers around him, and his fingers gently around hers so there is only the warmth of his hand for hers, the loveliness of her fingers on him, and his need to *be* for her. To reach her, like a fuse of the world.

A dizzying burst.

He bends down. Presses his face to her breasts. And it's the hardest thing: not to pick her up and get her out of there.

He slumps into the chair; lets his head tip back. Remembers. On her stomach, the rain of him. He reaches forward and rubs slowly, until it's a translucence, until her skin shines in the dim of the room.

He rebuttons her nightgown, his fingers labouring again. At the end of the row, one missed. She'd laugh. He smoothes sheet and blanket. He touches the ends of her hair. He kisses her lips, her forehead.

Imaginary Time

I

Every detail is clear. The wild flowers in the mayonnaise jar. Their leaves blackening in the water. The remains of toast and honey on the plate on the floor. The print of Van Gogh's swirling *Starry Night* coming unstuck from the wall by her bed.

'She won't get up.' Maggie's eyes are filling. 'You tell her.'

He has returned, distracted, hot, from he can't remember where. 'Tell her what?' Why is there stone dust on his trousers?

Carver wipes his face on his shirt, then goes to his daughter's bedside. 'Christina?' Her face is slack, her chin fallen. Her cheek is creased with marks from the pillow. 'Christina, get up. You're too old for these games.'

He lays his hand on her forehead and sinks to the edge of the bed.

'What? What is it?'

He pulls Christina to him. She's still wearing the T-shirt and running shorts she had on the night before. He touches her cheek, neck, breast, wrist. 'She's cold, Maggie. And on a day like this of all days.' As if his elder daughter is only perverse. He slaps her cheeks. He rubs her arms and legs, as if he's pulled her from the Chicago river in January, not from a cotton sheet. He shakes her by the shoulders until her head lolls.

'Dad, don't. Don't.'

Somewhere a bell starts to ring.

A doctor is at the front door. The MD from emergency the other night. Carver tries to tell him to go bother people who are actually sick, but Maggie ushers him in. He's young, resolute. He approaches Christina's bed and, as he opens his mouth to speak, Carver sees that his tongue isn't a tongue. It's a brass clapper and the doctor's mouth is the ringing bell.

He can hardly hear himself think. In the corner his second daughter stands terrified.

'Do you want to kill her with that face, Maggie?'

There are tears of frustration in her eyes. 'Open your eyes, Dad.' He can just make out her words, urgent over the clanging of the bell. That's what she's saying. 'Open your eyes.'

He does. To the middle of the night and the phone ringing next to his bed.

Again.

Maggie's in the hallway. She's running for the kitchen. He throws back the covers, pulls open the door, and shouts down the stairs before she can pick up. 'Leave it, Maggie!'

She stops just short of the phone.

'We're not answering.' Behind her, pulling on a faded T-shirt.

She's spooked, he can see she is, but her hand is on the receiver. 'I want to know who it is.'

'You'll only encourage them.'

'Them who?'

He looks at the kitchen clock. 'Them who are crazy enough to call us at four in the morning.'

The ringing doesn't stop. She *told* him. She told him, whoever he was, not to call again. 'Hello?'

'Maggie, give me the phone.'

'Yes, it is.'

. . .

'This is his daughter.'

'Who is it? Maggie –'

'Just a moment, please.' She puts her hand over the receiver. 'Dad –'

He grabs it. 'Who the hell is this? Do you have any idea what –'

. . .

'When?'

. . .

'Now? You mean right now?'

. . .

'I understand. No . . . Naturally.'

'Dad? What is it? Is she okay?'

'Christina?'

. . .

'Christina, it's me. It's Dad.'

. . .

'*Yes*. Dad.'

. . .

'You weren't feeling well, sweetheart. We had to make sure you were okay.'

. . .

'Sure, she's here. She's right here beside me.'

. . .

'Nobody feels like themselves, ladybug. It's the middle of the night.'

. . .

'Of course I'm not angry with you. Why would I be angry?'

. . .

'I was shouting?'

. . .

'But, sweetheart, when have I ever hit you?'

. . .

'Come again?'

. . .

'Listen. Christina? Listen, the nurse said not to keep you talking. You need to rest now. We'll be with you the moment you wake up.'

. . .

'No, you're talking fine. You're just overtired. It's not even morning.'

. . .

'Don't cry. Christina? Can you hear me? Don't cry. We're coming. We're almost out the door.'

. . .

'Dreams. That's all, honey pie. Just dreams.'

2

When she wakes, no one.

The door opens. A hand pulls back the curtain at her bed. The lay sister places a shallow bowl of water on the table by her bed. She folds back the embroidered coverlet and removes the sheepskin rug. She lifts Christina's limbs, one by one, and examines her as she washes. Her eyes, Christina thinks, are like holes in the ice on the river in November.

She checks, as instructed, for marks, bruises and emissions. The girl is accustomed. She sits up without prompting. The nun unlaces her shift and scrubs: back, breasts, stomach. Odour is the source of disease. She observes how her charge stares through the window, as if mesmerized by glass.

In the distance, the green edge of woodland.

She rubs Christina dry and raises her shift. She pulls at her hair with an ivory comb.

The bishop is clear. There are to be no exchanges. The girl will understand she is to converse with no one but her confessor.

La Merveilleuse, they're calling her. The Astonishing.

She is ordinary enough.

And the bishop, she decides, is kind. With few airs, given his station.

His father, they say, was a cabbage farmer in Picardy.

Maggie is afraid she will no longer know her sister.

The night nurse has already warned them about the changes Christina might experience. Fatigue. Depression. Impulsiveness. Hallucinations. Memory loss. Muscle spasms. Twitches.

Aphasia. Dyspraxia. Attention deficit. Changes in sexual behaviour. Frustration. Self-absorption. Aggression.

She said nothing about this.

Maggie is seated on the edge of her sister's bed. Her father hovers at the threshold. 'It's early days,' the day nurse whispers.

'She won't speak to us. She says she doesn't know who we are.' As if to say, Are you stupid? Can't you see how things stand? Nervousness, Maggie remembers, makes her father sound arrogant.

Christina is resolute in an armchair by the window. 'Do you think I can't hear you?'

'Bear with us, Christina. I'm doing my best. Maggie's doing her best.'

(She knew. She saw the light of her sister go out.)

Christina frowns, impatient. 'Stop calling her that.'

'Stop calling her what, sweetheart?'

'Maggie.'

'What else would I call her?'

Maggie is afraid to intervene. She watches Christina scratch at her arm.

'There's moisturizer in the drawer, honey,' murmurs the nurse.

But she doesn't hear. She is staring at her father. 'You're doing it again.'

'Doing what again, ladybug?'

She rubs her forehead. There are dark shadows under her eyes, as if the deep sleep of three days has not been peace enough. 'Lying. You're lying again.' She turns to the nurse. 'These . . . people aren't who they say they are. They're not my . . . family.'

'Christina, you know –' he starts.

'Don't let them' – she looks at the floor, concentrating – 'discharge me. I won't go with them.'

Carver walks to the window and crouches near her chair. 'Christina, you asked us to come. Remember? On the phone. Early this morning.'

Her eyes flash. 'How do you know about that call?'

'It was me, ladybug. The nurse at the desk wheeled the phone into your room, remember? You spoke to me.'

She turns to the nurse. 'Someone's told him. I called my father last night. He's on his way. And my sister.'

'I'm here. Now. It's Maggie and me. Right, Maggiekins?'

Maggie slides off the bed. She takes a step forward, then stops. Her sister's eyes are wide, like they used to be when the basement door shut on her by accident. And her face is reddening.

'Why are you doing this to me? I've been sick. I'm in the hospital. Can't you see that?'

Maggie is afraid of her sister. From where she stands she can see her pupils are different sizes, as if one is frozen.

The nurse motions to them. 'You should go now. She needs to rest, and Dr Bishop would like to speak to you.'

Christina touches the nurse's arm, whispering. 'Don't give them my . . . details. Please.'

'Christina, look.' Carver pulls his wallet out of his back pocket. 'Look.' He takes out a faded snap: her mother in front of a cathedral in France.

She takes it in her hands. 'How did you get this?'

'I took it, sweetheart.'

'From who?'

'I *took* the picture, when your mom and I were in France. Before you were born. You know that.'

'Stop it!'

'Christina . . .'

Tears slide down her face. 'Why are you doing this?'

Maggie picks up her bag and runs from the room. This is not her sister.

Carver gets hold of Christina's hand. 'Maggie's just upset,' he says, grasping at meaning. 'She'll be okay. We'll all be okay.'

She pulls her hand away. Her face is hot. 'How many times do I have to say it? I don't *know* you!'

'Christina, please.'

Her nose starts to run. 'What do you want?'

He passes her a tissue from the box. 'We want you back home.'

'You're crazy.' She turns to the nurse. 'He's crazy –'

'Mr Carver . . .'

He pulls up a chair across from hers. 'What does your father look like, Christina? Tell me.'

'That's . . . none of your business.'

'Like me? Does he look like me?'

'I *said*, it's none of your business.'

'And your sister. Is she anything like the girl who was just here?'

She appeals to the nurse. 'Please. Call . . . security. Something is very . . . bad. Wrong.' She gets up. Stumbles.

The nurse catches her elbow before she falls. 'Remember what the nurse said last night? Take it slow.'

'Where's the . . .' She lurches into the clinical wastebin.

'The what, sweetie?'

'The . . .'

'*Slow.*'

'. . . the panic buckle?'

'Mr Carver, will you please go now? Or I really will have to call someone.'

'I told you. He *isn't* Mr Carver. Why won't anyone listen to me?'

'Christina,' he tries, 'please.'

'Just . . . just buck off!'

He stands. Goes to the door. 'You're going to be fine, lady-bug.' He can feel something hard swelling in his chest. 'Just fine.'

'I don't . . .' She steadies herself against the bed and stares. 'I don't . . . get people like you.'

Dr Bishop, Christina's neurologist, smiles at Maggie and turns over papers in a file. They're waiting for two of 'the team' who have been delayed in another meeting. Maggie stares at the picture above Dr Bishop's desk. It's big. In a gold-burnished frame. *The Creation of Adam.* 1508–1512. Michelangelo.

Her father broods in a leather easy chair to her right. On the side wall, behind him, are charts with coloured diagrams: cross sections of brain tissue that loom like overgrown pieces of cauliflower.

Dr Bishop feels sorry for her, she can tell. He can probably see she's been crying. 'Seen that one before, Maggie?' He nods to the picture.

'We did it in art history.'

'Like it?'

'Sure.' She smiles briefly.

'I bought it years ago. A trip to Florence. It's a reproduction, obviously, but not a bad one.'

Maggie nods, twisting the rings on her fingers. 'It's nice.'

'The thing is, after getting it back to Chicago, I realized why it had struck me. Well, *I* didn't realize. I read an article by an MD called Meshberger. He realized.'

'Oh.' She wishes her father would speak.

'You see, he realized that Michelangelo's God is the human brain.' He smiles. At his desk. He's shy as well. 'Forget Adam. He looks like a bit of a slacker, if truth be told.' He pushes back his chair, gets to his feet. He's gangly for a middle-aged man. 'Look at God. See that cloak? See its shape?'

She looks up. 'Yes.'

'It looks a lot like something else in this room.'

She wants his gamble to pay off. She looks to her right, to her left. 'That brain diagram over there.'

'Clever girl. The cerebral cortex.' He beams. 'Who would have thought?'

'Weird.' And he's right. She can see it too. The same shape.

'It's even pink, same as the cloak,' he says. 'Because grey matter isn't grey when it's alive. And see these?'

'What?'

'These folds in the cloak.'

She nods.

'They're like the grooves that characterize the cortex. See over there? They're called sulci. And this rise or bump in the cloak up here? A gyrus, or bump.'

'Are the angels anything?'

'Yup. Take this one here. Big eyes. Sad face. See him there, peeping out from the shadows under God's arm? That's the precise area we see activated in PET scans when someone is having a sad or mournful thought. And see all their legs and feet down here? Together, they make a brain stem. And this trailing veil, this swirl of green? The vertebral artery.'

'They didn't say anything about that in art history.'

'If I had a transparency of the brain, of a mid-sagittal cross section, one big enough to lay over this print, I could show you, and bore you, a lot more.'

'And God?'

'Well, he's reaching to the pre-frontal cortex, the most creative region of the brain; it's the part which makes us most impressively human. So he reaches for the brain's HQ and, presto, there goes the famous spark – which is also, coincidentally, the synapse's signature.'

'So is God just God? Or is he something too? Something in the brain, I mean.'

'He's what we'd call the old brain.' He winks. 'Hence the grey beard.'

She smiles, as you do when an older, avuncular man risks humour.

'Specifically, God's our limbic system.'

'Our what?'

'Limbic system – the ancient seat of our emotions. The source of our fears, our aggression, our sexual attractions, our instinct to nurture. Maybe also the source of transcendent feeling.'

The door opens. Two people walk in and introduce themselves to her father, who's jettisoned now out of his own thoughts.

'But how did Michelangelo know what was where in the brain?'

Bishop hesitates. 'We know he performed some dissections . . .'

'But he couldn't have got all that from . . . Not in the fifteen hundreds.'

'No.' He looks at her. 'He couldn't have.'

She chews her lip. 'Do you ever wonder if maybe we download stuff when we're asleep?'

'Download stuff?'

'It sounds stupid.'

'From where?'

'I don't know. From God, if there is one – Dad says there isn't – or the universe, or something.'

He weighs her words, taking his time, though his colleagues are ready to start. 'Our brains are certainly very active when we dream.'

'Christina used to say it. That she did.'

'Download stuff. Like ideas, you mean?'

She nods. 'Or pictures.' She looks at the carpet. 'She said it was like her dreams were windows in her head, and that she got glimpses of things. Real things. Do you think that happens?'

He studies her. 'I don't know, Maggie. I wish I did.'

Dr Bishop introduces her to Dr Sperber, a neuropsychologist, and Ms Keegan, a cognitive therapist. When Ms Keegan smiles, Maggie wonders why she also looks as if she might start to cry. She has one of those faces. And Dr Sperber has a beard that makes him look like he's hiding something. He's dressed more casually than Dr Bishop. A jacket, no tie. Through his open shirt collar, she can see a simple gold cross and chain. Her father, she thinks, will behave better if he doesn't see it.

He talks. They all talk. The burble of their words is like a radio she tries not to tune. Her head is already too heavy on her shoulders. Her neck aches.

She thinks about Michelangelo knowing what he couldn't know – either that or Dr Bishop is simply seeing what he wants to see, like you do with clouds when you're lying in the grass.

When the words stop, she watches Dr Sperber pick up the phone on Dr Bishop's desk. He asks the switchboard to connect him. 'Room 212, please.' He passes the phone to her father.

Her father takes the receiver, swallows and waits. Then: 'Christina?'

. . .

'It's even better to hear you, sweetheart.' He smiles. He looks at the psychologist. The psychologist nods.

. . .

'Of course we haven't forgotten you.'

. . .

'She's right here.'

. . .

'That's right.'

. . .

'Do you want a word?'

. . .

'Great.' He turns in his seat and passes Maggie the phone.
What will she say? What can he possibly expect her to say?
'I'll be outside, Dad. I'll wait for you outside.'

3

It's like an elaborate hoax.

'I can only be honest with you, Dr Carver. We can't say with any certainty.'

'But the tests will show something?'

'Something. Yes. But there are billions of neural cross-connections. Your daughter stopped breathing. She went into a coma. There are T-wave irregularities – cardiology still wants more tests. The quality and speed of any eventual recovery was always going to be difficult, if not impossible, to determine.'

'But she woke up. In less than three days.'

'Yes, and I'm delighted to say that she has bettered our predictions by far. Her short- and long-term memories seem relatively unaffected. There appears to be slight aphasia and some confusion, but it's too early to say. From what you've told us, it's possible she's suffered right-side lesions because she falters, particularly, when reaching for what we call emotionally potent language – a right-brain skill. So my guess is that "Back off" and "Fuck off" collapse into the one command "Buck off" in the pressure of the moment, and the panic button becomes the "panic buckle". Do you see? She's also experiencing mild dyspraxia, a motor impairment related, in her case, to visual and spatial orientation – again, consistent with right-side lesions. But it could all be far worse.'

'She doesn't know who we are, Dr Bishop.'

'No, not at the moment. But she can recognize your voice, which is why we're reasonably confident that we're looking at Capgras Syndrome. As I say, primarily a –'

'– misidentification syndrome. You don't have to be a neur-ologist to –' He stops himself. 'I'm sorry.'

'I understand your frustration, Dr Carver. But my job is to look at the whole picture. And almost everything is educated guesswork right now. Given the history, we can probably assume the cause of the Capgras, if it is Capgras, is organic: acquired brain injury; likely cause, cerebral hypoxia – possible lesions in the posterior area of the right hemisphere, where face recognition is performed. Or, as more recent research suggests, possible damage to the neuronal pathway that wires the primary visual cortex to the limbic system. As I was telling your other daughter a little while ago, that's the brain's emotional centre.'

'She looks at me like I'm some kind of conman.'

'You need to understand. She's not hallucinating. She sees you as clearly as I do. She also remembers without difficulty what her father looks like. The problem is, she feels no emotion when she looks at you. A galvanic skin-response test would most likely tell us what you know already. She looks at you and Maggie and feels absolutely nothing.'

'It's absurd.'

'It is. And Christina herself may even admit that it *sounds* absurd. There's no indication at this point that her logic or reason is impaired. But where there is no emotion, there is no recognition. And where there is no recognition, there is no meaning.'

'So she decides her family are impostors.'

'She's not doing it on purpose, I promise you, Dr Carver. There's simply no other way for her brain to make sense of her situation.'

'Except on the phone . . .'

'Exactly. Because the signal from her primary auditory cortex to the limbic region – the centre of the emotions, remember – is unaffected. Therefore, when she is required to rely only on her sense of hearing, she recognizes your voice and *feels* you are her father. She feels you are her father, so you are her father.'

'Even if I wasn't twenty minutes ago in her room.'

'You and Maggie now exist for Christina in duplicate. One version is true and one is false.'

'What if we prompt her with memories and photos? Say, some of her mother, whom she recognizes, *with* Maggie and me.'

'She'll recognize the three of you in pictures, I'm sure. But that's not the issue.'

'We can explain to her that this is happening to her. That there's a syndrome that affects her in this way. If her logic is unimpaired –'

'We'll try, of course.'

'Very gently,' adds Ms Keegan.

'But you don't hold out much hope.'

Dr Bishop looks at his desk, choosing his words. 'Dr Carver, it seems that, at our most fundamental, we are emotional beings. And truth is, first of all, a feeling.'

Carver rubs his hands over his face.

'Of course we'll consider certain cognitive techniques –'

'Reality testing and reframing,' notes Ms Keegan.

'And if necessary, in the long run, we'll consider certain antipsychotic drugs. Clozapine has yielded some good results, for example, as have some SSRIs at higher starting dosages.'

'Jesus.'

'I understand. It's a lot to take in.'

'You said the cause was *probably* organic. What else could it be?'

'Well, some argue there's a psychodynamic dimension.'

Dr Sperber, the neuropsychologist, leans forward. 'In the

case of Capgras, Dr Carver, not everyone in the patient's circle is perceived as a stranger. Often it's only the person or persons closest to him or her at the time of onset who are recast as impostors. In *some* instances, we've found that the Capgras patient has had ambivalent responses to that person or persons, feelings which are usefully explored.'

Carver hates him.

'Do you have any other questions, Dr Carver?' Bishop is a father too. He wants the man released.

Giles Carver closes his eyes. '*All* she did was run for the phone.'

4

He walks the surrounding streets. He asks passers-by if they've seen her, a girl, eighteen, about this tall. They shake their heads. They seem somehow ill at ease in his company. He's ill at ease in his own.

Two daughters lost.

He crouches down, out of the sun, in the shadow of the cathedral's west tower. Flies buzz.

And it occurs to him. She will have gone to the scriptorium. She will ask Brother Bernard if she may resume her duties. She will want to turn pages again.

And the bishop will find her there.

It is true then. What he said.

He has nothing. He has already disappeared. In a matter of days his life has become an emptiness – the negative impression on the wrong side of a mask or a mould. Without his wife, without his daughters, he is only the image of the man he used to be.

None of her fellow librarians sees her enter. And still, no one knows anything. Not Mrs McFarland. Not Helen. Not Miss Slack. She doesn't want Christina to become another strange and tragic story at coffee break.

Maggie finds a desk in periodicals and sits, hidden from view by a microfiche machine. The silence is good. And she likes the smell of old glue that permeates the place. It calms her. It makes her think everything will be all right. Her father will stop asking her to pretend. And in time her sister will slip out of the dream she's still dreaming.

★

It has been agreed. Christina's recovery and rehabilitation will be managed by the Skilled Care Unit. She will be moved from room 212 into a ground-floor room that features full cable TV, a cordless phone, hand-painted wall borders and a quilt hanging. The Skilled Care Unit also includes a recreation room, a private courtyard, two lounges for social activities, an on-site pharmacist, dentist and beautician.

As a patient of the unit, she will have access to a full range of rehabilitative and diagnostic services. Her medical team will be led by Dr Bishop, her neurologist. It will include Dr Sperber, her neuropsychologist, and Ms Keegan, her cognitive therapist. She will spend one night at the Chicago Sleep Lab, at Dr Sperber's recommendation.

There is only one problem. Christina Carver has informed the team that she is discharging herself. She tells them she's going home.

Giles Carver is sitting on a bench in Austin Gardens, hoping Maggie will at any moment pass, when his phone rings. Dr Sperber. Carver sits up. He feels his heart lift. Sperber is telling him that Christina wants to come home.

'Thank God.'

But the psychologist's words racket him back into the real. 'You forget, Dr Carver. She'll come back and find another you and another Maggie living in her family home. She'll leave more confused, more upset, than when she arrived.'

'Maybe at home things will be different.'

'I'll be frank, Dr Carver. They won't be. But if you're willing to let her risk some happy homecoming scene, she'll be in a taxi outside your front door in ten minutes and life for Christina will go from bad to worse.'

'Let me talk to her.'

'And tell her she can't come home? As far as she's concerned, she's walking and talking, and that qualifies her as a going concern. What will you say when she demands to know why she can't come home?'

'Tell me what to do.'

'Help us proceed with involuntary admission. In the short term, that's to say *now*, a quick petition for emergency admission will buy us twenty-four hours.'

'You mean commit her.'

'By tomorrow we'll probably be able to persuade her to admit herself voluntarily.'

'She's not crazy.'

'No. But she is vulnerable. You saw that yourself this morning. And, in light of the Capgras, the one place she won't rest easy is at home.'

'So tomorrow you get her to admit herself, and she tries to leave again in a few days. Then what?'

'According to the Mental Health and Disabilities Code, voluntary admission is by no means the same as informal admission. Under its terms, Christina will not be able to walk out any time she wishes.'

'You're going to have to spell it out, Sperber.' He can feel his blood pressure rising. His gums start to throb. 'Because it sounds to me like you're about to trick her into locking herself up.'

'No, we want to outline her options. Most patients will choose voluntary admission if they understand that involuntary admission is inevitable.'

'So you give her a rock and a hard place.'

'If you want to see it like that.'

'And you need my permission to proceed.'

'Strictly, no. But we prefer to have the support of the family.'

He stares at a blot of starlings on the afternoon sky. 'I don't know.'

'She's at the information desk now, Dr Carver. A taxi is on

its way. Emergency admission is the only course of action that will guarantee Christina the stable environment she needs to make a full recovery.'

Rubbing his temples. 'I hear you.'

'With respect, Dr Carver, that means what exactly?'

'I'll sign.'

'You give your consent?'

'Either way I feel like I'm letting her down. But it's not about what I feel.'

'The situation will, in all likelihood, normalize within a week or two.'

'And in the meantime?'

'We'll stay in close touch.'

'And Christina?'

'She'll probably try to phone you. She'll ask you to come and get her.'

'And I do what?'

'Don't answer.'

'What?'

'If possible, switch off your phone.'

Carver feels the day dissolve. 'It's her lifeline to her family.'

'Give us twenty-four hours at least. Forty-eight if you can.'

In periodicals, the wheel of the microfiche machine is clattering away. Two elderly men take a seat at her table. Maggie's safe haven is gone, and her headache is back. How long has she been here?

Her eyes are heavy. She can feel her mother taking her into her arms. She's saying, *Poor lovely thing. You're just a button on a thread, aren't you?*

Yes, says Maggie. Yes. I'm barely holding on.

Make up with your sister, sweetheart. Don't stay mad.

She got mad first.

Try, Maggie. Try for me.

The phone in the foyer is free. She finds St Thomas's number on the scrap of paper in her wallet.

It rings and rings. At last, someone picks up and puts her through to the nurse's station on the second floor. 'Room 212, please,' she says. 'Can you connect me to room 212?'

'I'm sorry. That room is currently vacant.'

Vacant?

'Who was it you –'

Maggie hangs up. She feels like someone in deep space, trying to hold on to her family – to mother, father and sister – when gravity is gone.

In Beauvais there has been discussion. The bishop, the abbot of St Germer and Brother Bernard inform her that her father has left Beauvais.

'Why,' Marguerite asks, 'why would he leave Beauvais? It is not possible.'

Her father, they begin again, has left Beauvais. It is understood he will seek commissions in Paris. *Soyez tranquille.* She will not go without. Arrangements have been made. The bishop, in his largesse, has found her a home. She will join the Dominican Sisters of Fanjeaux.

Fanjeaux?

Far from Beauvais, it is true. Yet Fanjeaux, the abbot tells her, will afford her ample opportunity for reflection. It will help her to begin again. She will have a new family, new sisters.

Maggie casts the scene in her mind's eye. At 3:45, Mrs McFarland will phone their house. She will leave a message, wondering where Maggie was today. Hadn't Maggie wanted the holiday shift? Didn't Mrs McFarland give it to her rather than Helen? Perhaps Mrs McFarland will knock on their door on her way home from the library. 'Just passing,' she'll say. 'But ach aye, if only I knooo you couldnae worrk today, we might have coped, hen. I can only hope you're nae tooo pooorrrly.'

Maggie doesn't feel poorly. It is easier this way, she tells Mrs McFarland, standing on the threshold of her own daydream. It is easier to slip from life. Less painful, she says.

'Oh you're young, Maggie. So young. You dooon't know what pain is.'

Pain is her sister's cold stare and her one frozen pupil.

Pain is the secret phone number on Tina's hand, and the nameless man on the phone.

Pain is a father who doesn't know how to talk to her if he can't charm her; who likes her best when she pretends; who doesn't want her as she is.

'The world comes right in the end, Maggie,' Mrs McFarland is saying. 'You mark my words.'

But Mrs McFarland doesn't know the world any more. She's out of her element; she's out of her century.

'You're a good gerrrl really, Maggie Carver. I was saying as much tooooday to Miss Slack.' Mrs McFarland cocks her permed head. She hears something at the margins of this, Maggie's daydream. A man's voice? 'Tell me, hen.' Her eyes dart. 'Is there someone else here in this wee rrreverie of yours?'

It's her father's voice, louder now. 'That's right,' he says. 'My daughter. Margaret Constance Carver.'

Maggie smiles, pleased that Mrs M has finally noticed. 'Yes, Mrs McFarland. My father's in the next room on the phone.'

'Goodness, I wish you'd said!' Her hand moves quickly to her hair. 'I didnae realize your father was here, having a *prrrivate* conversation no less. And there's me, mithering away like . . .' She peeks round the corner, into the next room. She draws breath at the sight of Dr Giles Carver, a man in his prime, taking action in a family emergency.

The cord of the phone is taut in Giles Carver's hand. His back is hunched over the phone on his desk – a red phone, Maggie decides. 'What do you mean "Give it time"?' he shouts. 'She's a missing person now!'

Her father cares. See how he cares.

Mrs McFarland looks to her, then to her father, and back to her again. She fans her face. She covers her mouth with a liver-spotted hand. 'Oh dear, Maggie. Oh dear, dear, dear, dear, dear.'

Maggie looks at the ground and smiles. Hasn't she been disappearing, little by little, for days? But now, now it is accomplished. She is a missing person. Her father has just said so to the police. This is how it will be.

'Ooooooh, Maggie. What have you done?'

She shakes her head and smiles again. How can she explain?

On her own, she will be fine. On her own, she can steer a steady course in an unsteady world.

5

It turns out you're that kind of commuter. Giles Carver occupies an aisle seat. He's unaware of you behind him, reading over his shoulder. Today's paper. Thursday, September 6. He has things on his mind.

Maggie made one withdrawal on Monday minutes before her bank closed for the day. $386.56. Her savings for France. She left one dollar in the account. That's a good sign, he was told. It suggests prudence, said the beefy cop. An optimistic outlook, adds his partner. They told him it was important to maintain routine; that she is eighteen years old and, from what her teachers say, a level-headed girl.

Usually he gets his paper in Oak Park, on the walk home. But today he picks it up at the station in Geneva instead. He needs the distraction for the journey home. He doesn't want train time on his hands. He turns a page and shakes the thing into submission. He glances at headlines.

There. An article in the far left-hand column: 'Scanning Mystery: Columbia Computer Scientists Investigate the Rise and Fall of the Gothic Cathedral'. The fall of one in particular: St Pierre in Beauvais, France. He's got the picture of Jen in his wallet, standing in front of it, holding two dripping cones.

Once the tallest building in Europe, taller than even the Pantheon in Rome, its towering choir, you read, collapsed in 1284. In spite of its eventual reconstruction, the structure remains a mystery. Or, in other words, a cause for concern. Nobody can say exactly *how* it stands.

There are theories about the fall of 1284: a failure to account for gale-force winds off the English Channel; a lack of roof support; an inherently unstable foundation; insufficient buttressing; an unexpected rate of settling; greater attention to opulence than structural soundness.

In June, the Columbia team arrived in Beauvais with a laptop and a laser scanner. For ten days they bounced beams off the 700-year-old stonework. Then they returned to New York to produce 3D-range scans and imagery of the cathedral. There's a copy of one in colour with the article. Golden, unearthly, St Pierre seems to float free of its foundations in a digitized night.

The scans, you read, will permit a degree of structural analysis that has not been possible before now. The team will return next summer to complete the modelling. The mystery of St Pierre's collapse, of its ever insistent flux, might yield up its secrets at last.

Good luck. Carver closes the paper. The irony isn't lost on him. The renovations at Wilson Hall have been going on for, what, three years now? These days scaffolders seem to outnumber scientists at Fermilab, for, like St Pierre, its lofty inspiration, Wilson Hall also defies symmetry floor by floor, axis by axis. That piece of concrete in 1993 was an interesting case in point: a piece of a fifteenth-floor support joint plummeting past his office window.

He checks his cellphone for messages.

Nothing. Not from Maggie. Not from Christina.

He has ignored Sperber's advice. How could he switch off his phone with Maggie gone?

Will he find her? she wonders. Will he try? Or is it as they tell her? Has she truly died to the world?

Marguerite has seen no one since the day she arrived. Only the pale freckled hand that pushes her daily meal past the curtain. The curtain is permitted until vespers, when the oak door of the room is closed upon her. On the air sometimes: the smell of lavender, off the fields of Fanjeaux. But no window.

And it is true. What she has always known. She can survive within herself.

He wonders where Maggie slept. Friends. Surely she has friends. School friends anyway. When he realizes.

He doesn't know.

Since Jen, the three of them have been all for one and one for all. ('Are you with me – or are you with me?' '*Dad.*' 'Well?' 'I'm with you.' The old call and response.) They have conjured their own world. They have looked upon others as if they were short-lived illusions, less real somehow than they three.

For the first time he can see the effects of his own faulty magic: Maggie's strange interiority; Christina's secretiveness, hidden too well behind her good cheer; his own clanging loneliness. (Jen gone. Nat forced out. His charm all but used up.)

He can see collateral damage too: his eight-year isolation in supergravity, playing the wounded maverick – playing it safe, ironically – when all along he's known that only creative, chancy dialogue can yield anything worth a damn. As Ed Witten proved. And there was Nat too. Wasn't she still struggling to recover her life, her livelihood, after her gamble for him?

But it's too late to know, to see. He can't turn things around fast enough.

Christina will know by now that he gave his consent for her involuntary admission. Betrayal. How can it seem anything but? And Maggie's punishing him by running away. She must be. Because nothing is as he promised.

The room is plain but clean, apart from the dead and dying bugs in the light fixture. There's one double bed. A pair of yellow-and-brown pleated curtains. A framed picture of grazing cattle. A TV too big for the bureau it sits on. A Better Business Bureau calendar tacked to the wall. A small bathroom with a cracked toilet seat and a stammering fan.

Through the wall, she can hear the family in the next room. Someone is bouncing a ball off their common wall. Someone else is taking a shower. The TV is on, a rerun of *I Dream of Jeannie*.

The smack of the ball. The groan of the hot-water pipe. The shouts of Larry Hagman at Jeannie in her bottle. Each sound elongates in Maggie's head, stretching the container of its moment like a soapy bubble blown slowly through a plastic ring. One moment after another. She remembers this from childhood: time lengthening to its secret proportions.

She is about to change the month on the wall calendar but doesn't. It's still July. She still likes her job at the library. She's still saving money for France. She doesn't know yet that Christina has a secret.

From her window, the vast laughing face of the Happy Griddle is a leering moon in the gathering dark. It won't let her forget: her sister's cold stare, her father insisting that everything is fine, her motherlessness.

6

Christina's confessor does not raise his voice.

'Something or someone,' he repeats, 'has made away with your spirit.'

'No.'

'No?' He leans back in the chair.

'I believe not.'

'Yet you are spiritless.'

'These are heavy days.' She turns her face to the window. 'It is difficult even to breathe in this heat.'

He folds his hands in his lap. 'There is a name.'

'There is no name.'

'You gainsay me.' His eyebrows mimic surprise.

'I know no name.'

'You are without family, without connections.'

She meets his eyes. 'This is what I am told.'

'Yet you reject the efforts of His Grace, your spiritual father. And you reach not for Christ's forgiveness.'

'Is my need so great?'

'It is your heart which must tell you that.' He smiles, sardonic. 'It seems we await your heart.'

As the bell rang for matins on the morning that everything would change, Christina panicked and her heart faltered.

We hardly remember that the word 'panic' is the legacy of the shaggy-legged god Pan.

Pan was born into turbulence. His mother was an Arcadian nymph who abandoned her infant son at birth after first laying eyes on his wild and bearded face. His father, Hermes, was more robust. He picked up the child, wrapped him in a hare's pelt and carried him back to Olympus.

God of procreation and the natural world, Pan's image was often a suitably phallic post draped in a mantle, a mask and leafy boughs. A shape-shifter, he also took animal form, usually that of a goat – hence the trademark horns and cloven feet. In the minds of the ancient Peloponnese, Pan was many things: magical, libidinous, terror-awakening, though not necessarily malignant.

Clothe Pan liberally in our cultural suspicions, and he emerges as the duplicitous demon lover of Western folklore: 'They had not sailed a league, a league,/A league but barely three,/Until she espied his cloven foot,/And she wept right bitterlie.'

But think back again to the ancient world. For before demons were 'demons', they were *daimones* – Greek for 'spirit-energy'. Even our word 'devil' derives from the primeval root DV, which in Sanskrit is found in two forms, DIV and DYU, the original meaning of which was not 'to corrupt' or even 'to tempt', but rather 'to kindle'.

In his 'Treatise on the Descent of the Soul', the classical writer Apuleius describes for us these 'kindling' beings: 'As they are media between us and the Gods, in the place of their habitation, so likewise is the nature of their mind; having immortality in common with the Gods, and passion in common with the beings subordinate to themselves.'

Is it this passion then that we fear? Are we scared stiff of its transformations? Is this why, through centuries of consensus, we have demonized the *daimone*? A figure who, in Latin, Apuleius reminds us, corresponds to Genius.

Daimone. Demon. Pan. Wild man. Incubus. Outcast angel. Each speaks to us of the terrible force of change.

★

'The impression of a body?'

'Sometimes.'

'A parasomnia. You're familiar with the term?'

'Yes.'

'Since . . .' He glances at her file.

'I was thirteen.'

'But you've had problems, during sleep, since you were . . .'

'Seven.'

'About the time of your mother's death.'

'Yes.'

'Tell me what you remember about the night you collapsed.'

'I've told you.'

'A bell.'

'Yes.'

'The phone was ringing.'

'Apparently.'

'You'd been asleep for . . .'

'Hours.'

'And the phone woke you.'

'I don't remember waking.'

'And you don't remember running?'

'I just remember a bell.'

'Ringing?'

'Yes.'

'What else?'

'I couldn't move . . .'

'When you heard the bell.'

'I've already said.'

'Why do you think you couldn't?'

'I was asleep, I suppose.'

'Was someone with you as this bell rang or were you alone?'

'I have my own room.'

'I mean, was there the *sensation* of someone?'

'I can't remember.'

'Guess.'

'I'd be making it up.'

'Fine. Make it up. Someone familiar or not?'

'Familiar.'

'Did you want to run?'

'I panicked.'

'So you wanted to run.'

'Yes . . . And no.'

'No because . . . You wanted to stay?'

'I could say anything and you'd write it down.'

'Let me worry about that. You wanted to stay with that person?'

'Yes. I think I did.'

'And?'

'I also wanted to run.'

'Why?'

'I don't know.'

'Just talk. Why did you want to run?'

'I've always been a good runner.'

'And for you, running is about . . . ? Pick a word.'

'I don't know . . . Energy. Speed.' She looks up. 'Flight.'

He nods, pleased, she thinks. 'And since your coming to on Tuesday, no sleep disturbances? No "visitations"?'

'No.' She crosses her legs. 'None.'

'Good.' Dr Sperber studies her. 'Though I still want to get you checked into the sleep lab as soon as a bed is available. Just a few routine tests.' He replaces his pen's cap. He nods to the sketch she has stuck to her window. 'You're drawing again?' He doesn't ask her why she has taped it so that the picture faces the glass and not the room.

'No.'

'Why not?'

'I'm not so good at silk-flower arrangements.'

'Have you seen the fountain in the courtyard?'

'Yes. Have you?'

He slides his pen into his breast pocket. 'I'll see you tomorrow, Christina.'

'I've already told you I can't explain it.'

'Explain what?'

'How they can make themselves look like my family.'

'I know you can't. I understand.'

'And I understand it's your job to say you understand.'

He smiles, amused. 'I'll let Dr Bishop know that the aphasia has clearly resolved itself.'

When the call comes, she lifts the phone from its charger and walks to the door where the laundry staff huddle on their cigarette breaks.

'Find me,' she says. 'Find me.'

Her room is on the ground floor. He'll know hers, she says, when he sees the sketch stuck to the window: the river, sparking with light. The oak trees grave as witnesses. And a figure – 'You,' she laughs into the phone, '*you*' – taking the embankment in slipping strides. Still unfinished. He'll see it. He can't miss it.

She leaves her window open to the night. She closes the curtains and the venetian blinds. She turns off every light. She puts a towel at the bottom of her door to soak up the crack of light.

Then, sleep's undertow. Until the bed's creaking and Angel's pulling her to him so they lie, breathing like one.

His neck is salty against her lips. 'Are you here?'

'Of course I'm here. I said I'd be and I am.'

She pushes her face into his chest. 'There's something wrong with me.'

'There's nothing wrong with you.'

His warmth. His solidness. His voice in the night. She runs her toes through the soft hairs on his calves. 'They say there is. Not in so many words, but they might as well.'

He reaches past her, groping in the dark for a bedside lamp. She grabs his wrist. 'I told you on the phone. You can't.'

'I'll be me.'

'What if you're not?'

'I will be.'

She turns and clambers on to him, sinking into his chest. 'Promise me you won't fall asleep,' she says.

'I won't. Now let me turn on the light.'

'Because I won't go to sleep if I think you might.'

'I won't.'

'You have to be gone before I wake up. Way before.'

'I get the picture.'

'I couldn't bear not to know you.'

'You're thinking too much.'

'Dr Sperber says my reason is unaffected.'

'So you're still unreasonable.'

'I'm afraid a lot lately.'

'You'll get better.'

'It's not like me.'

'Good to know then how the other half lives.'

'And I bump into things.'

'Which is where lights help, I find.'

Her cheek is in the cradle of his neck. 'You smell of outside.'

7

'Give it more time, sweetheart,' he's saying into his cellphone. 'It's only a week since you –'

'I want to come home.'

'What does Dr Sperber say?'

'Let me talk to Maggie.'

'She's not here, Tina. I'm at work. What's that Ms Keegan like?'

'I don't belong here.'

'There's still the MRI tests. And the sleep lab. That's tonight, isn't it?'

Dead air between them. He can see her rubbing the place behind her ears, like she does when she can't find the words. Then, 'Dad, please. Please don't leave me here.'

'It's not for long.' Don't say it. Don't say it, sweetheart.

'He was here again.'

He winces. 'Christina, I can hardly hear you . . .'

'I'll be at the information desk, Dad. I'll wait –'

'You can't just walk out, sweetheart. There are rules.'

'I don't care any more.'

'You know what the signal's like out here, ladybug. If my phone cuts out, I'll –' He hits the CALL END button. Turns on his swivel chair. Sits, head between his knees, defeated.

Last night: to hell with Sperber, he decided. At last she was phoning. Thank God she was phoning. Four messages yesterday. Two on the answering machine. Two on his cellphone. It was Sunday. He was going crazy sitting in the house by himself.

He argued his way in after visiting hours.

Her door was open but he knocked anyway. She was watching TV. Some reality thing.

But the look in her eyes: like he was a rapist or something.

She leaves behind the pastels of the Skilled Care Unit and talks her way past security. At the information desk, she lies. She says she has an appointment with Dr Bishop.

The receptionist checks the extension. 'I'll phone to let him know you're on your way.'

'That's okay.' Christina moves away from the desk. 'He knows.' She hadn't expected the woman to pick up the phone. She hoped she'd simply point her in the right direction. She has no idea where his office is.

She takes a quick right down a nearby corridor, then a left. She finds herself suddenly in a pale green waiting room where people pace in thin, hospital-issue bathrobes, clasping the fluttering edges against the threat of two fans. Clearly no one is permitted shoes, though many still wear socks or pantyhose in spite of the day's heat – something which, Christina notices, makes them look more uncovered, more vulnerable, not less. Each holds in his or her hands a small paper cup. A few grimace as they sip. Those nearest the door look up at her, startled, grey-faced.

'Excuse me,' she whispers.

She is not sick. She should not be here. She does not need St Thomas's.

'Would patient Christina Carver please come immediately to the information desk?' It's a hospital-wide announcement. They know she's missing from the unit.

She moves through the outpatients clinic and down another hallway, past consultation rooms where the curtains on the windows of the doors haven't been closed all the way. She sees half a man's naked chest. One bright pink nipple and an outstretched arm. Overhead a CCTV camera follows her movements. How long before someone finds her?

She feels like a rat in a laboratory trial. She turns back and, expecting to arrive at outpatients again, stumbles instead into a long, skylit corridor. There's a carpeted hush. Royal blue and a good weave. A man with a golfer's tan and Grecian Formula hair nods and smiles to her as he passes. On each door, a nameplate gleams.

In his lab in the west tower of Wilson Hall, Carver stares at sprays of particle showers and data from hundreds of collision events. He squints for hidden symmetries; for the faint tracks of vanished particles; for the trace of something, anything, that will make him care today.

He gulps coffee nervously. It's not even noon. He moves into his office, turns to the latest Fermilab newsletter and finds himself reading it in its entirety. He stands, walks to the window and stares out over the grounds, watching traffic zip along the main ring road. A bus pulls up in the parking lot – another batch of college students filing in for a tour before the annual shutdown.

From up here, the ring of the Tevatron's tunnel is just visible through the prairie grass. Four miles in circumference. A magic circle, he used to tell his girls.

She has learned, with difficulty, the art of compromise.

'With your permission, I'm going out today, Dr Bishop. I need to get out. I will not attempt to go home. I will be careful. I will not overdo things. If I have a problem, I will ring the day nurse. I have her number here, see? I will be back in my room by five in plenty of time. I'm not due at the sleep lab till nine. My taxi is booked for eight-thirty. I won't forget.

'But I cannot stay day in, day out in the Skilled Care Unit, Dr Bishop. I do not want to learn origami. I do not want a make-over.'

David Bishop leans back in his chair and smiles, reluctantly.

By noon Christina is on the train. By 1:30 she's running up the steps of Wilson Hall, dodging a sprawl of visiting college students. She stumbles twice, as if her body is still not her own, as if her feet have not yet remembered the experience of stairs. She stops outside the main doors, dizzy, faintly nauseous, but it has never felt so good to be in the open air.

At reception, she's getting her breath back. Sunlight floods the atrium ahead. 'Would you let Dr Carver know his daughter is here, please? Christina Carver.' He'll just have to see her to realize that everything is okay, that *she's* okay. Whatever the doctors have been telling him. They'll start afresh.

The receptionist looks up from the switchboard. 'I'm sorry, Christina. I have a note here. Dr Carver is unavailable all afternoon. Was he expecting you?'

'No.' She feels stunned. 'No, he wasn't.' Abandoned all over again. 'Could you call through to him for me?'

'Sorry. It's priority calls only to the tunnel.'

'The tunnel?'

'Yes. He's down there this afternoon with the Beams Division.'

The leader of the college group is anxious behind her. His students are drifting away, in the direction of the cafeteria in the atrium. 'Could I catch up with him in the tunnel?'

'Not without authorization, honey. And I can't give you that. Would you like to leave a message?'

'No.' She moves away from the desk. 'Thank you.' She bumps into someone by a display cabinet. She moves towards the cafeteria because she doesn't know where else to go. In an hour and a half, maybe two hours, she'll have to turn back. Dr Bishop will phone her room. Her gamble will have failed.

'Excuse me.' A guy with very large blue eyes is waving a hand in front of her face. Concerned. He looks concerned.

Suddenly everything – the whole world – is on the other side of a pane of glass. She looks up.

'Are you here for the tour?'

'Pardon?'

'The tour?' He's mistaken her for one of his fellow freshmen.

'Yes,' she hears herself say. 'Yes, I am.'

'I nearly missed you. Everyone's everywhere. Okay. Dr Holtz says we're to meet on the steps in five minutes. And like he said on the bus, you'll need to wear one of these.' He passes her a radiation badge to pin to her top. 'They won't let you into the tunnel without it.'

Giles Carver has gone to ground. Thirty feet under the prairie he talks cold-leak repairs with a Tevatron operator. He gets the latest on the luminosity figures. He chats with Mike, one of the operators. He asks after his wife, who's been diagnosed with lymphoma, a lower grade than Jen had. He says, yes, sure, he'll juggle again for charity. Why not? He appears cheerful. He almost *feels* cheerful.

'Say hello to your girls, won't you?' says Mike.

First stop on the tour: the main control room of the Accelerator Complex. 'The brain of the place,' says the Fermilab guide, 'if only after many dozen kicks of caffeine.' He nods to some of the operators, shy of celebrity at the coffee machine. A guy called Gary from the Beams Division looks at Christina as if he can't quite place her.

In the central detector's assembly hall they stare up, way up, at the 500-ton colossus of the detector, 'a remarkable example of twenty-first-century wizardry' that nevertheless, thinks Christina, looks like the dream-come-true of some nerdy child. Soaring over thirty feet into the assembly hall, its bright red, blue and yellow components are as cheerful as Lego.

Their guide relays the detector's vital statistics before the heart of its central chamber – located behind a big telephone dial of a portal – is opened for all to see. The chatter stops. Christina looks up. Even the operators seem to go quiet. 'This,' says their guide with a smile, 'is what we acolytes call the tabernacle of quantum mystery.' The chamber is crammed full of gold-plated wire – 'sense-wire', he calls it. 'It's here that we register the glimmerings of the subatomic world.'

And he's right, she decides. It's actually beautiful. Sudden radiance. Like the golden glory of the heavenly host in a medieval painting. That's what she'll tell her father later. She'll say it to annoy him because he's an atheist, suspicious of anything that smacks of the Church. When she used to ask why, he'd say, 'Ask Galileo.'

The group arrives at gate A24. Christina stays near the front. She needs to be able to see. 'Please stay with the group,' the guide reminds them. Together, in the vaulted half-light, thirty feet underground, they will walk the four-mile ring.

They step, one by one, into the tunnel. The guide draws their attention to the accelerator, 'Where time turns back on itself. Where the earliest moments of Creation crack open again in the collisions of streaming particles.'

Technicians and operators squeeze past. Maintenance workers, too, are busy, checking ventilation ducts and shafts.

She squints into the flickering fluorescence, searching for a glimpse of his profile, for the back of his head, for the determined stride of his walk.

*

He keeps moving. He's fine if he keeps moving. He checks his phone, then remembers – no signal. He's out of range.

And relief washes over him like some sweet depressant.

Only half a mile to go and still no sign. She's tired. Dizzy again. She should have eaten something on the train.

'Remember, we're thirty feet underground,' the guide explains. 'If you recall that just one cubic foot of soil weighs about a hundred pounds, you'll appreciate that the construction of the Tevatron tunnel was no mean feat in its day.'

And hot. She's sweating now. The noise doesn't help. A high-pitched, tuning-fork type of noise. Is it only her or is everyone hearing it?

She looks around. She's the only one with her hands pressed to her ears. She concentrates on her breath, on slowing it down. But the harder she concentrates, the faster it gets. And her palms are sweating against her head.

'Sorry about the sound effects,' their guide calls, grinning. 'They're checking the tunnel blowers and cleaning the supply registers today,' he says. 'Basically, they're trying to lower the system's pressure. The general aim is to pull more air.'

A U of C student, someone says. 'Our last panic attack of the season.'

Giles Carver looks up from the huddle of Beams Division operators and watches with the others as she disappears around the final concrete bend. 'You okay?' one of them calls out, but she doesn't turn. 'She'll be at the gate in no time,' says another.

'Guess I shouldn't have mentioned airflow,' confesses the guide as he reaches them. And from the back of her, Carver thinks, from the back of her, the girl could almost be Christina.

Or it's his conscience – fucking with him again.

8

He leaves early. He can't work. Why kid himself?

He picks up the West Line before rush hour. As usual he gets out at Oak Park but this evening he doesn't turn up Oak Park Avenue. He sticks to North Boulevard instead, takes Harlem and turns on to Lake. Just past the intersection, he looks over his shoulder and takes you in.

He's wise to you. At last.

You pass William, Monroe, Jackson, Lathrop. He turns up Lathrop unexpectedly. Then it's Quick Street. The tennis club. The library, where Maggie's name has been erased from the duty roster. It's muggy. The weather these days won't break. But he doesn't slow down. Instead, he strides off in the direction of the common, determined to prove something to himself once and for all.

You've engendered something. A break with routine. Enough, it seems, for happenstance to kick in. In the far distance, you see him. Angel, his jacket slung over his shoulder.

His face is upturned. He's following a plane out of O'Hare, its jet stream trailing like a thought. What he wouldn't give. He and his dad almost flew to Ontario once, but it turned out that the cousins with the lake all their own weren't cousins after all. That's what his father told him in the end.

Carver's head is down, unaware. He's trying to summon the moment; to stop, to turn around, to ask who the hell you are?

You see them approach one another, each on the path that cuts a sharp diagonal across the common's green: Carver, stubbornly out of place; Angel, craving open space after the dust of the railyard.

Yes. You have the wide view now.

You watch them pass, less than an arm's reach from one another. It's one of those myriad moments of significance that never unfold; that charge the day-to-day with a hum at a frequency we'll never hear.

Carver looks back, searching. Where did you go? He's oblivious of course to Angel, now just a few feet ahead, in his immediate foreground.

It's only at 11:00 that night that the tongue and groove of cause and effect snaps back into place. A call from 'Mr Ciacci, Head of Security at St Thomas's,' says Mr Ciacci.

Giles Carver's chest tenses.

They picked up someone on the grounds late last night. In the area of the Skilled Care Unit. Not that there was any trouble. Not that she was even aware. A coincidence perhaps.

Yes, sir, says Mr Ciacci. That's right. By her window.

Here in the sleep lab, there are few windows and none that can open.

Christina can't sleep. She has woken twice. On the monitor at the sleep technologist's station, she opens her eyes wide to the infrared night. The on-screen timer reads 23:42:36. Below it the date flickers: 09-10-01. Above her bed a microphone awaits the undulant rhythm of her breath.

She turns her head to the right, to the left, then to the right again. She rubs her arms as if to comfort herself and is surprised by metal – the saturation probe on her finger. She pulls the blankets higher.

Upon arrival she was asked to complete a questionnaire. 'Please summarize your feelings of the last twenty-four hours.' Homesick, she wrote. 'I've been feeling homesick.'

She did not mention her escape today from the Skilled Care Unit. She did not note her panic attack in the tunnel, or her failure to find her father. When required to tick a box – anxious, restless, sad, depressed, calm, alert, well or happy – that best described her current state of mind, she opted for restless. She imagines Angel at her window at St Thomas's tonight – shut out.

There are four electrodes on her scalp, two at the corners of her eyes, three on her chin, two on her ears, and an airflowthermister on her upper lip. There are two cords on her chest, near the clavicles, for the EKG. Another on each leg, for the measurement of muscle tone. She's already told one of the nurses at St Thomas's. Her legs have started to ache. She needs to get outside. She needs to run. The nurse said they could probably get a treadmill for her room. Or a stationary bike. Which would she prefer?

Time passes. Her sleep technologist skips from channel to channel. On 4, there, Christina. Asleep at last. He slips out of the office and buys himself a weak cup of coffee from the machine in the corridor.

He will confirm Christina's entry into delta sleep before forcing arousal. He would expect to see slow waves, with a frequency of only one half to two cycles per second. And yes, he would expect to see the pens of the polysomnograph sketching the shape of stalagmites on the page, close narrow peaks in the cave of sleep.

He sips his coffee slowly. Christina, remember, has caught his imagination.

Is that why he is unable to read the data properly? Suddenly, bells are ringing. He moves from computer screen to amplifier; from video monitor to oxygen saturation monitor. Coffee spills over a keyboard. We've been here before.

He rips a recording from the rolling paper output of the

polysomnograph. The last three minutes of her sleep. Why can't he interpret?

The automatic writing of the twelve pens is wild. The EEG says delta. No, delta moving into theta. Non-REM into REM. Deep sleep into dream. She is only dreaming. The oculogram confirms it. Yet airflow indicates arousals. Chest and abdomen effort is maximum. Nothing will correlate.

He makes a dash for her room and throws open the door. Her blanket is on the floor. So are the cords that were connected to her legs and chest. He doesn't understand. He goes to her bed. Beneath her lids, her eyes pulse in dream. Where is she?

(Flat on her back as debris rains in on her from above. She's turning her face, trying to breathe, spitting grit and earth from her mouth, when someone wanders past. A thin man in an open bathrobe. 'Tastes awful, doesn't it?' he says, grimacing.)

The technologist covers her once more. He listens at the door for a moment as she cries in her sleep.

He checks his other patients. Normal. He fills out an incident report, minimizing discrepancies. He thinks of the girlfriend he once had who threw out every wristwatch she wore; who seemed to turn off street lights as she passed. He writes 'ghost in the machine' and overcompensates with a spree of exclamation marks.

Later, when the call comes through from St Thomas's to his supervisor, he will regret the cavalier tone of his report. He will nevertheless be clear. There was nothing significant to report. There is nothing further he can add.

He'd just left her room – evident from the tape. He'd looked in on both Mrs H and Mr R. By the time in question, he had not yet returned to the monitors.

Twenty seconds of footage. 'What appear to be radial distortions.'

No. He cannot account.

9

Vespers is over. Pilgrims drift into St Pierre under lean bundles and worn blankets. They will end their day under vaults of midnight blue. They will bed down under golden stars that bid everything rise.

Maps, frail in their pockets, are marked with holy wells, public houses and monasteries that offer ale and shade. They know the toll of searing heat and receding horizons. They know the curses of farmers and mad bark pullers. They know the price of clump-soles, brass buckles and reliable oxhide.

Under a scaffold, below the west tower, a dog starts from sleep. It stands – fur raised, ears flat, muzzle drawn back to the gumline. It darts forward, back, then forward again, barking up at its owner. Through the open portal, a dozing pilgrim takes aim with his boot.

The mason, still at work on the façade in the last of the twilight, hardly hears the din. Because suddenly he can't steady his chisel on the mark of the stone, and the strangeness of it sparks a low panic in him. He glances at his hand. Flexes it. He remembers his father, a mason same as him, who got so bad with the palsy he couldn't hold a spoon to feed himself or even a bowl from which to suck. When it occurs to him.

His hand isn't trembling.

The whole world is.

Through the cab's open windows: a drone. Fighter planes patrol the skies, angry as bees in a jar. It's the driver who tells her, on the way back from her night in the lab. 'The Arabs,' he says over the radio reports. 'You wait.' Traffic is gridlocked. In the soaring corridors of the city, suddenly she can't find any space, any sky.

When she makes it back to her room, she throws down her bag and switches on the news. At O'Hare, chaos. Every flight, grounded. In the city, the Sears Tower is evacuated, all 110 storeys. On Michigan Avenue, passers-by gather at the windows of WGN and stare as the north tower collapses all over again on two widescreen TVs.

Is it *real*?

In the Loop, businesses shut down and people struggle homeward. Trains and buses heave. And already at supermarkets and gas stations, there are tailbacks of cars – people stockpiling food and fuel.

All seven of Chicago's Muslim schools are closed. Municipal workers are searching waste baskets and dumpsters. Every post office, every mail room, is on alert.

Fear, she thinks. It's everywhere.

First a storm of stone and glass. Now, a stale hot mist that clings to the town.

What is disaster, nod the diviners of Beauvais, but trouble in the stars?

It is true. The vaults of heaven are fallen.

On the grape terraces, the harvest is thick with chalk dust. In the streets, it settles slowly in teeth, noses and ears. It sits on every loaf of bread, on every garden bloom, on every market ware. It shrouds each pilgrim hauled broken from the ruins.

The bishop's residence is in uproar. His retinue gathers like crows in the corridors, cawing despair. The kitchen staff are raw-faced with grief. The people of Beauvais are dumb at the sight. How is it possible? The cathedral down.

IO

The bishop gives up blessing the shattered dead. He sits at his table, turning over in his hands a fragment of carved and painted stone. 'A detail,' he announces to his serving nuns, 'from the highest keystone in all of Christendom.' His low laugh turns to a cough.

Blanche pours cool water into a goblet. Mathilde polishes his spoon.

'A mason's boy found it. What were the chances? I ask you.'

Blanche shakes out the cloth. 'What a shame it's broken, Your Grace.'

They behold: the solitary eye. The edge of a nose and a cheek. Still, the full O of the mouth.

'Nine of these faces peered out from the keystone, Blanche. I commissioned them myself. Hair of gold leaf. Three clusters of three. Do you find it beautiful, Mathilde?'

Mathilde starts. The bishop has not addressed her before. 'Angels may only be beautiful, Your Grace. It is as you say.'

'When I wish to hear my own views, Mathilde, I speak to my prelates.'

'If I may, Your Grace, the expression, what remains of it that is, appears somewhat wild.'

'You are not mistaken, Mathilde. I too find the eyes over-large – the eye at any rate.'

'Then there's the mouth. Forgive me, Your Grace, but I didn't know angels had teeth.' She bends closer. Blanche too draws near.

He smiles tightly. 'Those are not teeth, Mathilde. They are graven letters.'

'Words, Your Grace?'

'Indeed. The carver has charged the angel's mouth with speech.'

'He speaks?'

'He does.'

'Up so high where no one can hear?'

'Precisely, Mathilde. Precisely.'

THE TENTH ANGEL.

How dare Giles of Beauvais make of his cathedral a heretic's mouthpiece? How dare he curse it with his Arabist ideas?

And Blanche observes: the knuckles whitening; the gold ring of office tightening on his finger; the dark flash of amethyst. She understands the glories and dangers of a man of God. 'Mathilde, leave the wine,' she says. The younger woman nods and slips from the room. Blanche lifts serving lids. She slices cold chicken from the bone, even as the bishop feels envy tighten in his jaw.

Envy for a showy heretic. Envy for a man who has a strength of belief he himself will never know.

'I want word sent to my chief prelate.'

'I believe he is expected.'

'I require assistance.'

'It is only right.'

'Monsieur l'Ymagier will return to Beauvais.'

She stops.

'As a guest of this house.'

'Your Grace?'

'And when he is found, he is to be offered this' – he looks at the fragment of keystone – 'as a token of my faith.'

Air on her face. At her feet still, the window's broken glass. The missile too. A large stone.

It is even as her confessor warned. She is at risk. She is not wanted in Beauvais. She is her father's daughter.

From the other side of the door, mayhem. Raised voices. People running throughout the house.

She will do it. She will leave the bishop's residence. She will flee Beauvais. She will sleep at the edge of the pigherds' camp if she has to. She will feed herself on honey and truffles; on wild ginger and the roots of water lilies. She will leach the bitterness from acorns.

She thinks of her father at Fermilab. On the fourteenth floor. Did he go in today?

She goes to the window to breathe.

A sliding window. A light screen only.

Tomorrow. She will find a way out tomorrow.

Before she starts to believe there is nowhere else for her. Before she gives in to fear for good.

'Watch lest you cut yourself.'

She turns from the window, a final shard of glass in her hand.

It is the bishop himself who stands at her door.

He observes her. He contemplates, too, the miscellany on the floor. Her morning loaf. A pair of slippers shoved into another pair – harder wearing. The offending stone – he had the report. A rolled rug, for warmth as the nights draw in.

He enters and takes a seat, as if this is their day's routine. 'I will say little, Christina. Of course you may come or go as you like. Perhaps I may even be of assistance, as I was to your sister.' He folds his hands in his lap. 'But I reproach myself, for did I not promise your father I would shelter you until his return?'

'He does not return. I am without family. I have been assured.'

'Life reveals itself even by the day. Your father's commission in Paris is now complete.'

'Commission? There was no –'

'And naturally, given the devastation of the cathedral, I have deemed Beauvais's need the greater.'

'He comes then?'

The bishop stands and smiles. 'I ask you, how can he not?'

II

'Thank you for coming.' Dr Bishop is hauling a large armchair over to his desk. 'Giles – may I call you Giles? – please, make yourself comfortable.'

Carver takes a seat, checking his phone for any sign of Maggie before reluctantly switching it off. It's Thursday. Two whole days since the world went crazy and still he's not heard from her. He can hardly bear the thought of her out there, alone.

He blinks. 'That's right,' he's telling Dr Bishop's secretary, 'black, no sugar.' Dr Bishop takes his seat behind his desk. Dr Sperber, already instated, shakes his hand. 'Right,' says Bishop. 'Shall we get started?'

Carver feels the nerves prickle at the back of his neck.

'Naturally, Giles,' begins the neurologist, 'we felt it important to meet again to review Christina's progress. Certainly she gets stronger from day to day, which is terrific news. My colleague, Dr Newman in Cardiology, will speak to you himself, but he informs me they've ruled out the need for a pacemaker. There is, I understand, some T-wave irregularity, but he feels Cardiology can monitor her as effectively on an outpatient basis.' He reaches for the paperweight on his desk, a carved replica of some kind. He seems to meditate upon it.

'As for the coordination problems, the physio's report indicates there is no longer cause for significant concern. And, encouragingly, the most recent MRIs show either clearing or reduction of the lesions in the right motor cortex. A few unspecified ones remain, but we've deemed them clinically silent. She's been very lucky. I do need to tell you that we're still assessing signalling abnormalities in the temporo-parietal lobes but –'

'I want my daughter back, Dr Bishop. We will live in the dark if we have to.'

'With respect,' notes Dr Sperber, 'that's not a solution.'

Carver ignores him. 'At home things will be different. I know they will be. She can't go on living among strangers here, cut off from the world.'

Dr Bishop puts down the paperweight. 'The Capgras, as you know, is still an issue.'

'Like I say, I think things will be different once she's home.'

Bishop looks at his desk. 'There is something else.'

Carver looks up.

'It's the particular reason we asked you here today.'

'Is it that guy? Has he done something?'

'No, no. Nothing of that kind. And security is dealing with that issue, as I believe Mr Ciacci explained.'

'What then?'

Dr Bishop looks to Dr Sperber.

Dr Sperber reaches for his coffee and stirs it slowly. 'There were irregularities in the data collected at the sleep lab on Monday night.'

'Irregularities.'

'Some due to random power surges, possibly.'

'And the others?'

He shrugs. 'They've proven more difficult to characterize.' He puts down the mug, opens his briefcase and lays a videotape on Dr Bishop's desk. 'There are distortions in the video data.'

'What do you mean, "distortions"?'

'Our media and imaging lab is analysing the original now.'

'What kind of distortions?'

'New closed-circuit cameras were recently installed in each observation room at the sleep lab. They changed suppliers: a new, small company tendered for the job. I know little about it, but our head image analyst here tells me that sound video footage depends upon a series of almost tedious pre-calibrations. To quote his memo . . .' Sperber unfolds a piece of paper, fishing for his glasses in his breast pocket. '"Neglecting lens distortions introduces a systematic error build-up, which causes recovered structure and motion to bend."' He looks up. 'I am also told that footage may be manipulated to achieve certain distorting effects.'

'What are you talking about?'

'Augmented reality. That's what they call it. With the right tools one can, I understand, turn a video clip into a virtual funhouse of waves, bends, ripples, gaps. It's all possible.'

'Let me see the tape.'

'With respect, you're missing the point, Dr Carver. The tape isn't at issue. There are distortions. We know that. However, as of yet, we can't say how or where they originated. Nobody watched this tape through at the sleep lab. It's routine to pop it in a confidential envelope and forward it to the supervising psychologist, along with the rest of the data. Given the anomalies in the EEG and EKG output, and those that Dr Bishop's team have picked up here, I watched the tape through this morning to see if I could spot anything.'

'What does the sleep lab say?'

'What can they say? They have a receipt from a courier. The tape left their office first thing on Tuesday morning. For reasons we may never know, it only just arrived here, on my desk, today. Two days later. God knows, there are delays everywhere, and were, especially, on the eleventh. I believe it arrived in the hospital's mail room only late Wednesday – yesterday – afternoon. It still should have been processed by them much faster. But they're under instruction. They're opening every rigid package that comes through, especially those without return addresses. And especially those marked confidential.'

'Is there evidence it's been tampered with?'

'No, although, as I say, I'm curious to see if our media and imaging people pick up anything.'

'Why are you telling me all this?'

'You told St Thomas's head of Security you were being followed.'

'Yes. I'm being followed.' He feels himself bristle. 'Usually on my way home from work. By someone who could be anyone. But there's no evidence of any connection to St Thomas's.'

Dr Bishop intervenes. 'I'm sure you're right. We're simply trying to weigh up all available information.' He folds his hands on his desk. 'I had an unusual phone call today, Giles.'

'Go on.'

'I wonder if you've heard of a Christian organization called Aquinan Services.'

'No.'

'Well, it was established in Chicago in the mid nineteenth century. It has flourishing ministries in Illinois, Michigan and Iowa. Its members, the Sisters of Aquinas, are dedicated to the ideals of St Thomas Aquinas – that is to say, to the advancement of learning and scholarship, especially as they relate to the physical and spiritual needs of the wider community. Their well-endowed parent organization, Aquinan Services, Inc., is this hospital's largest sponsor. Today, the CEO of that organization, a Mr Joseph, contacted me with a request.'

'I don't see what this has to do with Christina.'

'Both he and Sister Paula Wright, the mission director of the Sisters of Aquinas, are acquainted with her story. The sisters, I'm told, would like to pray for her. He asked me if I could tell him a little more about Christina.'

'Acquainted with her "story"? Acquainted how?'

'Christina's admission was not a secret, Giles. The challenges our patients face are discussed at various levels here at St Thomas's. However . . .'

'However?'

'What surprised me was Mr Joseph's specific reference to her visit to the sleep lab on Monday night. As Dr Sperber says, we've only just received the data ourselves, so the timing strikes me as odd. If it was one thing or the other – the video *or* Mr Joseph's phone call – I wouldn't be giving any of this a second thought.'

'But you are.'

'I suppose I am. Which is why I decided to ask Dr Sperber about the sleep lab observation. It's why I then felt I needed to get the three of us together. These are strange times, sadly.'

'I don't get it. Why on earth would either Aquinan Services or the Sisters of Aquinas be interested in Christina's trip to the sleep lab?'

'I really don't know. But I have to say: my impression, fleeting as it was, was that Mr Joseph was trying to confirm the timing of her visit, as if he was looking for some kind of corroboration, perhaps under the guise of polite inquiry. He said that Tuesday morning must have seemed to Christina – even more than to the rest of us – like waking into a bad dream. He asked if she had trouble that morning getting back to the hospital from the sleep lab, what with all the chaos downtown.'

'You think there's been a leak.'

'I wonder if there has been. Certainly it seems that some confidential details are out. Anyway, the ostensible point of Mr Joseph's call was to make a rather unusual request. He approached me, as the supervisor of Christina's team, and asked, in short, if he and Sister Paula could visit with her.' He flexes his fingers. 'Naturally, I said I would speak with you first.'

'I still don't get it.'

'No, and I wish I could enlighten you. The hospital's director wants me to receive them as warmly as possible, but if you are against the visit, for whatever reason, I will do my best to put them off.'

'Christina won't want to see them. Why would she?'

'No . . .'

'Although,' adds Dr Sperber, leaning forward, 'it might be worth remembering that it was their funding that made the new MRI purchases possible. Christina has been one of the first patients to benefit. We shouldn't run away with things. All this could be nothing more than an excellent photo opportunity for Aquinan Services.'

Dr Bishop nods. 'Or even something more sincere. Mr Joseph asked me to tell you, on Sister Paula's behalf, that, should the offer be of assistance, she is prepared to provide a home for Christina until such a time as she is ready to go home. They have a place called' – he checks his notes – 'the Aquinan Center for Living. "For special young women who –"'

Carver looks up from the rim of his mug. 'Let me see that tape.'

12

Mr Ciacci loosens his tie. Behind his desk, the shifting frames of his security monitors carve up the world. 'Good to see you again.'

Angel pulls up a plastic chair, sits down, spreads his legs.

'You smoke?' Ciacci reaches into a drawer.

'It's No Smoking.'

Ciacci smiles, extends the pack. Angel takes one, pulling a disposable from his pocket. It's dead. Ciacci lights up, then throws him the box of matches. He leans back, drumming his fingers on the metal desktop. 'You won't regret coming in today.' He opens a file. 'You've got my word on that.'

Angel takes a long drag. He'll say whatever it takes. He'll say, 'Yeah, I'm with her. No, her family doesn't know. I *am* too old for her. I know that.' He won't say it's wrong.

Ciacci is squinting at some faded print. 'Don't misunderstand me. I'm not turning a blind eye. I had my friends down at the cop shop dig out some old paperwork. I've done my homework.'

Angel leans back. Smoke streams from his nostrils. He can do this.

Ciacci blows crumbs off his desk. 'I see we grew up in the same neighbourhood practically. I used to jimmy car windows for the Fitch brothers – I think they lived on Ashland. Your street, right? The older one would be about your age. Know him?'

'I moved when I was twelve.'

'I see that.' He taps ash into the can by his desk. 'The

Thurlow Home for Boys, 1978 to 1982.' He squints hard, as if weighing his options. 'I'm going to be blunt with you, because we both want this over. That's why you're going to forgive me when I ask you what the hell you were doing outside a girl patient's window with this kind of shit on your record?'

Angel looks past him. He cannot react.

'Me, I've never been a spiritual man, but from where I'm sitting, "Angel", this isn't looking like divine inspiration.'

'I didn't do anything.'

'You raped a minor.'

'I was a minor.'

'Just. And that's the only reason you're sitting here today enjoying the view. Mr Dognini was in no doubt about what he saw you doing to his fourteen-year-old daughter. What was it you used to call him again?' He glances at the notes. 'The Dog Catcher.'

'He used to tie me to a banister in the basement.'

'You were resourceful. I'll give you that.'

'She'd open my fly.'

Ciacci kicks a desk drawer shut. 'Maria Dognini was autistic.'

'I didn't know what the fuck she was. I thought they were saying "artistic". She used to come over after school some-times and wait for Dognini to finish his shift. She'd sit at the kitchen table making things out of clay. Birds and things. If Dognini went out, he'd tie me in the basement. I'd hear her up there. I was sixteen.'

'And all hormones, from the sound of it. She told the police she used to take you in her mouth.'

'Go jerk off somewhere else, will you?'

'Pretty thing, I guess.'

'No.'

'She passed the time though.'

'Who the fuck are you?'

He turns over a page. 'You got her to untie your wrists.'

'I didn't *get* her to do anything.'

'But she wouldn't undo the others.' He glances at the notes. 'The ones around your legs and upper arms. You asked her, but she wouldn't. She knew you weren't allowed out of the basement. So it was a case of close-but-no-bazooka. God, you must have been angry. Tied up like a . . . well, yeah, like a dog, I guess.'

Angel throws his butt into the can.

'And I can understand. Cos this has been going on for a while, hasn't it? Sure you're angry. Who wouldn't be? Angry enough, in fact, to pick up that skinny retard of a daddy's girl and stick her right on it.' He nods at the paperwork. 'That's how the Biography Channel sees it.'

'You don't know what you're talking about.'

'You're right. Anger couldn't have been the half of it. You must have felt what? Shame? Fear? Loneliness? The gut-wrenching kind, am I right? Or do you just have a thing for girls with special needs?'

'That's not how it was.'

'Tell me then. Tell me how it was.'

Angel locks eyes. 'I liked her.'

'The truth is, I don't care whether you did or didn't. Because we got you, Angel. On a new camera that overlooks the rear grounds.' Mr Ciacci turns in his chair, hits a switch on the console and summons a swathe of green lawn. He doesn't take his eyes off the screens. 'I also have a nurse's statement, reporting an interesting anomaly, as we say in the trade. A Sue Patterson and a Donna Young attended Christina on the night of September 2. That was a Sunday. The night before she woke up from the coma.

'At the time, I thought it was probably nothing. Around eight-thirty that night the two nurses gave her a sponge-bath, then dressed her again, fastening a long row of buttons on her nightdress, ones that, according to the report, went right up to her neck. Little pearl buttons, they said, with loop buttonholes. Women seem to remember these things, don't they? Anyway, the duty nurse messed up on the roster. Sue Patterson ended up working a double shift. So, coincidentally, she was also the first to attend Christina in the morning. And she noticed almost right away.

'She noticed that someone had dressed Christina again. How did Nurse Sue know that? I'll tell you how. The top button loop was button-less. The buttons had been buttoned wrong. The sequence was out by one. It seems that whoever dressed her again didn't have the patience, or the time, to start again from the beginning.

'Now granted, by the time the nurse filed the incident report almost two days later – it was the Labor Day weekend, remember – all the tapes of that Sunday night had been wiped. But when we picked you up the other night, I remembered something. My head's like a computer, Angel. I remembered I'd seen you in here. In fact, I was sitting in this very chair talking to Mr Carver, as it happens. On that same Sunday night. Know how I know? I'll tell you how. I'd had to leave my own Labor Day barbecue just as I was about to sink my canines into one mother of a burger.' He shrugs. Picks up a quarter sitting on his desk and flips it. 'Heads or tails?'

'What?'

'Heads or tails?'

Angel stares.

'Heads. You come anywhere near either this hospital or Christina Carver ever again, Angel, and I won't be talking to you. Tails. Whaddya know? Same thing. No, I won't be talking to you about your sorry fucked-up past. I'll be on the phone to Metra. I'll be telling them they got a rapist working their tracks. Why, you got to be on and off those passenger trains all the time in your line of work, am I right? Then, I'm on the phone to the city police. Maybe you don't know Illinois law, so I'll paint you the picture.

'Anyone believed to be a potential sex predator may be "evaluated" by a social worker or mental health employee as a first step on the road to commitment. The main thing to remember is this, Angel: the state rep and the judge only have to find that the person in question has a personality disorder – I told you I did my homework – a personality disorder that makes him "likely" or "substantially probable" to engage in an illicit act. Once that person goes "inside", he isn't likely to get "outside" again, not here in the state of Illinois anyway. I've seen the stats.'

He stubs out his cigarette in the can and reaches for the air freshener on the shelf behind. 'So, like I said before, I know you'll be glad you made the effort to come in today.' He pulls a stick of gum from his pocket, throws its wrapper on his desk and launches it into his mouth. 'Now, if you have no further questions, Angel, I'll be only too happy to show you out.'

13

She opens her eyes to the dark. She can smell the night, sultry through her open window. She can't tell what time it is.

He sits down on the edge of her bed.

Half awake, she moves over, makes space for him. Then remembers. She's leaving. Tomorrow she's leaving. She'll tell him tonight.

He touches her shoulder. 'Christina?'

She reaches up, puts her arms around his neck.

'Sweetheart.'

Her father's voice. She lies down again, pulling the sheet over herself.

He raises the light blanket and tucks it under her chin. 'I've startled you, darling.'

'Dad.'

'Yes,' he whispers. '*Me*.'

She can smell the Noxzema on his face. She can see his shaving brush in the bathroom drawer at home. 'It's late. What are you doing here?'

'The doctors say you're doing a lot better.'

Her words slur with sleepiness. 'I could have told them that.'

'I wanted to see for myself. I wanted to see *you*.'

She waves a hand in front of his face. 'Hello?'

'I know. But we'd better leave the lights off. Visiting hours were over at least an hour ago.'

'Where's Maggie?'

'She misses you.'

'I miss her too.'

'Listen, ladybug. Do you want to get out of here? Do you wanna blow this popsicle stand?'

'I can come home?'

'Not just yet. But you don't have to stay here. I've got an idea.' She's waking, slowly. 'How'd you get in here?'

'They know me at the information desk. I said I was just going to leave some fresh clothes in your room.' He taps a bag on the floor with his foot. 'That's them. And I said maybe I'd take a peek at you while you slept. Neither of which, I hasten to add, is a lie.'

She turns her face away on the pillow. 'You took your time, Dad.' He can feel the force of her frown in the night. 'You really took your time.'

'I know. I'm sorry. Really sorry. Dr Sperber told me it was for the best.'

She tugs at the blanket where he's sitting on it. 'How could it ever be for the best?'

'I know, ladybug. I know.'

'You *don't*. It's been scary.' She faces him again in the dark. 'I couldn't even walk before now without crashing into things. And there have been people . . . Weird people.'

'I was stupid. Really stupid. And wrong.'

'Really wrong.'

'I know. But I'm here. I'm here now. And I have a question.' He reaches for her hand. 'Something I need to ask you.'

'What?'

He whispers into her ear: 'Are you with me . . .'

She can just make out the glimmer of his smile as he hesitates.

'Or are you *with* me?'

'*Dad.*'

'Well, are you?'

She hesitates, turning to the darkness of the window – open as usual in case Angel comes. 'I am. Okay. I am.'

In the motel room, Maggie lies, stomach down, in the dip of the bed. Though it is hot, the windows are only open a crack – there's too much noise from the motel parking lot. Large families slamming SUV doors at five in the morning.

She has made sure the DO NOT DISTURB sign is prominently displayed. Yesterday she phoned the motel's reception desk and asked that the housekeeping staff ignore her room; bad flu, she told the receptionist. Take-out containers, rolls of toilet paper and paper cups from the bathroom dispenser amass on the floor.

She flips from CNN to *Twenty-Twenty* to the public service announcements: precautions one should take in readiness for a city-wide emergency. She knows everything there is to know now about batteries, back-up generators, bottled water, blackout screens, canned food, carbohydrate bars, first-aid kits, flares, seat-belt cutters and window punches. She has not been able to turn off the TV since Tuesday morning.

Christina dresses in the dark, then unzips the bag her father has brought. She tips its contents out on the bed, goes to her top drawer and lifts out her mother's nightdress and her own sketchbook. She lays each flat on the bottom, then stuffs the clothes back in.

'Where does the door at the end of your corridor go?'

She turns back to his voice. 'To the courtyard.'

'Is there a gate or something?'

'No, it's all walls, to hide the parking lot.'

'The door's open. Someone's stuck a rock in it – I guess to let some air through.'

'My window. There's my window.'

'I wouldn't want to chance it. How high are the courtyard walls?'

'Six or seven feet maybe. There's a bench under one of them. Over to the right, past the fountain.'

'Could you do it?'

She reaches: for her old self, for her old ease in the world. 'I could do it.'

'Okay. Because it seems, sweetheart, I'm about to abduct you. Officially, under the terms of your admission, Dr Bishop is your guardian.'

'Everything's crazy.'

'We need to go one at a time. Here are the car keys. You'll see it in the lot. There are only a few cars out there. I want you to go first – just to be sure you're okay. But I'll be right behind you.'

Her hand is on the door when she turns back.

'What is it?'

She goes to the window and untapes the sketch. She opens her bag, lifts out the pad and carefully slides it in.

As she opens the door, he avoids the widening span of light. 'Just climb in the back, open my door, and put your head down on the seat. I'll be right behind you. Promise. But keep your head down till we get there, okay? Don't look up.'

Maggie flips channels. As of September 11, says one local report, Fermilab closed to the public.

On Channel 17, she stops. *Dr Zhivago*.

It's near the beginning: the bit where Lara paces in the dress shop, not knowing whether her mother is dead or alive in the bed upstairs.

He gives her a head start, then goes to the door and peers into the dark of the courtyard. He can hear her footsteps on the pebbled path. Close to the fountain, she trips a floodlight and backs quickly into the shadows. He waits, gripping her bag in his hand, until he hears her land, safe on the other side of the wall.

'I'm so sorry,' says Omar Sharif, turning to her in the flickering dark of the motel room. 'We did everything we could.'

And tears flood Maggie's face.

Giles Carver opens the driver's side, throws the bag in, and picks up the keys. 'You okay, ladybug?'

'Yup.'

He switches on his cellphone again, in case Maggie tries to call. 'Grab some sleep back there, why don't you?'

'Where are we going?'

'I'll tell you when we get there.' And as he turns the key, he starts to breathe again.

Maggie wipes her nose with her hand and heaves herself out of the dip in the bed. She's all out of tissues. Through the crack in the curtains: the Happy Griddle's neon grin. It won't let her sleep.

She finds the bag into which she stuffed some clothes. At the bottom, *Jane Eyre*. Her mother's book.

He switches on the air conditioning, glides on to Washington Boulevard and hangs a right on to Route 43. Street lights and store signs blare. He glances in his rear-view mirror. Her head's down. He feels like he's plucked her from some danger even he can't fully imagine.

Not that he doesn't have his suspicions. The leak. It has to be Sperber.

It was his line about the MRIs and the generosity of Aquinan

Services – there was something too oily, too complicit, about him in that moment. He'll check. He'll find a way. Watch. Sperber will turn out to be a born-again Christian, a pair of fervent eyes for Aquinan Services, a mole sniffing for some twenty-first-century miracle. God knows, he's righteous enough. Charmless enough too. Carver can see it now, the moment of conversion: some woman, her buttocks shaking for Jesus, backing into him at a Billy Graham rally. Probably the first woman without a serious head injury to show interest. Of course he felt saved by Christ.

Yet if Sperber did send Aquinan Services the video or copy it for them, why would Mr Joseph need to probe David Bishop? The time, the date – it's all there in the recording.

But Aquinan Services have to be sure. *They* need to know the video hasn't been tampered with. They need to check and triple-check its provenance. Because, who knows? Maybe Sperber's not a closet charismatic, after all. Maybe this isn't about God. Maybe it's about beachfront property in Florida. Maybe Aquinan Services looks upon that video, and now Christina too, God help her, as some kind of investment.

Wasn't there that girl outside Boston? Audrey. Little Audrey. The one in the coma who was supposed to heal people? Hundreds, it was said. They had to put out Port-a-Potties on the front lawn of their suburban Worcester home. They had to get a football stadium for her annual mass. Ten thousand attended in ninety-degree heat. Forty miles away in Brookline, his own mother had thought about going until he asked her if she was out of her mind. 'Look at this stuff,' he said, scanning the website. Audrey videos. Audrey T-shirts. Audrey fridge magnets and mouse pads. The Audrey Event CD.

He gears down, changes lanes. Somewhere behind, a horn blares.

So Mr Joseph watches the sleep lab video – or at least the

crucial twenty seconds – care of Dr Sperber. He talks to Sperber. Yes, certainly, he says, he can appreciate its value to Aquinan Services.

But a good investor, thinks Carver, knows you don't take the word of the salesman. You scout around. You read the labelling. The Truth has a shelf-life, and in this case it is precisely one day. Twenty-four hours. 09-11-01. For significance, too, can expire. Mr Joseph knows that the date could make all the difference between Christian revelation and video glitch.

Yet, like most of us, Mr Joseph is also aware that clocks and calendars may be manipulated. And his company can't pay out wads for a recording that could be subject to error or retrospective analysis. The data needs to be secure. The day has to be guaranteed.

But Mr Joseph only has Sperber's word for it. Joseph realizes he has to go to the top, to Dr David Bishop. He needs the date of Christina's visit to the sleep lab confirmed by someone without a vested interest.

He goes behind Sperber's back and calls Bishop, seemingly out of the blue. He never dreams Bishop will think to take it further, to cross-check. He never dreams his two sources will compare notes. Hasn't he made the phone call seem almost incidental? A friendly by-the-by chat. A few shared chuckles, perhaps, about the repartee at the last board meeting at St Thomas's. Only then does Joseph change the subject to that of Christina . . .

And who, let's face it, would be suspicious of a charitable organization? Who would speculate about the motives of nuns?

Carver stops at a set of lights. Okay, he thinks, playing devil's advocate with himself, then why doesn't Sperber just lie to David Bishop about the anomalies in Monday night's data? It wouldn't be difficult. Why doesn't he simply neglect to mention the twenty seconds of footage? Bishop might never see the tape himself.

The lights change. He shifts into first.

Why doesn't he?

Because he has to play it carefully. Christina has to be booked into the sleep lab again – because, everything else aside, the data that night *was* anomalous. Unreliable. The sleep lab people were talking power surges. As Christina's now legal guardian, Bishop might ask to see the tape for himself.

Besides, Sperber can't really know how much Mr Joseph gave away in his phone call to Dr Bishop. Joseph was stupid enough to ask about the sleep lab, wasn't he? Stupid enough to probe the date; to relate the timing of Christina's visit to the shock of Tuesday morning's events. David Bishop is a sharp individual. What other miscalculations did Mr Joseph make in that call? What else, Sperber has to ask himself, might David Bishop not be telling him? What else might he suspect?

So Sperber realizes it's too risky to lie. Better, in any case, to play to each audience. To talk radial distortions to the very reasonable David Bishop and revelation to the die-hard Christians. And who doesn't want revelation when they're looking the 'infidel' in the face? Who wouldn't clamour for a Christian miracle in America's heartland when share prices are falling?

Carver makes a mental note to check the holdings of Aquinan Services, Inc. No doubt, he'll find a surprisingly broad portfolio. Where else would a Christian outreach organization get the cash to launch themselves as *the* major sponsor of a state-of-the-art primary care and research facility?

In fact, he begins to realize, it's possible that Sperber, Joseph and maybe even Sister Paula Wright concocted the whole video story. It's possible they 'cooked' the tape themselves to get the results they wanted. 'Augmented reality'. Isn't that what Sperber himself was saying? Maybe the whole show of concern in Bishop's office was nothing more than Sperber's alibi. It's highly unlikely, Carver decides, that *any* head of media and imaging is giving that tape so much as a cursory glance, let alone a 'distortions' analysis.

On the other side of Carver's windshield, the turn-off for Bridgeview suddenly looms into view. He brakes hard. In the back, Christina rolls forward, frowning hard in her sleep.

14

The doorstep is dark. The peephole slides back.

'Nat, sorry it's late. It's me. Giles.'

A woman's voice. 'Nathalie isn't here.'

He talks into the door. 'I'm Giles Carver, a friend of hers. Who am I speaking to?'

'A neighbour. I'm babysitting Aarif.'

He glances back to the car in the driveway. Christina, asleep still.

'She might not be home for some time.'

'I understand. Could you open the door perhaps? I'm a friend. I used to work with Nathalie at the university.'

The porch floods with light. And only then does he see. He backs down the stairs to read it in full.

'SAND NIGGERS OUT.' A filthy scrawl across the aluminum siding.

'My God.'

The door opens. A small, plump woman in her fifties appears, her eyes nervous.

'Thank you, Mrs . . . ?'

'Mazin. Nathalie isn't here.'

'What's happened?'

'You don't watch the news?'

'I'm sorry. My daughter's been ill . . . I –'

'Last night three hundred teenagers drove into Bridgeview and ran riot. They honked horns and waved flags. They chanted slogans and hurled bricks. And worse.' She nods to the front of the house. 'Nathalie and Aarif were in here, terrorized.'

He feels all the adrenalin of the night drain from him.

'The police came in riot gear and stopped them from marching on the mosque, but only just. They were still permitted to "demonstrate". They were still permitted to shout, "Kill the Arabs!"'

'Where's Nat?'

'Two officers turned up this morning to investigate the vandalism – not that there was much to be done after the fact. It so happens they also noticed her library books on the table – books on Islamic philosophy and so on. They seemed curious. They asked her what she did for a living and she told them. A physicist. An associate professor. They asked her how long she'd been living in the US. They wondered what she was doing in a foreign country all by herself. They seemed bemused, Mr Carver. Then tonight two different officers in an unmarked car turned up at the door and told her they needed to speak to her at the station.'

'What reason did they give?'

'Some kind of visa violation. It's happening all over Bridgeview. Things, Mr Carver, are happening all over Bridgeview. The FBI has even been down to our public library. They're trying to access records: who checked out which book and for how long. It would be funny if it wasn't so serious.'

Aarif wanders out in his pyjamas, dragging a *Canadiens* hockey shirt behind him like a blanket.

'Hi, Aarif,' he calls. 'The bedbugs biting?'

He approaches the door. 'I told my mother I didn't want to play soccer with you any more. I told her.'

'Aarif,' chides Mrs Mazin.

'You're right. Now hockey, that's the game. Can you skate yet, Aarif?'

The boy pushes at Mrs Mazin's arm. 'Where's my mother? Why isn't my mother home yet?'

'Sssh now. She'll be home soon.'

'She told you not to open the door.' He raises his arm and pummels her side.

Giles stops his hand. 'Can I do anything, now, for you or Aarif?'

'What can be done, Mr Carver?' She sighs, adjusting her headscarf. 'People have enough religion to hate, it seems, but not enough to love.'

There is nothing he can say.

A white man in a baseball cap passes the house on foot. She retreats slightly behind the door. 'To bed now, Aarif. I'll come tuck you in in a minute.'

Giles looks at his feet. Tears prick his eyes. 'Tell Nat I'll call her in the morning. And, again, Mrs Mazin, I'm very sorry about the hour.'

She nods, closes the door. Only when he turns does he see: Christina, wide awake and glaring at him through the car window.

He stops where he stands, an animal in the headlights, until Mrs Mazin remembers the porch light.

She won't discuss it.

'I'll get you a flight. You can go to Boston. Grandma and Granddad Carver would love to see you. Remember how you wanted to see Walden? And art – they've got that great museum of fine art. Or we could think about a hotel. I'll find you a special one.'

She stares out the window. She speaks only to say that if he doesn't drive her back to the Skilled Care Unit immediately, she'll get out at the next set of lights and call them herself.

In less than half an hour he's pulling up in front of St Thomas's bright foyer. The back door slams before he can turn around in his seat.

He sits, watching the slim line of his daughter recede. He sees her approach the information desk. She seems to say something to the receptionist about the bag in her hand. Then she turns the corner and disappears.

This, he thinks, is what you get for holding your children to you instead of allowing them to outgrow you. This is what you get for being more charmer than father; more suitor than guardian.

Tomorrow, he decides, he'll try to see David Bishop. He'll ask about medication: the anti-psychotics. He'll admit he doesn't know what else to do.

15

At the town gate he dismounts, awkwardly.

'I prefer not to meet His Grace with the dirt of the world on me.' He nods to the water trough inside the gate where two cows lap. 'Tell him I will be with him shortly.'

His keeper – young, burly – looks uncertain.

L'Ymagier smiles. 'Do you think I would wander off here, in Beauvais of all places?'

He is alone for the first time in days. He stands and stares at the hole in the horizon where the towers once soared. He washes quickly, not easy with his hand in the sling. Then he slips into the warren of cramped houses that teeter against the town walls.

A word. A hello. His only chance.

How could he not take it? A wooden likeness. The spirit of her caught in a tree. He found it days ago under the tumble-down roof where his father once hauled sacks of char. As if it had been left for him.

He knew immediately the planes of her face. The rise of her breast. The fineness of her hands. He touched her hair, pale at his fingertips. Cruel magic.

Sometimes he let himself lie next to her. On a bed of earth. In the balm of shadow. As if she might stretch her wooden limbs and turn to him.

The evening the towers fell, he felt the ground shudder. Swallows skidded skyward from their nests. A cloud of bees retreated into the carcass of a dead tree. A pigherd drove his beasts towards the town.

And for the first time he felt it. He alone was alone.

The sign above Athalie's door wobbles from a nail. The rebel eye in the flaming heart. The secret sign of ecstatic contemplation.

A secret no more. L'Ymagier can see where the bolt has been forced.

He shoulders the door, crunching glass underfoot. Smashed phials. He almost trips over a heavy stick.

He bends, taking it in his good hand, and pokes at the vast heap of cooling embers. Her father's volumes; borne on his own back all the way from Egypt to France. Disguised as a brutish hump, she'd told him once. 'No one questioned it, for naturally we're a coarse breed.' She'd laughed. 'Yet together they must have weighed five stone.'

In the draught from the open door, ash stirs.

That evening, as chalk dust fell like pollen from the sky, he went to the pigherds' camp and felt his voice burble in his throat. Where is the girl?

La Merveilleuse, they said with a laugh. The one who rises up to knock a cathedral down.

In the morning, he followed the pigherds' trails through the wood and across the grape-growers' terraces. And he saw it was so, what they told him: the sky vast again.

Nearing the town walls, he stopped short at the sudden clamour of pickaxes and the urgent shouts of labourers. It was not yet light. He would know the house, the lame pigherd had said, by the soaring spray of water.

Yes.

A locked gate but he hurdled it easily.

Many windows. He touched his palms to the transparency of glass. He beheld the faces of women, trampled by sleep. He observed the form of a man weighed down by fur, even in the warmth of the season. At last her, alone on the far side of a room – laced and still in her sleep. Half obscured by heavy curtains. Yet he had only to see her to understand.

She needed release.

He found the stone easily, a good weight in his hand. Then he stepped back, raised his arm high and broke the cool spell of glass.

A serving nun shows l'Ymagier through to the pleasure garden. The bishop sits in the shadow of the fountain. Bright marble fish dart at the pool's bottom. On the fountainhead, a fisherman lets down his nets. His own work.

The bishop stands and runs a finger across the rim. 'As you can see, Monsieur l'Ymagier, the dust is still settling.' A smile flickers at his mouth. 'And to think I had Blanche clean it but yesterday in anticipation of your visit.' He extends his ring.

Giles of Beauvais bends low and kisses it. Then he reaches into his rucksack and, with some difficulty, passes the bishop the surviving piece of keystone wrapped in chamois leather. As instructed.

'Well,' says the bishop, 'what think you of my keepsake?'

(A cul-de-sac, not far from the stonecutter's workshop, where he'd found work at last. His feet kicked out from under him. His left arm hauled free and pinned to the ground. A message: the bishop asks that you accept this token of his faith. The stone brought down at speed, shattering every bone. The fragment of his angel's head left rolling with him on the ground.)

'Do you reflect?' queries the bishop when he does not reply.

Giles of Beauvais stares at the ground. 'Sadly, I see now that the quality is poor.'

The bishop surveys him. 'I would be inclined to agree.'

It is hard not to step through to the other side.

Christina sits by the windowless window, turning the mossy stone over in her hands.

It is hard to believe that her father will indeed come.

First she is told he has left her and that Marguerite is sent away. Now the bishop talks of a Paris commission and her father's imminent return. She cannot believe it. And yet, if she goes and he does come? If she flees now and they never meet again? And how, on her own, will she find Marguerite?

'That hand looks bad. Your carving hand, am I right?'

'Yes,' says l'Ymagier, adjusting the sling, avoiding his gaze.

'An accident, I suppose.' The bishop dips his hand in the fountain's pool.

'Yes.' He wills the words from his mouth. 'I was careless.'

'Broken?' says the bishop.

'Entirely,' says l'Ymagier.

The bishop calls into the house. 'Mathilde, you may serve now. We will dine in the garden. And please tell Blanche that Monsieur l'Ymagier will require help cutting his food.'

Sometimes, in the dizzying quiet of her cell, Marguerite still hears her. *Marguerite, are you awake? Marguerite?*

Yes, Christina. Yes. I am. I hear you. I'm awake.

The bishop looks up, taking a piece of venison in his mouth and chewing thoughtfully. 'I am sorry you will not carve again.' He waves at the fountain and smiles. 'Like magic. Isn't that what people always said?'

'It is a craft.'

'Indeed. But which sort? Now I myself am a practical man. My concern is not enchantment but insurgency: ideas with the power – if I may coin a phrase – to topple a church.' He lifts his serviette, wipes his mouth.

'I understand.'

'And I understand that you, of course, are no longer a *free* mason. You cannot travel at will as you were wont. It is doubtful, Monsieur l'Ymagier, given your injury, that you are even yet a mason. The situation is, frankly, difficult. Were I to grant you freedom to leave this house, you and your daughter would be pelted with cathedral rubble before you could make it even as far as the town wall.

'Why, just the other morning, the day after the collapse, a stone was hurled through her window as she slept. There was glass everywhere. I regret to say it has not been easy to keep her safe. Especially when she will not unburden her heart to her anointed confessor.' He sips his wine. 'If, on the other hand, she were to confess – '

'With respect, Your Grace, confess to what?'

'If she were to ask for Christ's forgiveness in the holy sacrament of confession; if she were to appeal, *publicly*, to the Holy Mother Church; if she were to pray for the Church's *intercession* on her behalf . . .'

L'Ymagier stares at his plate.

'. . . then I am confident you and *both* your daughters would find peace at last. In fact, you have my word on it. My only interest is the stability of my diocese, and at the moment, Monsieur l'Ymagier, as you may have noticed, I have a cathedral on the ground.'

He pours himself water, waves his hand. 'You have not eaten.' He frowns. 'I forget myself.' He pushes back his chair, walks to the top of the pebbled path. 'Blanche! Did I not say you were needed?'

He returns to his seat and reaches for a dish of leek and courgette. 'Speak to your daughter.' He looks his guest in the eye. 'Counsel your daughter, Monsieur l'Ymagier – as only a father may.' He smiles broadly. 'I know you will. In fact, I rely upon it.'

He looks up. 'I believe that was a drop of rain.' He pours more wine. 'The farmers will be glad.'

16

A drop of rain at last. Outside Something's Brewing.

Yes. You have a funny sense of déjà vu.

Giles Carver is talking at you, edgy, self-conscious. Or he is until he finds himself suddenly at a loss. Out of his depth. He turns, starts to walk away – that Milky Way wrapper flapping from the sole of his shoe – when the words move through you, catalysing the moment. 'You can't leave her there.'

Giles Carver stops short. 'What did you say?'

Say it. 'Your daughter.'

'What do you know about my daughter?'

'You can't leave her there.'

He stares, bewildered.

The rain comes at last. A downpour in an Indian summer. Commuters, on the home stretch, dive for doors and bus shelters. They huddle for cover under awnings and news-papers. Across the street someone darts out of a shop to save a table of second-hand paperbacks. In a moment, he'll walk on again, lost to his thoughts, to whatever it is he won't say out loud.

Remember. Don't lose him.

'And raised a Catholic, you say?'

'Well, baptized one, at any rate,' says Dr Sperber. 'Her father, I believe, is lapsed.'

'That's not an issue,' says Mr Joseph.

The elevator door opens. The three of them step on to the

ground floor. 'I think she enjoyed your visit last time more than she let on. After she let her guard down, that is. It's been a tiring time for her.'

'Of course,' says Sister Paula. 'She's weathered a lot. Which is exactly why we want to help, if we can.'

'And that brings us to our other question,' says Mr Joseph.

Dr Sperber smiles. 'About a boyfriend, you mean.' He opens a door and ushers them through.

Sister Paula smiles graciously. 'The Aquinan Center for Living, Dr Sperber, is really a place for guided retreats and educational advancement. We've found that the greater the girl's independence from family and friends *in general*, the healthier her transition.'

'I understand. And, I must say, from the literature it looks like a beautiful place.' He motions them down another corridor.

'It is,' says Sister Paula. 'Truly. And that's what we'd like to make clear to Christina. The Center occupies close to a hundred acres of protected woodland. There's a spa, a set of stables, a Neo-Gothic chapel, not to mention a good and growing collection of contemporary art. But, most importantly, we have an accredited learning programme. We offer classes with top people in everything from bee-keeping to horseback riding; from landscape painting to conceptual art. The Center was established forty years ago and our members have gone on to play key roles in all areas of American civic and family life.'

'Well, if she does have a boyfriend,' says Dr Sperber, 'we haven't seen him here.' He lowers his voice as he approaches her door. 'But she's . . . how shall I put it?' He knocks politely. 'Reticent on the subject.'

'Perhaps I could try,' says Sister Paula.

★

Inside Something's Brewing, you stand at the counter, dripping.

At last the kid behind the counter is pouring the coffees, punching the register and taking your money. He's explaining something about stamps and loyalty cards when a cellphone goes off.

'Of course it's me – who else were you expecting on your old dad's phone? No, sweetheart, I'm not sure where she's got to . . .' Carver's voice is light, easy, but when you turn to look, he's staring at the ceiling, his face strained. He remembers his surroundings, turns to the wall. 'Of course I haven't left you there. No, listen, Christina. I keep saying. No one's *left* you anywhere . . . Well, what does Bishop say?'

You cross to the table and lower the tray.

'I'm just asking, Christina. I'm just asking if he had anything new to say. Maybe something about medication? No, of course he's not God. I'm merely . . . Well, don't worry about them . . . Again? As in again today? Well, who authorized that?' He pushes his hand through the wet thickness of his hair. 'What sort of questions?'

He meets your eyes briefly.

'Okay. Christina. Christina? Listen to me. Listen. I'm coming now. Are you listening? Yes, right now.' He reaches for his coat, sliding one arm awkwardly in. 'No . . . Like I said, ladybug, I don't know where Maggie is but . . . Christina, listen. I'm leaving now.' He glances at his watch. 'It's six-fifteen. I should be with you by seven. Quarter past at the latest. Do you have a clock in your room? Good. So I'll be there soon.' He shuts his eyes, like he's making a wish. 'The video's yours for the choosing on the way home. Anything but *Dr Zhivago* again.' He forces a laugh. 'A benign dictator? *Me?* Are you sure we're talking about the same guy here?' He winces – he's just said the wrong thing. 'That's what I said, didn't I? Okay . . . Yup. Bye . . . Bye, ladybug.'

He flips his phone shut. 'Have to be somewhere.' He slides out of the booth. Studies you for a moment. 'See you around.'

By 9:00 his keys are on the kitchen table, the blinds are pulled, and he's peeling off the damp skin of his coat.

'No change,' said the duty nurse, as if it wasn't obvious: his own daughter, his first-born, picking up the phone and calling Security.

When he hits the button on the answering machine, the message. At 6:10. Just before she tried his cellphone. *Maggie? Dad? It's me. Will you pick up? Are you there?*

Christina: speaking to him from whatever place it is that passes for the Beyond these days.

17

Gone.

When l'Ymagier opens the door of Christina's room – the bishop only moments behind him – she's gone.

Running: up the hills, through the vineyards, lungs straining, rain streaming, her heart climbing in her chest, as if it could lift the whole of her with it.

'Gone,' Dr Bishop breathes into the phone. 'She was on camera about an hour ago, moving in the direction of Maple Avenue, but I'm afraid it wasn't picked up on time. The truth is, Giles, we have no idea where she is.' And Carver, phone in one hand, steering wheel in the other, feels life kick-start within him.

Her father's line is busy. Maggie hangs up. She'll try again later. She goes back to her booth at the Happy Griddle, asks for a refill and opens *Jane Eyre*. The last chapter, and still no word from her mother.

No exclamatory comment. No passing thought. No fragment of her voice.

So she's going home. Back to her house and her sister's teacups dangling gladly from the trees in the backyard. Back to her father who was loved by her mother, whom *she* loves, who must love her, who *does* love, if haphazardly. Back to her room, where she'll close the door and stand before the old lacquered bookcase – the last surviving piece of furniture from her parents' first apartment. Back to the creased and faded spines, two rows deep, and the layer of dust, silent as a first snow. *Wuthering Heights. Villette. The Rainbow. Women in Love. Dubliners. Bleak House. Hard Times. The Awakening. The Scarlet Letter. The Age of Innocence. Gone to Earth.* And there, there: her mother's delicate, erratic handwriting alive in a margin, waiting to be found.

The window to her right is smeared with the syrupy finger-prints of children. Rain's coming down now, bouncing off the asphalt in the parking lot. And she suddenly realizes: she's not even sure what town she's in.

In the purple blaze of a lavender field, Marguerite stops at last, caught in a sudden downpour.

How good it is to be in the weather.

How easy it was to slip past the curtain. How easy it always would have been. It was only fear that stopped her, the fear of being any more lost than she has been.

Yet she has never felt easier than she is now, here, in the middle of nowhere.

Standing in the rain. Before two surprised lavender pickers.

Her face upturned and wet.

Making a spectacle of herself.

At the airport he shakes out the umbrella they've crowded under and scans the overhead monitors. Flight AC 784 to Montreal is departing, unexpectedly on time, at 12:35. He loads Nathalie's luggage on to the cart. As they push into a sea of delayed passengers and security checks, he takes hold of Aarif's hand.

'What will you do?'

She smiles. 'I don't know. Work in the bakery for a while. Read palms. Sell magic carpets. Dabble in extremist groups. You know me. I like to stay busy.'

He smiles. 'When will I see you?'

'When you can. When you can do it, Giles. That's when you'll see me.'

'Soon then.' His hand finds hers. 'I'll see you very soon.'

Christina stops for shelter in the ashmen's ancient lodge. Her legs are mud-splattered. Her tunic and shift are soaked through.

He will sense her in the wood as easily as he does the movement of deer. At times, he will watch her. Watch out for her too. She knows this. He will leave food. She will not go hungry.

She stops at last, out of breath, and bends, anchoring her hands on her shins. Rain trickles down her front. Her T-shirt sticks to her. Her hair is hot at her neck. She checks the plastic bag with her sketchbook, pencils and charcoal, and pulls the handles tighter against the weather.

And as she breathes, it comes to her. All of it. The dream from the night of the tenth, as she lay wired up in the lab.

It was the Tevatron tunnel. That's where she was. She was lying in the tunnel, only it was open to the sky, and earth was raining in on her. 'One hundred pounds per cubic foot,' she could hear the Fermilab guide saying somewhere behind her. 'That's how much it weighs.'

She was spitting grit from her mouth, trying not to choke, when the thin man in the open bathrobe wandered past. 'Tastes awful, doesn't it?' he said.

She's remembering now. 'My legs,' she pleads. 'I can't move my legs.' But he doesn't turn around. When she reaches out to feel her thigh, she touches solid wood.

Someone's shouting from high above. *Angel*. It's Angel. She turns her ear, trying to hear over all the noise of the world falling in. He's telling her that it's not what it seems, in spite of her useless legs, in spite of the grave. It's hard to catch every word. 'Listen to me, Tina!' he calls. 'Listen.' And suddenly she knows where he's calling from.

He's there at the very top of Angel's Flight, high above all the winking lights of the Near West Side. Where she would love to be. 'What are you doing down there?' he says. 'What did I tell you? You are fucking *made* for the world.' And she *longs*. She longs to be there, up high, looking down on the expressway, a slipping current of unending light. 'You can do it, Tina. I'm telling you. You can do it.' And slowly, slowly, as if magnetized by his words or his voice or his will, she feels herself rise . . .

She finds the key for the lodge's padlock under the usual stone. The door is swollen with the damp. She forces it with her hip. It is a moment before her eyes adjust to the dim light; before she spots it, in a heap in the corner, under a dribbling leak, next to the rusty signalling lanterns. His jacket.

She picks it up, shakes it out. In ballpoint, immediately above her own writing, words: 'I love you. Know that.'

In the sudden shadow of the ashmen's lodge, the words come back – 'And the devil wept, saying: I leave thee, my fairest consort, whom long since I found and rested in thee; I forsake thee, my sure sister, my beloved in whom I was well pleased. What I shall do, I know not' – the story Marguerite copied long ago by stealth in the days when a story was only a story.

Christina shakes rain off the bag and lifts out the pad. A train rushes past on the West Line, and she watches from the rain-dashed window, her heart still drumming for him.

She won't see him again. That's what he's telling her. She knows it is.

She opens the pad to the loose sketch and reaches for a stick of charcoal. She sits down cross-legged on the broken floorboards, under the best crack of light.

Within minutes she'll focus it: the kinetic life of him as he comes down the embankment; the private stillness of his face. She'll get his eyes too: melancholic, luminous. She'll finish the sketch.

It will be the first time she will have got a figure – a person, that is, and not a still life – right. It will be the first time she gets the contradictions of the human form down on the page. It will be the first time a drawing will feel truly like her own.

Later, she'll head back through the wood, slipping into his jacket, a new, strange skin in the torrent of rain. The smell of his cigarettes will rise up, fleetingly, around her. She'll realize she's hungry; that her blood sugar is low. As she walks, she'll already be tasting it: the bread hot from the toaster, the trickle of butter, the richness of honey.

18

Entanglement is the thing.

Einstein, for one, didn't like it. For him, the ability of one particle to instantaneously affect the physical properties of a once-related particle on what could be the opposite side of the universe was nothing less than 'spooky action at a distance'. Physicists today are more relaxed with the idea, if only because, unlike Einstein, they worry less about its metaphysical side-effects.

Entanglement between particles, we now understand, exists everywhere and all the time. Once any two (or more) particles have interacted, it no longer makes sense to consider one in isolation, no matter how great their separation. The physical realities of these particles, such as their momentum and spin, are now decidedly *shared* properties.

But the story of the entangled world does not stop at the subatomic. The latest research is a bolt from the blue: researchers have located entanglement here, in our big, wide, macroscopic world. While the discovery of entanglement between holmium atoms in a magnetic salt may not be everyone's idea of a heart-stopper, the implications are far-reaching. The results suggest that, if we only knew where to look, we would find the effects of entanglement elsewhere in the everyday world.

Some go further. Some believe we will, in time, discover entanglement everywhere. Some argue we will find that entanglement is a consequence of anything with claims to a physical reality. Consider your own body, for example, and the countless interactions between the electrons in all of its atoms. Wouldn't it be surprising if it were anything less than a mass of entanglements?

What about two related bodies? Or two bodies in relationship? Wouldn't two masses of entanglements tangle? And what about two kindred consciousnesses? After all, entangled atoms make molecules. Molecules make biology. Biology makes life and all its attendant mystery.

But even here, it seems, entanglement doesn't end. For recent research has uncovered an uncanny connection between past and future time.

Think photons for a moment. Think polarization. Picture it: you're measuring a given photon's polarization.

Done. Great. Phew.

Polarization measured. You've got your result.

Now measure the polarization again. Same photon.

The news?

The second measurement you take or, more precisely, the influence of the act of this second measurement on the photon, could well affect how that photon was polarized earlier.

Yes. *Earlier*. For time too, it seems, can become entangled.

As for worlds—

You bump into Carver by the revolving doors. He laughs as if to say, Of course, who else? He's on his way out, having seen Nathalie and Aarif off.

You're on your way in. Your stay is over. You're flying back. No baggage to check. You travel light.

He's unexpectedly chatty. Relaxed even. He turns back and walks with you towards departures. 'I'll follow you for a change, if you don't mind.'

It shouldn't surprise you. Did you think you could remain

detached from events? Did you think you could resist entanglement?

He makes a joke about the riddle of the video footage, about his career in supergravity 'of all things', about 'the tired jests of the gods'. 'There's no one,' he says, 'like your own children to puncture your vanities.'

He's hedging. Play along. There's time yet. You have fifteen minutes before you board. And you can see a difference in him, a change that began the day you confronted him outside Something's Brewing. Man of science though he is, he seems at last to be coming round to the idea that he can't conjure the world; that mystery persists.

Of course he'll never know what he can never know: that early one morning in 1284, as the church bell rang for matins, Christina of Beauvais's body shut down in the panic of too much feeling. That, even as that bell rang, his own daughter collapsed on the kitchen floor of their home, her heart faltering as she picked up the phone.

He'll never know that, just as he himself was made outcast for his physics, so a thirteenth-century man called Giles of Beauvais risked all for a radical metaphysics; that the imaginator's vision, like his own, was of a cosmos that is endlessly unfolding.

Giles Carver will never know that four girls moved as one into the world.

Nor does he know anything of you. He knows only that you've dogged his steps; that you've watched with a keen eye; that you've read him strangely well. And though he'll never say it, he also senses, in some vague way, that you, the Observer, have been the making of him – even if he does regard it merely as a turn of phrase.

He's laughing again. He's telling you he's even relinquished, at last, the puzzle of the late-night phone calls. He jokes. He'll crack the mystery of the singularity itself – the secret of the universe's first spark – long before he figures out who was on the phone the night Christina collapsed.

You've made it through the crowds as far as the departure gate. You take a final gulp of the drink you've acquired en route. You have to go. Yet there's still something you need to know.

He's trying to explain something called a graviton, a 'spin-two particle', the theoretical carrier of the force of gravity. Elusive. Exotic. Half dream. You're beginning to wonder if you've come all this way for a science lecture. Yet he's working something out. Something in his own head.

Because he knows. At the end of this day, the force of your expectation isn't something he can avoid.

'What most people don't get is this: gravity is actually a hell of a lot weaker than most of us ever would or could imagine. Take the electromagnetic force – just for the sake of comparison. It's a thousand billion billion billion billion times stronger than gravity.' He smiles. 'Forget that. Think of this. It takes nothing more than some aerodynamic thrust to get an entire jet off the ground. Nothing more than magnets to suspend high-speed trains above metallic tracks. Right? No. Forget engineering. Think of the human body. You need only a very ordinary set of muscles to overcome a *planetary* force, routinely, on a daily basis. We do it all the time, every time we heave ourselves out of bed.'

You drop your cup in a waste bin. As he talks, you adjust your watch. Soon you will be in another time zone.

'But the weakness of gravity has stumped everyone for ages, right? Why should one of the four forces of the world be so paltry compared to the other three? Nobody gets it until a couple of voices come along and say, "What if?" What if gravity isn't just "thin on the ground"? What if there's a leak? A flow of gravitons, in other words, from our familiar world to worlds *within* our world – to dimensions within our dimensions.'

You hear the boarding call again. Time's running out.

'Okay. Take it a step further. What if it's not a leak? What if it's a transmission instead, like some M-theorists suggest? Some kind of signal between all these planes of being. It isn't impossible. That's all we can say right now. But to say that is to say more than I, for one, ever dreamed of.'

And he can see it again in his mind's eye.

You too can see it in his mind's eye. At last. The mystery of those twenty seconds. In real time.

Look.

The images are grainy. The light is greenish on the infrared footage. The video's on-screen timer reads 01:37:14. Below it, the day pulses: 09-11-01. Under the fixed view of the camera Christina looks like a girl in a box. Her face is unusually pale. Her covers are in disarray. She's been restless in the night.

What surprises both you and Giles Carver as his daughter rises – three inches, six, a foot and a half – is how unremarkable it seems. How quiet. How untumultuous.

Her face calms. Her mouth falls open slightly. Her breath is as shallow as a child's. The sheet and blanket slide from her on to the floor, but she hardly stirs. Only her right foot twitches briefly in the air.

('You can do it, Tina. I'm telling you.' Angel's voice.)

Below her, EEG wires dangle with her hair, blonde now after the long summer. Her right hand rests on her chest. Her left hand drifts below her, as if she is trailing her fingers over a river's cool surface. Her back remains effortlessly straight.

She is as light, as weightless, as a bird on a warm uprush of air.

Ten seconds. Twelve. Fifteen. Then her slow, ineluctable return to earth.

Only twenty seconds. Yet you feel as if you've just surfaced from a slow-plunging dive.

Your final boarding call is flashing.

Giles Carver blinks, turning back to you. 'It's a mystery,' he says. 'We don't know where gravity comes from or where it goes.' He looks at the floor, trying to hide whatever it is he's feeling. 'But, whatever the case, it's always about pull.' He looks up. 'Do you see? It's *always* an attractive force.'